Confined to a Wheelchair in the prime of
his life, Charlie Pyrmont craved not only
to be normal again . . .
.. *but to be Immortal.*

I0592480

THE
IMMORTALITY CONNECTION ©

JAMES WILLIAM DAVIS

James William Davis

Published by James William Davis
17 Wedgewood Crescent, Beacon Hill NSW 2100
©

Copyright 2012, James William Davis
International Standard Book
ISBN 978-0-646-98821-4

National Library of Australia Cataloguing Publication entry
Author: Davis, James W.

Title: The Immortality Connection / James William Davis.
ISBN 978-0-646-98821-4

019 01-2023 Book 1 Immortality.doc
M-Submit 2022 July Submit Cover.pdf

Cover Design and Layout by James William Davis.
©

Born in 1944, James William Davis branched into writing inadvertently during his time in the film and television industry. Story telling became a driving force in his working life, albeit mostly with a camera or an editing device. Now he likes to hone his craft using the written word, that essential step prior to all other forms of expression.

James William Davis

Books
by
James William Davis
Series of 13

THE IMMORTALITY CONNECTION

MIND SET

ZER**O**ZONE

HOLIDAY HORROR

GHOST WRITER

OVERKILL

WITHOUT SOPHIE

CHAPTER ONE

By the time Charlie Pyrmont's 28th birthday rolled around, he should have been dead already.

Five years ago he suffered his first big heart attack while working on the roof of a house; *suffered* probably isn't the right word, because Charlie himself had been heard to claim, *thanks to modern science the whole thing was an absolute breeze*.

Charlie had a lot of faith in science.

Had he known the grief that science would bring to his uncertain future, he might well have wished he'd died on the operating table. But then, the following bizarre story would never have emerged.

He was totally astounded at the way surgeons were able to introduce a small *Stent* into his blocked artery, allowing obstructed blood to once again return to the heart. His wife Silvia wasn't fascinated in the least; the heart attack had only served as a grim reminder. Although in their early twenties, premature death was

1

ostensibly still on the cards. Young people tended not to dwell on such depressing thoughts, but an unexpected heart attack had a way of changing that. There would be many life changing issues contributing to this new preoccupation.

At first, blissfully unaware of the future, Charlie remained positive, even in the face of what some unthinking people had to say regarding heart surgery and its possible failure. Mostly though, largely negative comments hadn't come until well after he'd returned to the relative safety of home.

One particular afternoon, he was informed by a well-meaning friend that not all of these so called simple operations went smoothly. *They poked the Stent right through my uncle's artery*, his friend told him. *They had to rush him into another theater for open heart surgery; he's lucky to be alive.*

Charlie wasn't unthankful for being alive, and certainly not lacking in appreciation for what had been done for him by the doctors, but right or wrong he firmly believed luck had very little to do with it. He often referred to *luck* as the *L*-word.

Silvia made the mistake of mentioning the 'L' word over dinner one night and he lightheartedly picked her up on it.

'Thirty or forty years ago I'd have been dead, and that's a pure fact. Luck didn't save me,' he affirmed pushing his point. 'It's the times we live in.'

Silvia understood, but didn't particularly have anything to add to the comment, but she knew better than to ignore it, so she waited for him to continue. 'Well go on, tell the story?' she finally had to prompt.

Clearly she was leading him on, so he playfully told her, 'Modern science; who knows what they'll save us from in the future.'

'Good point *Chas*, who knows?' she said cryptically agreeing. 'But come on, there has to be a limit don't you think, babe.'

'No. Why should there be?'

She mulled it over while eating, then said, 'Let's say you're right, *that there is no limit*! It would mean people might live forever. Do you really believe that?'

'Sure, why not.'

Silvia's mood suddenly changed for the worse and it came as a shock even to herself. She labored over her food and swallowed hard. An involuntary tear crept onto her cheek forcing her to cast her eyes away to the glass of wine on the table, which she nervously pivoted between restless fingers.

'What are you crying about?' Charlie asked with a grin, trying to make light of it.

She wiped her face with the back of her hand and took a sip of wine like it was really needed.

'Are you okay?' He asked reaching across to touch her arm.

She gave him an awkward smile. 'Sorry, I'm being a bit of an idiot,' she answered managing a light laugh.

He let her arm go and returned to his meal. 'What's got you so upset?'

She flicked her eyes around the room searching for the words. 'Well, this wonderful world you talk about won't be around for *us* will it, and it sure as hell won't help our parents.' She sculled the remaining two thirds of her wine and refilled the glass.

She was on the edge of tears again, and Charlie knew not to encourage where the emotions were taking her. 'I'm the idiot,' he offered, 'let's change the subject.'

She had more to say, but an unsteady voice betrayed her fear. 'You managed to dodge a bullet this time; it doesn't guarantee you will next time. The future you're talking about will be long after we're pushing up daisies.'

Charlie was somewhat stunned by her sudden gloom and felt awkward watching her cry. 'I think you've had too much wine, *sweetie*.' Making light of the situation was all he could think to do.

She jumped up from the table and emptied the rather expensive vintage into the kitchen sink. 'No, Charlie, I've had too much stress. I just needed a little wine to relax.'

He saw she needed consoling, not quirky remarks. Easing in, he enveloped her in his arms from behind. 'Life's short, sweet, let's not worry about how it ends.'

She turned and kissed him hungrily. Just two years of marriage—and recent events—had molded Charlie and Silvia into one entity, not always agreeing, but never in fear of separation. Always *in love*, only death would ever tear them apart. Or so they believed with absolute probability. They were an attractive couple and such solid commitment after only two years could easily be considered a little premature.

He gripped her shoulders and held her at arm's length. She was beautiful; on the surface, and below it, and, normally, with a happy-go-lucky personality.

She had the sundrenched body of an athlete too, moulded by years of surfing in her youth, resulting in honey-blond hair that flowed over bronze shoulders in soft naturally formed waves. She had fire if the occasion presented itself; fools need step clear at times like that.

He loved *everything* about his wife in fact.

He wasn't the only one, her sincere warmth, sense of humour and easy-going-nature were traits noticed by everyone she met. For Charlie, the easiest thing to like about Silvia was that she loved *him* and made mention of it in large and small ways every day.

'I don't think I could ever live without you,' she told him pressing her head into his chest.

'We're together and that's all that matters. You're worrying over nothing.'

She certainly felt this was true. He was her man and he was here, a man with a big heart. A heart that was unfortunately diseased before its time. A few inches taller than her, he was a real *catch*. Deep brown eyes, dark wavy hair and lips made in heaven for her to kiss. He was long legged, muscular and with a firm round butt that drew her eye. Not just hers. She loved his hairless chest and his straight, bulky ribcage; his abs, his biceps. He was her stud.

She was secretly gushing in her mind.

Better than all else, he was an angel of a man, a nice guy. As sick as he'd been in recent months, he was *her* guy, a guy who needed her love and care more than ever.

It would take diligence and dedication to diet to keep him alive and well, he deserved her help. She promised herself that she would at least try and play her part in humoring his silly talk of living forever in the future.

Whatever keeps his mind at ease, she thought.

Her future though was far more grounded, and in no way unconditional. She really wanted to start a family, something they had both been putting off due to unforeseen circumstances.

Their decision to postpone having children had nothing at all to do with finance however, they were outrageously rich, thanks to wealthy families on both sides of the fence, but their immense fortune had come suddenly, and by tragic means.

Both their parents had recently been prematurely plucked from this world in the same plane-crash while on a joint holiday.

The *In-laws Excursion* they called it.

The passenger jet went down over the Australian Outback while Charlie and Silvia were overseas in Europe. The news of the crash came to them in their hotel suite in France, savagely ending their honeymoon and bringing them home to Australia to take care of four funerals on four consecutive days of hell.

Although the funerals were well attended by many high society friends, the extended families were minimal by fact of their nonexistence. Silvia had only one distant aunt who lived in Canada; and Charlie, just one brother who had one child to a wife he'd divorced a year after Charlie's heart attack. With such a small network of distribution, the double inheritances left the newlyweds extremely well off, multiple millionaires.

They were both only twenty eight, and with their affluent teenage years still ringing in their ears—albeit fading slowly with the march of time and tragedy—the money could not have meant any less. Wealth certainly could not have replaced their dead parents. Charlie's father wasn't his real father; his biological father had died when Charlie was only nine years old. Money came Charlie's way then too.

On top of the devastating plane crash, Charlie's recent health alarm brought about the undeniable peal of their impending mortality. Death's door hung over them in a constant cloud of uncertainty. Not an environment to bring children into - not yet.

This was all five years ago.

They'd stuck religiously to the medical routine and maintained their resolve to hold off having children. Most decisions were centred on Charlie's condition. He was diligently taking his prescribed medication and she was preparing the healthiest of meals, low in fat, low in cholesterol, high in vitamins and the rest. Time was slowly pushing grief into the background. With all of the drugs, outside of a few side effects he felt quite well. That is until a familiar niggling pain in his throat forced him to down tools while working in the garden. When Silvia saw him come in the back door looking like a ghost, she immediately knew what was wrong, but asked anyway. 'Are you feeling all right?'

'No. I've got that damn burn in my throat again.'

'Sit down and relax.'

Charlie made his way over to the couch and did as he was told without argument. He heard the water running and a moment later she was back with the glass.

'Here, drink this.'

He took a sip, but knew he needed more than water. 'I think I'll lie down on the bed,' he said after a few more sips.

'Have you got pain?'

'It's getting that way.'

'Use your spray.'

'Is it on the cupboard?'

'Yes, it's on the cupboard,' she sang as she always did when she was worried.

Silvia walked with him into the bedroom and made sure he used the *Glyceryl Trinitrate* under his tongue. He was in quite a bit of pain now and hoped like hell the medication would soon take effect.

'Are you feeling all right?' she asked again.

'Not really. The pain's getting worse.'

'Do another spray.'

Charlie didn't even feel like sitting up, nausea was swelling from the depths of his stomach and taking over his entire body; cramps and phantom pains were the only distraction from overpowering sickness.

Two more squirts under the tongue, head back and hope.

After ten minutes he was feeling even worse and the pain was intensifying. Two more squirts - then another two. As he found out later, this was about three doses over the limit. The result was Charlie's blood pressure went into a death spiral, bringing on wooziness.

As before, the decision to ring the emergency service was made quickly, Silvia knew that's what had saved him the first time. As if things weren't bad enough though, Charlie began to feel bilious and started lifting himself from the bed to make it to the toilet. That's when he felt the true effects of low blood pressure. Immense weakness prevented him from even standing.

She struggled to keep him on his feet. 'Charlie, what's happening?'

'Get me to the throne - before I *shit* myself,' he told her convincingly.

Weakness sent him staggering to the left. He hit the wall and slid down, coming to rest on the floor, almost unconscious, sicker than he had ever felt in his life.

Fearful of losing him right there and then, 'Oh, Charlie,' was all she could think to say . . .

The ambulance arrived to find their patient exactly where he had collapsed, barely conscious. They helped him out of his shirt and began the task of stabilization. Breathing became a little easier with the fitting of an oxygen mask.

Thirty minutes later he was lying comfortably in the hospital, already wondering when he could go home and marveling once again at the technology that had saved him.

In the week that was to follow, new challenges would present themselves. Yet again, fortune would not go the way they yearned.

The day after Charlie was admitted, the doctor came in for a chat to explain the situation. 'We've looked at your x-rays and there's a bit of a problem,' the doctor said holding up the mysterious black and white film to the light. 'We can't fix this with a stent unfortunately; your best option now is open heart surgery, that's the only way we can reach the blocked artery.'

This was devastating news for Charlie. The last thing he wanted was a length of stitches turning him into a Frankenstein reject. Scars weren't his thing. Images of people proudly showing them off didn't impress him, he had little to no desire to become a resigned member of the 'Zipper Club'.

'Silvia,' he told his wife. 'Get on the Net and search for Keyhole Surgery.'

She didn't like where he was heading. His talk of miracle cures still pervaded her mind. His fantasies about it frightened her. She was worried sick over what he might decide to do next and wanted to tell him to wake up to reality, but couldn't bring herself to say it. Had she known the benefit of that advice, she wouldn't have held back. If she had spoken her mind, deep heartache that was set to tear their world apart might have been avoided?

'Chaz', just do what the doctor wants.'

'Cool advice sweetie,' he quipped sarcastically, 'if you're not the one being opened up with a power saw.'

'All right,' she gave in, 'if that's what you want. I'll check it out tonight, okay?'

It was definitely *okay*, but in the meantime Charlie would do some of his own research from his hospital room. He had a phone brought in and spent the rest of the day ringing around. By midafternoon the small table near his window was smothered in scribble notes. With disappointment he discovered no one in Australia was doing keyhole surgery on hearts.

Silvia returned to see Charlie the next day with some information she'd found on the Net and it momentarily lifted his spirits. But, after reading through it, he felt as skeptical about it as she did.

A doctor in America has been doing Keyhole on hearts for several years with great success—so the report said.

Of course the American surgeon's success was very much self-professed, as you'd expect on a site wishing to round up customers. There were testimonials, but who was to say what deals with the doctor had been made, and America was a long way from home.

'Just go ahead with the operation,' Silvia advised. 'The doctors here know what they're doing.'

'I'm getting a second opinion,' Charlie warned her.

'From who . . . ?'

'Thompson; I've already rang him.'

Dr. Thompson was the man who had performed the stent operation after the first heart attack, and Charlie felt he could trust in his impartiality.

When the doctor came over to the hospital to talk with Charlie, Silvia made sure she was there to hear what he had to say.

'I've checked the x-rays,' Thompson told them, 'and I agree with Doctor Bramton; Open Heart is the only way to fix this.'

Charlie's spirits submerged. 'I guess that's it then,' he said resignedly.

'You're in good hands, Charlie; Doctor Bramton is doing exactly what I would have done myself, under the circumstances.' He drew an imaginary picture in the air as he explained. 'The affected artery is around behind the heart and too hard to reach with a stent; too dangerous in fact. It's not a risk I'd take.'

None of this was what Charlie wanted to hear, but it was fast becoming clear that he was about to join the millions of zipper club members, who had reluctantly, or otherwise, allowed themselves to be opened up like human sardine-cans.

On the afternoon before he was due to go to surgery, he smiled at his wife and said, 'I guess this is the right thing, then turned to the window deep in thought.

Silvia could see the worry written on his face. 'Have you spoken to Les yet?'

'Yep, this morning . . .'

'Well—what did he say?'

'You know my brother; - don't worry he says, you'll be sore at first; - time will pass and you'll be right-as-rain.'

Time was beginning to pass — as promised.

Charlie had been given a complete body shave and was now being led into the operating theater.

This is it, he thought, *no turning back.*

He remembered very little after that. Twilight-dreams descended on him as he emerged from the anesthetic. He couldn't expel the idea he was now lying inside some sort of trailer. He would eventually discover that this was one of many hallucinations that always happen at night. He'd be alone inside a sea of drapes, somehow sensing there were people behind them—waiting, and it would only be a matter of time before a nurse or doctor would come through to check on him. One by one they came, parting the curtains like a presenter on a stage. Ask mysterious questions; fiddle with instruments, and leave.

His most vivid recollection of these hallucinations was when the surrounding drapes adapted into deep seething walls with ever changing shapes.

He wasn't afraid of them, just intrigued.

'How are you feeling?' one female nurse asked him.

He looked up, but without his spectacles could only make out a blurry face.

Over the next couple of days, as the anaesthetic wore off, pain reigned supreme. Hallucinations devoured his senses, he couldn't tell if a desk in the corner of the room had recently been brought in, or if it had been there all along. The nurse who sat at it seemed to know all about what he was feeling—especially the pain.

'The button in your hand will administer morphine whenever you need it,' she told him. 'Just hold it in for a few seconds and the pain should go away. Let me know if it doesn't.'

The short time spent on morphine was comparatively comfortable, pain coming and going in self-controlled waves. The more persistent pain wasn't to arrive until after he was transferred from intensive care to the ward.

Several visitors came to see him during the week he remained in this suffering state and most would repeat the cliché, 'How you feeling?'

I'm feeling excruciating pain, he wanted to tell them. Instead he'd politely settle for, 'Not too bad, wee-bit painful.'

A bit painful - on the first day, he'd been so sick that he had to throw up. His chest heaved involuntarily and it felt like his zipper would split open, spilling his heart into the bathroom basin.

He spoke to his brother Les, for the first time since the operation, and asked if it had been quite this bad for him when he'd had his operation.

'I didn't want to say anything before,' Les admitted with a grin. 'But I went through the same hell you're going through. I *know* what it's like believe me.'

'I believe you,' Charlie agreed sarcastically.

'Give it time. In a few months you'll feel like new. It's been twelve years for me and I've been fine, no problems.'

Charlie wanted to believe things would turn out as well as they had for Les, but it wasn't to be. In fact he wouldn't have to wait twelve years for another problem, not even twelve months. The worst—and the best, was yet to come.

CHAPTER TWO

Charlie sat beside his large living room window overlooking the reserve. He glanced over at his wife and discovered her watching him, but felt too depressed to open a conversation.

'The doctor told you there'd be days like this,' she said recognising the depths of his despair.

He clamped his security pillow hard against his chest and coughed . . . 'Man; that really hurts.'

'Of course it does; you've had a big operation.'

In the valley below, a massive screeching choir of white cockatoos captured his attention, he watched the flock swoop up toward the house and disappear over the roof as though performing aerial pageants.

An empty feeling of envy devoured him.

Six months later, Charlie couldn't deny he felt a lot better than when he had first come out of hospital, but he was still experiencing strange inexplicable pains in various parts of his body. Sometimes the pain was under his ribs. At other times it seemed to be in the wall of his chest. On one occasion the discomfort was more like a cramp; on another, like a savage attack of *shingles*. It was confusing and more than a little worrying.

'These pains don't make any sense,' he told Silvia. 'I felt better a couple of months ago.'

'You're due for another blood test, so we'll go and see Chambers tomorrow; see what he says.'

Silvia always went along with him on the GP visits, because she didn't trust Charlie to remember what the doctor told him.

Charlie didn't mind though; he knew—and had been warned by the doctors—that his memory wouldn't be the greatest after surgery.

Charlie struggled up from the couch with the pillow against his chest.

'Think I'll take a shower.'

'Okay,' she said placing some breakfast dishes in the sink. 'I'll get you a fresh towel.' Silvia went to the linen closet while Charlie made his way slowly to the bathroom. 'You make a start,' she called after him. 'I have to get a towel from the dryer.'

'No problem. Take your time.'

In the downstairs laundry she stopped the unfinished drying cycle, took out a towel and closed the door on the rest, anxious to get back upstairs and make sure Charlie was safe.

When she'd made her way to the bathroom he had already stepped into the shower. The room was filled with an abnormal amount of steam.

'How hot are you having that shower?' she called out.

Charlie didn't answer.

She pushed through the blinding steam to turn on the exhaust fan, and tapped on the misted cubical to raise a response. Charlie still didn't answer; she tried sliding the door to the shower open.

Something was stopping it.

'Charlie! Can you hear me, sweetheart?'

She pushed the door harder and it opened reluctantly, releasing her husband's leg onto the floor outside the recess. While reaching in to switch to cold water she managed to scold her arm in the process. She had to wonder why Charlie wasn't screaming in pain. Once the steam dissipated she realised that Charlie had collapsed. His legs were glowing red from the near-boiling water, and he appeared to be semiconscious.

'What happened to you; did you slip?'

In some sort of stupor, Charlie made no attempt to answer.

'Why get in the shower with the water so hot? Your legs are red raw.'

Silvia placed her arms under his shoulders and tried to raise him up into a sitting position. He was a dead weight. 'Can you try and stand.' It was then that she realised he couldn't move at all. Grabbing the towel she placed it across him to keep him warm, and then went straight to the phone to ring for help, wondering all the while what else could possibly go wrong in their lives.

Within a very short space of time, paramedics were there checking Charlie's vitals. 'He's had a heart attack recently,' one of the officers observed looking at the raw zipper on his chest.

'Six months ago,' Silvia told him.

The paramedic raised his voice. 'Can you hear me, Mr. Pyrmont?'

Charlie moved his eyes a little.

'I'm fairly sure he's had a stroke,' the emergency guy guessed.

'Oh no,' Silvia breathed.

'Let's not get too worried. Quicker we get him to hospital the better.'

The ambulance raced to the Northern District's Private Hospital with siren blaring. Five minutes later Charlie had medical staff swarming all over him in an effort to stabilise his condition.

Silvia had sat in the waiting room for over an hour before a doctor came out with news. 'He's had a reasonably substantial stroke I'm afraid.'

'I don't understand. I didn't think it was possible to have a stroke after a heart attack.'

'A popular misconception,' the doctor revealed. 'It happens, but not very often. Your husband is one of the unlucky ones.'

A weird thought crossed Silvia's mind, and she was exceedingly glad Charlie hadn't heard the doctor label him unlucky.

'How bad is he?' she asked with hesitation.

'Bad enough; it's probably a bit early to predict, but he may have some permanent paralysis.'

'Will he be able to walk?'

'Possibly not at first, only time will tell how well he recovers. A lot will depend on how much help he gets in the early stages. This is going to be hard on *you* as well. It'll take time and effort.'

'There's not much in the way of extended family,' she volunteered. 'He only has one older brother. That's fine, I'll look after him.'

The doctor couldn't help thinking that this attractive young woman's commitment to her husband might easily be put-to-the-test in the long term; he was no longer the man she married. This was the new Charlie.

'Does he know what's happened?' Silvia wanted to know.

'For sure; in fact he's quite alert mentally, and that's the best thing about his condition right now. Usually people who have good faculties straight after a stroke do better than those who don't. So, there's quite a lot to be thankful for if you consider it like that—Keep your spirits up if you're able, he'll need you to stay positive, because he may struggle to do so.'

'Is he talking?'

'Perfect. His speech is totally unaffected. In about twenty minutes, I'll get you to go in. Have a good talk with him. It'll help you both.'

The doctor placed a sympathetic hand on Silvia's arm and told her they'd talk after she'd been in to see her husband.

When she walked in she was shocked at the number of tubes that had been connected to Charlie's body, but she managed a brave expression.

'I guess the 'Zipper' is the least of my problems now,' he told her as she reached his bedside.

She kissed him on the cheek. 'You're alive, and that's all that matters . . . How are you feeling?'

He thought, *there's that damn cliché.* 'Unlucky,' he admitted without thinking.

His unconsidered comment slightly astounded her. 'Not as unlucky as you could have been,' she breathed with relief.

Charlie opened his mouth to say something, but his face went stone frozen — tears welled into eyes full of new fear.

She understandably assumed he was feeling a bit emotional about everything, but that all changed when a nurse ran into the room and urgently began checking the machines that surrounded Charlie's bed.

'What's wrong,' Silvia asked in a panic.

'I'm not sure; he might be having another stroke. It might be wise to step out, Mrs. Pyrmont, things could get a little crazy in here in a moment or two.'

Silvia moved over near the door to keep out of the way. Her heart rhythm leaped, pounding against her ribcage like a drum, raising a hot blush to her cheeks and a lather of cold sweat to her entire body. All colour drained away from her as people came running in and began fussing over her husband's tubes and machines. Someone pushed up Charlie's sleeve and straightaway injected him with something.

Just arriving in the corridor outside the hospital room, Charlie's brother, Les, did a double take when his sister-in-law came darting out looking as white as a winter frost. 'Silvia, what's up?'

'It's all going wrong,' she blurted tearfully.

She fell into his arms and he held her while she sobbed. He was brought close to tears himself.

As the weeks passed, Silvia Pyrmont appeared to be heading for a complete breakdown. Her cheeks were drawn and her skin appeared pale, it was as if she'd spent a lifetime away from any form of natural light.

'I think you've been working too hard, *Sil*,' Charlie said almost apologetically, 'why don't you get off your feet and rest?'

Silvia turned toward the voice and looked squarely at her husband. She broke into a pitiful sob and it ate into Charlie's heart. 'I don't understand why you're so upset. You should be pleased I survived *two* massive strokes - not to mention two heart attacks.'

She still wasn't used to seeing him in the wheelchair close to helpless. *His speech is still fine*, she thought on the bright side, but then quickly lapsed back into depression.

He commanded the motorised wheelchair across to the table where his distressed wife sat holding her face in her hands. 'Hey, the worst is in the past,' he told her as he stroked her trembling arm.

Silvia spun round and held him as best she could. 'I'm sorry, sweetheart. If anyone should be crying it's you.'

'Well I'm not, so what does that tell you.'

Driven by her husband's newfound will to overcome adversity, she calmed herself down and wiped away the tears. She kissed him and ran her fingers through his hair. He was still her handsome husband in spite of everything that had happened. 'I'll always be here for you.'

Charlie had no doubt she meant every word, but deep doubts sank into his soul as he thought about the great burden his predicament provided for his young wife.

In the countless afternoons that followed, she'd sit by the bed as Charlie took his regular naps and study his peaceful face . . . the doctor's words repeating over and over in her head—

I'm sorry Mrs. Pyrmont - you need to know, your husband will never walk again . . .

She'd cry while he slept - afraid of the future.

CHAPTER THREE

Charlie did have a new found inner strength at first, but after a year of being trapped in a wheelchair, his emotional armor began to show distinct cracks.

'Come on, let's get this under you,' Silvia instructed as she placed a hospital style bedpan on his lap.

Charlie lashed out, using his good right arm to shove it onto the floor in disgust. 'For God sake let me decide when to take a shit!'

Silvia was so shocked by the outburst that she hardly knew how to respond. After a moment she bent down and picked the pan up and took it from the room.

'I'm sorry, sweetheart,' he called feeling guilt ridden. 'I'm a bit cranky.'

She didn't answer; he turned to the window, to the valley of bush-land that was happily soaking up the light rain that had been falling for the past couple of days. 'We really need this,' he said with a slightly raised voice.

He received no response.

He focused back on the mist that had settled on the valley floor. 'I hope Les isn't out in this, there's a fog moving in.'

Since Charlie's incapacitation, his brother had been staying over most nights to help Silvia with chores and dealing with Charlie; he lived only a couple of suburbs away.

'He rang to say he's staying home tonight,' she told him.

He turned, relieved to find his wife standing at the entrance to the room, recomposed. 'Oh, fine, that's good,' he said.

'It's nearly news time. Do you want to watch it?'

As though it didn't matter, he answered, 'Yeah put it on if you want.'

The news reader faded onto the screen in the middle of an overseas bloody war. Another terrorist bombing with scores of people killed or injured came next. Silvia turned away from the screen and found Charlie vacantly staring out at the rain. 'Are you watching?' she asked casually.

'I'm listening,' he lied. Wars and terrorists didn't really interest Charlie.

When a commercial break came on, Silvia decided to go out into the kitchen and start dinner. Charlie muted the sound. A peaceful quiet settled on the room . . .

Now he could hear the rain on the window's canvas awning. 'The sound of rain reminds me of when I was a kid in our country house,' he reminisced, speaking to himself as much as to his wife. 'Rain on the tin roof, with Dad's old cinema projector rattling away on the verandah, while we watched the films on the bedroom wall.'

He let himself sink into that blissful memory.

'Back on,' she told him as she came back into the living room. He didn't even know she'd left.

Charlie stabbed at the audio button, destroying the peace. A timely decision as it turned out . . .

There's been a breakthrough in Stem Cell research, the news reader droned on . . .

Charlie's ears pricked - this was interesting.

'Professor Sagle, who heads an Australian team of researchers, claimed five years ago, when he first snapped his spinal cord, that he would one day walk again.'

Professor Sagel appears on the screen:

'Doctors were adamant it would be impossible for him to walk or even have the slightest movement in any part of his body.

'Today, he proved them wrong, by willing his index finger to move

'Intense physiotherapy has been attributed to this latest development, but Professor Sagle believes the area of spinal cord repair will be the new reality in the near future—'

Charlie killed the sound again; he was incredibly excited by what he had just heard. 'How about that then,' he said slapping the arm of his chair. 'See, what did I tell you, pretty soon these doctors will be able to make paralysed people walk again.'

'You can't pin too much hope on news reports, Charlie,' Silvia warned him.

'I'm not. But it-goes-to-show, there's a lot more to learn and they're getting smarter every day. Someone out there has the answer - I'm telling you.'

'I just think you shouldn't rely on miracle cures. You could end up very disappointed.'

'That's a defeatist attitude, Silvia.'

'I think it's a practical attitude.'

'Give me a break,' he moaned screwing up his face.

'The way you're talking, it sounds like you'll have this miracle cure by the end of the year; it's just not going to happen.'

'Oh, you're sure about that are you? It's a matter of understanding how the body works. My body used to work, so it stands to reason it can again. All that's needed is to find the right person, someone who's close to a breakthrough.'

'Turning people like you into a guinea pig you mean; is that what you want for yourself?'

'Sure, I don't mind; what have I got to lose.'

His talk of cures was exasperating her all over again. 'Bloody hell, Charlie, you've been told what to do, but you haven't once been to the hospital for *physio*. Why you don't do what they tell you is beyond me.'

'I know only too well it's beyond you, Silvia,' Charlie responded with an acidic tone.

She faced him and saw disappointment, and a little anger.

'Why the hell are you getting so upset, Sil?'

'Because, I know you.'

Without a word, Charlie turned his chair around and went back to the living room.

'You don't have to get the *shits*, Charlie,' she called, but then decided to leave him to get over it.

A moment later, receiving no comeback, she began feeling guilty for taking the wind out of his sails and tried to amend the error. She stopped what she was doing and began walking back in to join him. 'Charlie, if you want to look into it, there's no harm I guess. I just don't want you getting your hopes up that's all—'

Silvia realised why he hadn't been responding when she reentered the living room—he wasn't there. On checking the other end of the house she discovered that he'd taken himself into the office and locked the door.

'Charlie, what're you doing?'

'I'm working. What's wrong?'

'Why's this door locked?'

She heard him moving around ahead of opening the door.

'What's the problem?' he asked impatiently.

'No problem,' she said as nonchalantly as she could. 'You don't normally lock the door that's all. I don't like you locking the door. If something happens I can't get in to help you.'

He softened. 'Sorry, sweetheart.'

'Charlie, this attitude of yours is worrying me.'

'I'm fine. I just want to work on the computer for a while.'

'You can leave the door open you know, I'm not going to steal your secrets.'

'How can I be sure of that,' he joked. 'I don't want you finding out about my girlfriends.'

'You're still a handsome bugger, Charlie Pyrmont, I wouldn't be surprised if you did have a couple of girls on the side.'

'You're safe my love. Now go away and let me work.'

When the door closed, her bemused expression turned to concern as she heard the latch locking from the inside once more. No matter how hard she tried to put the worry to the back of her mind, she just couldn't. Over the next few weeks he spent more and more time locked in the home office working on the computer, sometimes all day long. He was sensitive about it too; she dared not say a word for fear he might immediately jump-down-her-throat.

One night over their evening meal he made a sudden announcement. 'I've joined a stroke club.'

There was something in the way he said it that made her wonder if it was something she should be pleased about, or—for that matter—have any say in.

'Really?' she queried sounding less worried than she was. 'What brought this on?'

'What do you mean, isn't that what stroke victims are supposed to do?'

'Don't be like that, Charlie,' she pleaded. 'I'm just surprised you didn't mention you were thinking of it.'

'I wasn't until today.'

Silvia thought Charlie sounded overly bombastic and out of character.

'And where *is* this club - if you don't mind my asking?'

'The first meeting is tonight; not sure where. They told me to be ready around seven.'

'Someone's picking you up, *here*?'

'So they said.'

Charlie could see Silvia wasn't comfortable about it. 'This is what you wanted, isn't it; - for me to take an outside interest?'

'Of course I want you to take outside interests. I just like to know what those outside interests are—that's all.'

'I just told you; it's a stroke club. They meet, they have coffee - and they talk. What the hell are you worried about?'

Silvia started to say something, but the doorbell stopped her.

'That'll be them,' he said rolling back from the table.

Charlie was more anxious than she had seen him in a while. She followed him to the front door and in true form began wondering if there was anything he needed to take with him.

'Have you got your phone?'

'Oh, right. I'd better take that I suppose. Can you grab it for me?'

Silvia picked up the phone from a small table in the living room and automatically checked its interface. 'The battery's flat, Charlie; you should have charged it if you knew you were going out.'

The doorbell rang again.

'Don't worry, I won't need it. Give me a kiss and open the door, sweetie.'

Silvia opened the door to a man wearing a black suit and a black chauffeur's cap, with the words: Special Vehicle Transport Service written across the front of it.

The pleasant young man smiled dutifully and said, 'Hi I'm here to pick up Mr. Pyrmont.'

'He's ready it seems,' she said as though wanting to pass on her confusion.

Charlie came around from behind her in the wheel chair and held out his hand in a polite greeting. '*G'day*,

I'm Charlie,' he announced, giving permission to use his first name.

The chauffeur acknowledged, accepting the handshake. 'Charlie, I'm Arthur, pleased to meet you.'

Silvia watched the limousine pull away from the house through tactfully parted curtains. A solitude like she'd never felt before descended on her. She couldn't shake the fear that this might just be the beginning—of what? She wasn't sure.

The black limo made its way up onto the highway leading toward the city. Most of the peak hour traffic had taken a breather prior to the next wave of people heading out for the night. Like most big cities, Friday nights in Sydney always came alive with the sudden energy that workers somehow couldn't muster in the dying hours of their working week. Inside the special vehicle, Charlie's wheelchair was strapped down in a position just behind and to the left of the driver, so that passengers may make eye contact in the rearview mirror. Charlie could see the guy's smiling eyes fading in and out to the rhythm of the passing lights.

In the distance the mosaic of the city's colors were chewing into the last glow of a summer sunset.

'So where's this meeting?' Charlie asked the driver.

In the small framed mirror, Arthur's eyes flicked away from the road for a moment. 'Can't tell you; I'm sorry,' he said to the reflection. 'They only hire me to drive.'

His answer was polite, but Charlie wasn't sure what he meant. 'You mean you're not *allowed* to tell me?'

He chuckled, realizing the ambiguity of his answer. 'No, I mean I don't know.'

Charlie waited; *surely the driver has to know where he's going?*

'My job is to pick you up and take you to the foyer of the *Menzies*.'

'So that's probably where the meeting is.'

'Possibly not; I've seen customers leave in another car five or ten minutes later. It's not a hire car like this one—so, I'm afraid I don't have a clue.'

Charlie studied the driver's eyes in the rearview mirror, dutifully watching the traffic; relaxed and seemingly not put-out by the questions.

The eyes flicked onto Charlie, sharing the mirror with the road as he spoke. 'Everyone asks the same question . . . Don't worry about it . . . It's just the way these people operate. From what I can tell, it's a pretty classy operation.'

Charlie settled back to observe the trendy suburban houses flicking by, considering they were nothing at all like his beautiful big home overlooking bush-land. It made him think of the sad circumstances that led to his wealth. He brought his mind back to the present and responded to Arthur's comment. 'A pretty classy price too I'll bet.'

The driver snuck a glance at his obviously well to do passenger and gave a frowned smile in agreement, but by all accounts seemed to have no idea what pricey service his passenger might be paying for.

The special vehicle pulled serenely into the drop-off bay of the Menzies Hotel. Arthur waved an attendant over as he got out and rounded the vehicle to open the rear door on the curbside. A small ramp slid out and down to meet the pavement. The driver unfastened the restraining straps and rolled the chair out to meet the new carer.

'Good evening, how are you?' the middle aged man said, displaying all the professionalism of someone whose been making people feel welcome all his life.

'I'm fine,' Charlie chirped in proper response.

'Keith will take care of you now, Charlie; I'll see you next time.'

'If there is a next time I guess.'

'There usually is,' he said with a chuckle.

Keith gave Arthur a wink and pushed Charlie's chair into the cool air of the foyer.

'*You* seem to know where you're going at least,' Charlie observed making a comparison to the young limo driver.

'It's a good thing one of us does,' he joked.

People moving around the foyer of the hotel were a mixture of those being pampered and those doing the pampering, all on their best behavior. Charlie scanned the faces and wondered which one would eventually step up, smile and say; *hello I'm such-and-such.*

They made it all the way across the expansive foyer without this happening.

Keith set the chair at rest in front of the elevator and pushed the button.

'Going to a room are we?' Charlie asked wondering if he'd get a positive answer.

'Room 901 I'm told.'

'And of course you have no idea who I'm seeing, right?'

'All very covert,' Keith quipped melodramatically.

'I see that you know my name. You're with them are you?'

'No *sir-rie*, I work for the Menzies. You could be meeting Jack-the-Ripper for all I know.'

Charlie gave a bit of a smile as the lift arrived. 'The people you bring up here, they *do* leave, don't they?'

Keith pushed the chair into the elevator and spun it to face the way out. 'Most of them,' he answered with a poker-face as he set the doors in motion.

Charlie smiled to himself and thought, *Great!*

Keith knocked at 901 and a moment later it opened to reveal quite an attractive young woman dressed in a pale lemon business suit. Her lip gloss glistened as she smiled warmly at her visitors.

'Hello, Charlie,' she said holding out a slender hand. 'I'm, Debra Rowlands. I'm your orientation officer.'

Charlie grinned. 'Debra.'

She doesn't look like an officer of any sort, he thought.

'Thanks Keith,' she said sounding a bit like he'd just delivered a parcel. 'I'll take it from here.'

He tapped Charlie on the shoulder and smiled back at the woman. 'Catch you guys later.'

Debra allowed Charlie to use the chair's motor to take himself across to the window at the other side of the room. Spread out before him was a view of the city's ever changing north-side, with the iconic Harbor Bridge and Opera House in the foreground.

'So, you think you might join our university,' she mused as she joined him at the window.

Charlie beheld the slender woman inspecting the scene at his side. She had an air of confidence about her that was almost intimidating, arms folded beneath full, well presented breasts, *natural* Charlie decided. He knew the look of disapproval he'd get from Silvia if she were here to catch him noticing. Actually, just being alone in this room with an attractive young woman would be enough to put his lovely wife's nose out-of-joint. His being in the chair hadn't diminished her jealousy one bit. He didn't blame her for that; he had his own streak of wariness; hers often intrigued him because Silvia could hold up a candle to the best of them.

But, Debra Rowlands was definitely up there with the best. This young woman's confidence exuded patience, unwearyingly waiting before turning to face the gaze she knew Charlie was giving her. She gave off inviting vibes that made him feel obliged to initiate the conversation.

'I gather you're here to explain things to me.'

Her response was pleasant, albeit business-like. 'No, not really; first we have to make sure you're a suitable candidate. That won't be totally decided tonight either. Tonight is more of a warming; we see if we like *you*, and, if you like *us*.'

Debra relocated to a nearby lounge and sat sideways at its edge in a ladylike fashion, casually leaning back against the padded armrest. 'No doubt you have some questions, why don't you ask away.'

Charlie wanted to understand why they would send such an attractive woman to a meeting like this, unless of course it was to influence him in his decision. He wasn't about to make this his first question though, he forced himself to skip past the instant attraction and get down to business—that seemed to be what she was seeking anyway. 'You say you can cure the incurable.'

'Yes,' she confirmed without hesitation. 'We can.'

Charlie was hearing what he wanted to hear and she knew it, but he'd promised himself he would listen to her answers in order to form an educated opinion. 'What can you say to convince me this isn't just a giant con?' he asked bluntly, 'I'm assuming it comes with a hefty price tag.'

'I won't lie to you; assuming we take you into the University, it will as you say be very expensive. As for my convincing you our claim is legitimate, I'm afraid I can't do that here, in this room. Eventually—if you should get as far as beginning the program—you will actually be able to convince yourself without any trouble. Until that happens, we will not be asking for any money, but we *will* be asking for complete and ongoing secrecy. Do you think you can handle that?'

'May I ask why the secrecy?'

Debra leant further back into the seat and crossed her legs, brushing her thighs as though discarding crumbs from her lap.

'You might already have noticed we don't keep a high profile.'

'It's illegal - isn't it?' Charlie said pushing for confirmation.

Her eyes imperceptibly widened for an instant, then shifted to studying the back of her hand now at rest on her knee.

'Very,' she said as though she had decided on giving him a score of a hundred for his correct answer. Since they were getting down to business, she kept the ball rolling. 'Do you have a solicitor, Charlie?'

'Yes of course.'

'Does your solicitor have any dealings with your wife or brother?'

'I don't remember mentioning my family,' he said with raised caution.

'You didn't, but if we are to proceed with you we have to know everything there is to know. Your family in particular can stand in the way of success.'

Charlie was wondering who's success; his or theirs. 'You've already done a search on me it seems.'

'If we hadn't, this meeting wouldn't be taking place, we know you have no children, one brother and of course your wife, your only surviving family. We trust, because you tell us, that so far you haven't mentioned us to them. What we need now is an affidavit to that effect - and, we need you to sign a contract stating you will never divulge what goes on at the University.'

'I'll tell you this much,' Charlie said stalwartly. 'I'm not signing anything tonight.'

'I wouldn't expect you to. That's why I asked about your solicitor.'

She's ready for every response I give, he thought, *it's like she's heard it all before.* 'Okay, so I get an affidavit drawn up, show your contract to my solicitor, I presume he then talks to *your* solicitor; then, I make a decision about whether or not to sign on.'

'Partly right; at that point you won't be signing on, just confirming you intend keeping our little secret. A lot more work will have to be done after that before we accept you. If we don't, your affidavit still stands.'

Charlie was beginning to feel comfortable in the fact that his solicitor would be involved before any binding decisions, but he still had reservations about secrecy, especially considering if a scam or perhaps dangerous practices were to be uncovered. He really wasn't sure where he would stand legally—if he felt the need to uncover such a scam—in spite of having signed a contract not to do so. Of course his solicitor would know the answers to these questions.

'I have to ask; what are the risks. Is there anything life threatening?'

She sat forward on the seat again and clasped her hands in her lap. 'I can promise you there is no danger in what we do, unless of course you include the danger to ourselves. As I've said, what we do is extremely illegal right now, but in the future it will be common practice.'

He studied her pretty face for any sign of deceit and decided; *at least she believes what she's telling me.*

'I'm guessing you don't want to wait for the future,' she said recognising the beginning of acceptance.

Charlie definitely didn't want to wait around, but even though he'd managed to keep his search for a cure a secret from Silvia so far, the mandatory secrecy still concerned him. 'Why are you so concerned about my solicitor and the family?' Charlie asked harping back to earlier.

'Because your solicitor needs to keep the secret just as much as you do; and, sooner or later your wife and brother are going to get suspicious about what you are doing.'

'I think Silvia already is,' Charlie admitted with a degree of gloom.

'You can see my point then.'

She could see he did, but it seemed to her he had enough fire in his belly to handle his wife and brother. Here was a man who wanted out of his chair; at any cost. Just the kind of person they were looking for.

'All right,' Debra said quickly, getting to her feet. 'I think that will do us for tonight. We'll send you an email soon to let you know the next step, but basically it will be to sign the affidavit. Have a careful think . . . Don't proceed if you have any doubts, and be sure to let us know if our dealings are compromised.'

Charlie sensed that his comment about Silvia had slightly rattled his pretty young examiner, but he felt he had somehow passed the first test.

CHAPTER FOUR

If Debra Rowlands had known what was happening at the Pyrmont house in Beacon Hill - during the meeting with her potential client at the hotel - Charlie would never have been considered for the program past this point.

Silvia sat in front of the computer for several minutes before working up the courage to continue. Charlie's behavior over the past few months had been extremely bizarre. She wanted to know why. Was it connected somehow with the long hours spent in the computer room?

'Forgive me, Charlie,' she whispered. 'But I need to know what you're up to.'

She typed in Charlie's password to log on, it was no secret. The computer rejected the password and she typed it in again, carefully. Her fears were realised when it was refused for a second time. This confirmed her husband wanted to keep something secret. With Charlie's bad memory though, he had to have written the new password down. She began searching through the desk draws for a book, a note-pad, or somewhere where he might have recorded it. A little blue book labeled *emails* was a place to start;

. . . Nothing under, P; for password;

'That would have been too easy,' she complained under her breath;

Under, A - all familiar names; B to M - the same ... N - a couple of familiar names and—new; just new, with no explanation.

It was worth a try, Silvia punched in the word and the computer began to log onto Charlie's partition. The old password got her into his emails; there were twenty saved in the 'sent' folder, one of them caught her eye:

nlife@unihope

The message read;

I am interested in finding out more about your university, please send information.
chaspyrmont@bigpond.com.au
Charlie Pyrmont

The received folder was empty.

'My God, Charlie, what-on-earth are you getting yourself into.'

A Google search using the email address got her into the site that Charlie must have discovered. The email address now had a tangible title;

THE UNIVERSITY OF THE NEXT LIFE

She had no idea what it meant until she scrolled down and saw their claim in big bold letters:

IF YOU'VE GIVEN UP HOPE OF A CURE,
CONTACT: nlife@unihope.com

By the time Charlie arrived back home, Silvia had convinced herself not to mention breaking into his emails. He came home the same way he left, in the special vehicle hire car. She heard its arrival and was at the front door to watch him come up the ramp on his motorised chair.

'Everything all right?' he asked as he neared the top.

'I'm fine, how about you; did you enjoy yourself?'

The winding ramp took him seamlessly into the house. 'You sound a bit funny, sweet - are you sure everything is okay?'

'Why wouldn't it be?'

He went past her into the living room and wondered if she somehow knew what he had been up to. He swung the chair around. 'What's wrong then?'

In an effort to cover her real concern, she started fussing over items left lying around on the coffee-table. 'Think about it, Charlie. You give me two minutes notice to say you're going out, and for the past two hours I have no idea where you've been, or who you've been seeing. Not to mention no mobile phone. What if something had happened here, how would I have reached you?'

Charlie could see her point, but wanted to avoid made-up explanations. 'How about we deal with it tomorrow, I'm really tired . . . Do you mind.'

'All right,' she said heading toward the bedroom. 'Your bed is turned. All you have to do is get in it.'

He followed her and she helped him into his PJs . . . Nothing more was said until five minutes after the bed lamp went out.

'Goodnight, Silvia-sweetheart.' He sounded as tired as he'd said, but she wasn't at all happy with him.

'Night,' she responded after a second or two, her voice laden with annoyance.

She lay awake for twenty minutes, but Charlie couldn't sleep at all; his meeting with Debra Rowlands had been strange, raising scores of questions—and concerns—over how far he might be prepared to take things. He looked across at his wife in the dim light and wondered if he could ever bare to be without her, if that's what it came to.

The next day, Silvia decided to invite Charlie's brother over for a chat. Les let himself in the front door with his own key, and found his sister-in-law sitting on the lounge, more worried than ever.

'Hey, what's up?' He'd tried to sound cheery, plainly she was stressed. He took a guess as to why. 'Is he stuck in there again?'

'Sit down for a minute,' she requested quietly.

He put his case on the floor and sat opposite her; wondering what had made her so upset. 'Is Charlie all right?'

She wiped away a developing tear . . . 'Well, I'm not really sure to be honest.'

'Why, what's happened.'

Silvia searched for the words . . . 'Please don't tell Charlie, but I broke into his emails yesterday and I think I've found something that could be a real worry.'

'I had no idea you were so worked up about this.'

'I just had to find out what he's been doing.'

Les was waiting for more. 'And . . . ?'

'*And*, I found an email addressed to some sort of, university.'

'I don't get it. Why's he emailing universities?'

'Don't know. Perhaps I'm being paranoid . . . It's just that, he's been talking about alternative treatments and I'm scared he might do something really stupid.'

'A university shouldn't be a worry, should it?'

'That's if it *is* a university; the email suggests it might not be.'

'How do you mean?'

'Universities list themselves as such; I checked, and this one isn't, yet on their site they call themselves, *The University of the Next Life* - under *Rehab*.'

Les could see she was seriously concerned, and he had to agree the name sounded dubious. 'I'll have a talk with him if you like.'

She shook her head. 'I'd prefer to find out who these people are first. Don't mention anything to Charlie just yet.'

'Well, if that's what you want; shouldn't be too hard, we can just send an email. I'll send it.'

'That might not be such a good idea, at least not from either of us with the Pyrmont name. I'd rather they didn't know we're snooping.'

Les wanted to pull Charlie away from the computer and confront him straight away, but with his sister-in-law so stressed out about the whole thing, he thought it best to do things her way. Les was a few years older than Charlie and some might say not as handsome, in a strange way though they were alike. Les was shorter with less hair and more weight. He had a jovial face and a personality to match. Silvia liked her brother-in-law, because he was always there for them when help and support was most needed.

'Tell you what we'll do,' he said trying to sound positive. 'We'll get an investigator.'

The suggestion came out of left field for her; '*An investigator?* That might be a bit extreme. I don't think I could have Charlie spied on by someone else.'

'It won't be spying; just checking things out for us.' Les knew this wasn't precisely accurate, it was most definitely spying.

Silvia thought for a moment. 'I suppose, if you think they can do that sort of thing.'

'It's what they do, Silvia,' he assured her.

With Charlie close by in the next room, they had already been speaking in a whisper, but finally she lowered her voice even further, as though her echo might magically seep into the walls and be heard later. 'Whatever happens, Charlie must never find out we're doing this,' she told him earnestly.

Les leant back into his chair and measured his sister-in-law's ultimatum.

Hidden away behind the locked door of the home office, Charlie was staring at the monitor as though it were a new age window to the Holy Grail.

The latest email from the University was giving him instructions on what to do next. The last line read:

Contact us when you have taken care of the Affidavit.

CHAPTER FIVE

When Charlie Pyrmont came out of the Grace Building after seeing his family solicitor, he found Debra Rowlands' sleek sports car waiting in the disabled zone. A parking cop stood by watching her suspiciously. Garlanded out in a super tight, sleeveless light green blouse, fawn slacks and black stiletto shoes, she didn't appear the least bit disabled, especially given her completely impractical four and a half foot high sports car. She gave Charlie a warm professional smile as he approached in his wheelchair.

'You don't really expect to get me into that thing do you?' he asked with a chortle.

Taking on a smug expression she pointed a handheld remote at the car, setting in motion a metamorphosis. The wide, low door on the pillion side opened upward, gently coming to rest on the roof. This revealed a floor that was completely flat; ample room for a wheel chair. With a soft whir, the platform moved down, resting level with the pavement.

'Think you can get in now?'

He deliberated on the mechanical transmutation and gave a little twist of his head to show his surprise and approval.

The disappointed parking cop standing nearby, ready to pounce, put his pen back into the infringement book and meandered away, taking one last glance over his shoulder to make sure he hadn't been dreaming.

It was two o'clock in the afternoon, between two peak-hour periods. Debra and Charlie motored out of the city on the freeway—toward the inner suburbs—in traffic that was reasonably light.

'All good?' she asked.

'A little nervous.'

'Don't be. I absolutely promise you'll be made to feel welcome.'

Charlie smiled, but remained silent.

She gave him a quick glance. 'How did your solicitor react to the affidavit?'

'He was curious.'

'Do you believe he'll keep this to himself?'

'He'll have me to answer to if he doesn't.'

'And the Law Institute,' she promised, applying weight to Charlie's conviction. She gave him another quick glance. 'I know it must be hard, comprehending all this secrecy, but once you've seen what we're offering, you'll understand why we have to be so careful.'

'I'm not as worried as you might think, Debra, I'm prepared to do anything to get out of this chair - legal, or otherwise; I don't give a damn.'

'That's why you're here, Charlie. And, call me Deb.'

They made their way through the western suburbs; then wound over the Great Dividing Range, arriving in the foothills an hour later - and high on the mountain in a further half hour. Debra had chitchatted on endlessly, giving Charlie scores of success stories and referring to their intended destination as a property called, *Valley Bells*.

The first thing that he noticed as they entered via the steel gates of the estate was the placement of razor wire atop a high stone fence.

The car slid to a halt at a check point just inside the gate. In the distance he could see a large white house set amongst rolling hills dotted with cattle and sheep.

The security guard came out of a small booth, middle aged, shaved head, and bent to the window to inspect the occupants of the vehicle. 'Hi, Debra,' he said with a cheery familiarity, 'another customer?'

Aware he wasn't just asking for the sake of it, she made the introduction. 'John; this is Charlie Pyrmont.'

He began writing the name down in a little book he'd taken from his jacket. 'That's PYR?' he queried.

'Correct.' Charlie confirmed for her.

'How long you staying Mr. Pyrmont?'

Charlie turned to Debra.

'This is just a warm-up to see if he likes us,' Debra told the guard with a smile.

He let out a wheezed laugh. 'What's not to like.'

Debra grinned at him and prepared to move off. 'All right John, we'd better get on with it . . . Take it easy.'

The man gave Charlie a soft salute. 'You enjoy your visit Mr. Pyrmont.'

The sports car pulled away from the check point, and Charlie automatically saluted back as the man slid from view.

The winding driveway ahead was lined with neat rows of eucalyptus trees, the only sign of horticultural organization. Through the thick white trunks Charlie could see endless rolling hills painted in a soft swaying tapestry of tall autumn grasses, a constant banquet for contented livestock.

At the crest of a hill, the blue bitumen that had taken them three kilometers from the gate, gave way to a ribbon of dirt that looped through clusters of gum trees and out into a wide, gentle valley. In the distance the road reemerged and drew alongside the magnificent Colonial style house he had seen from the gate.

A plume of dust drew away from the front of the building as an exiting vehicle lifted the loose surface.

'Beautiful view,' Debra said with confidence.

'A few months out here might cure anybody,' His attention was on the bellowing trail of dust that was growing in their direction.

'You're about to meet, Benjamin Bright,' Debra informed Charlie as she joined him in his inspection of the approaching vehicle. 'He's the director and part owner of the company that runs the University.'

Charlie made a prediction as she brought the Lam to a standstill, their dust continuing ahead on course. 'I guess this is as far as I go until he gives his approval.'

'No, it's not like that. Benjamin just likes to meet people out here rather than in a stuffy office.'

Charlie was showing his nerves.

'Don't worry, you'll like him; he's kind of a cool guy.'

The car, a royal blue four wheel drive, pulled up near them and momentarily disappeared inside its own dust. Benjamin Bright exited the cloud with his hand already out in search of a hand shake. Dressed in faded, but neat blue jeans and a checkered long sleeved shirt rolled up above the elbow, he rivaled a modern day farmer. He strode across to Charlie's window and poked his arm in to accept his visitor's hand.

'Welcome to Valley Bells, Charlie . . . *Ben*.'

Charlie smiled 'Pleased to be here.'

'Well, we're pleased to have you . . . How about *I* drive you down to the house and explain a bit about the place on the way.'

Debra was already getting out of the Lamborghini to swap cars with Bright. She gave Charlie a petite wave. 'I'll see you down there, Charlie.'

The lanky thirty five year old director swung around the bonnet and gave Debra a passing peck on the cheek as she continued her way across to the other vehicle. Benjamin slid into the low seat beside Charlie and allowed the engine a little growl. 'Better keep these windows closed,' he said as he pressed the button.

Debra dutifully waited for her boss to take up the lead so as not to present him with her dust.

The Lamborghini moved away gently toward the shining mansion with the wrought iron railings.

Benjamin Bright launched into his spiel without so much as a single beat. 'The property is five hundred acres,' he volunteered. 'Apart from the University we run mostly Merino sheep for wool, but we also have a little bit of cattle; purely for breeding. It used to be a hospital, started in 1865 by my great Grandfather. His specialty was fixing broken limbs. The story goes, if he didn't like the way the bone had broken, he'd engage the patients in conversation to distract them while he quickly broke the bone the way he wanted it.'

'Ouch,' Charlie let out with a wince.

'I know, it sounds fairly drastic. But of course he would then reset the break and splint it. I don't think he got much thanks though - not at first.'

'I hope you don't take after your Grandfather,' Charlie joked.

Benjamin grinned. 'Maybe a little, but we fix a whole lot more than broken bones.'

He took a quick glance at his patient and knew from experience what he was wondering. 'I want you to feel relaxed about our program here Charlie. You're going to meet people who will convince you what we do is legitimate. Let me rephrase that; it's legitimate in the sense that its *'real'* - it's just not legal. I understand Debra has explained this to you.'

'Yes she has.'

'Everything we do is done one step at a time; at *any* time, if you feel you want out; you simply pack up and leave.'

Charlie thought of his wife at that moment, and how all of this was going to affect her; assuming he went ahead with it of course.

The car pulled into a covered area at the front of the house, which appeared just as majestic close up. The triple story mansion, with its wide verandahs, was intricately laced with gleaming white wrought iron railings. A small wisp of blue smoke traced a line from one of the half dozen chimney-stacks, fading into a layer of warm air higher in the valley.

A young man dressed in casual slacks and a white tee shirt came down the steps to assist in getting the new arrival out. There wasn't much to do, as usual the door remotely opened and the floor once again descended to the ground, allowing the chair to roll out with ease.

'Jack, I'd like you to meet Charlie,' Ben said as the man shook Charlie's hand.

'Welcome to Valley Bells, Charlie.'

'Charlie is here to look us over. Why don't you take him into Debra's room for now and fix up some refreshments.' Bright placed a friendly palm on Charlie's shoulder. 'I'll meet you there in about half an hour, all right?'

'No worries,' Charlie answered trying to sound as relaxed as possible. Both men could see that he wasn't.

Jack followed Charlie's powered wheelchair up a ramp that was set off to the side of the half dozen steps that led to a grand entrance. Once inside, Charlie could see that the interior of the building was just as impressive as the outside, and faithful to the era. The broad timber stairway which exited the large foyer on the right was unspoiled by ugly ramps; or *motor-tracks* for wheelchairs. The man stopped near an antique hat rack—the type with a seat, presumably for able-bodied people who wanted to sit while they removed or changed their shoes. Along its dozen or so hooks there were well worn hats, an umbrella or two, and some mud covered boots at the base of the bench-seat. From an unperceivable join at its center, the hat rack parted and revealed an elevator.

'That's cute,' Charlie commented.

'All of the mod-cons here.'

'Can we come up in the lift with you?'

Charlie looked over his shoulder toward the shrill voice and saw a small boy and girl, both about seven years of age, smiling with a plea.

Jack waved them on. 'Don't bother Mr. Pyrmont kids.'

'No, please; they can come for a ride, why not.' The two happy children responded to Charlie's invitation by rushing ahead into the lift.

'You might be sorry,' Jack warned him as he followed the chair into the elevator. The door closed and the boy and girl giggled happily.

'What are your names?' Charlie asked, doing his best to avoid playing down to them.

They answered across the top of each other giving priority to their own names.

Jack translated for Charlie. 'Joanne and Brian.'

'Well, my name is, Charlie.'

Joanne went slightly shy and said, 'I thought Jack said your name was Mr. *Pimmont*.'

Charlie couldn't resist laughing at the little girl's logic and at her attempt to pronounce his surname. The door opened on the second floor and the two laughing children ran from the elevator and disappeared into the corridor.

'I didn't know you had children here. Do they belong to patients?'

'Not those two, they're Ben's kids,' Jack told him as they moved away from the elevator. 'There are plenty of other kids here though, some are here permanently with patients - others come in from town. We run a day care center; it works well because the permanents get to meet other kids.'

Jack stopped the chair outside a tall, dark stained timber door. 'Here we are.'

He gave the door a couple of light raps and a moment later it swung open and there was Debra, smiling and welcoming as usual. Joanne and Brian ran down the hall laughing and Brian broke from his shell to call out. '*See ya,* Charlie.'

Debra put on a mock frown. 'I see you've met the terrors,'

The kids stopped to figure out why the adults were laughing—then, deciding they were just plain weird, went running off.

'All right, Mr. Charlie Pyrmont, let's get you started shall we.'

Charlie had a fish-out-of-water smirk on his face. 'You were quick - came up the stairs did you?'

She tittered and said, 'No, I materialised. That's one of the things we do here.'

Her humour got a cackle from Jack as he left them to themselves. Charlie didn't mind, he thought, *humour's a good sign.*

Debra Rowland's quarters was more like an office than a bedroom apartment, the living room boasted a state of the art wide-screen TV with all the surround sound bits and pieces. Against the window stood a large, impressive mahogany desk complete with a penholder that appeared it could be gold-plated. There was an intercom and an old fashioned blotting pad bound in authentic leather. Except for the *mod-cons* as

Jack had called them, the room replicated the mid eighteenth century.

Debra picked up a handful of photos from the desk and handed them to Charlie in his chair. He drank the dregs of a coffee he had been given and began viewing the picture on top.

'That one is, Margaret Simpson. She came to us a year ago; she'd had a stroke and couldn't walk or talk.'

The photo showed a young woman strapped in a wheelchair, presumably unable to even hold herself up in a seated position. She had a nice face with long blond hair. He slipped the top photo to the bottom to reveal a second picture of the same girl lifting herself forward in the chair, as if trying to stand up.

He flicked to the third picture and was presented with an image of her standing with a walking frame, the fourth, with a walking stick, followed by no stick at all, and finally, walking up the stairs at the front of the building, completely unaided and with a wide happy smile.

'Is there a chance I can meet these people?' Charlie requested outright.

'Not yet.' Debra said with equal bluntness. 'We have to be sure you're ready before we consider infringing on their privacy. We will afford you the same courtesy when the time comes.'

Debra dimmed the lights.

Margaret Simpson appeared on the wide-screen TV. . .

She is brought into the foyer in a wheelchair. A voice from behind camera asks:

'Margaret, can you tell us what happened to you?'

It's very apparent that Margaret can't speak . . .

Charlie felt the question had been a bit cruel. He faced Debra, who only insisted—with a point toward the screen—that he continue watching.

The image cuts to another location with Margaret still in the chair.

The same voice again. 'Margaret, can you tell us what happened?'

As before, her face is drooping on the left side, but she manages to speak. '*I ha - ta - stroke - at - werk.*'

'Are you feeling any better since you came to Valley Bells?'

'*Yea - I - I - can - tork - norw.*' Her speech is slurred, but legible.

The location changes; she is now in one of the corridors of the building. 'Margaret, how are you feeling?'

She answers with barely a hint there was ever a problem. 'I feel wonderful thank you doctor, how do I sound?'

'Wonderful, just wonderful . . . Now, show me how strong you have become.'

Margaret pushes herself eagerly to the edge of her wheelchair and uses her arms to lift her weight to a crouched position, then stands upright; albeit a little shaky. The images that follow show Margaret Simpson gaining in strength and capability until finally she is shown walking up the outside stairs.

Her face comes onto the screen.

'If you're watching this and wondering whether to join the University's program, please give yourself the time to absorb the truth of what these people can do for you. I was doubtful at first, and I almost turned away. I'm so glad I didn't. I guess you know we're all asked never to have contact with our families again, once we decide to sign on, it's hard, very hard. But, although our loved ones can never know where, or how we are; we are kept informed of *their* wellbeing at all times. I hope you'll forgive me for using the catch phrase, *this is your life*, but it is - isn't it. Good luck and I hope to meet you soon in person.'

The image fades to black . . .

Debra turned up the lights. Charlie was completely silent; *stunned*. If what he'd just seen was real; then it would be truly amazing. But he still had doubts—big ones.

She could see he was troubled. 'Charlie?'

He cleared his throat. 'Even if it turns out this is *not* some whopping big scam, I'm not sure I can turn my back on Silvia.'

Debra came and sat on a chair next to him. 'Believe me, I totally understand how you feel, everybody goes through the same fear. In the end, if you find you can't do this; you simply walk away. In the year and a half we've been operating, we've only lost one potential participant. Most people, once they realise what we're offering is not fantasy, and that their burden on the family will be removed, they take on the program wholeheartedly. I think you'll be one of those people.'

'I'll need a bit of time,' Charlie told her with a measure of guilt.

Debra went back to the desk, picked up another two photographs and handed them to him. The top photo was a picture of Debra herself, standing beside her beloved sports car, the Lamborghini. The second photo was Debra again, but this time she was strapped into a motorised wheelchair. Charlie couldn't camouflage his surprise.

'You were a patient?'

'I was completely paralysed after a car accident.'

'And they cured you?'

'That's right.'

'I had no idea. How long did this cure take?'

'It took a year. I was the first.'

Charlie wondered if she was making it up.

'You don't seem convinced,' Debra said cautiously, 'How about I show you something that might help.' She dimmed the lights again and a prerecorded excerpt from a local news show appeared on the screen.

The presenter speaks to his audience solemnly.

'We've all heard it a thousand times before—*speed kills*,—but all the constant warnings never seem to curb the increasing death toll on our roads.'

News footage of an accident comes to the screen. Debra Rowland's injured body is being taken from her wrecked car by paramedics.

Debra's voice-over laments from the TV—

'When I came around in hospital, I had no idea what had happened. Once they told me that I was paralysed, I was devastated. I truly wished that I had died in the accident.'

Her image comes onto the screen, sitting in a wheel chair.

'Do you really wish that you had died?' an unseen interviewer asks.

'Yes. I still have my moments, but straight after the accident — absolutely; without a doubt.'

'So, here you are in a wheelchair, presumably for the rest of your life. How are you going to deal with that?'

Debra thinks for a moment; then says. 'Given what has been offered to me in the way of rehabilitation, I really don't think I can.'

'You don't think you can deal with it?' he asked seeking clarity.

'I don't think I *can*.' She confirmed.

'What are you going to do?'

'Honestly. I'm basically looking for a miracle.'

'What sort of miracle?'

Debra looks straight into the camera.

'Scientific, crack pot, I don't care. If someone out there wants to experiment, just let me know, my body is at your disposal—

Like this, I may as well be dead . . .'

Debra froze the image on the TV screen and raised the lights. 'That goes on for another ten minutes, but I just wanted you to see that I'm a real person - show you that I had a real accident. Convince you that I was once paralysed. And now, as you can see for yourself, I'm as good as new.'

Charlie had to admit the TV show went a long way to convincing him that the University might be doing something valid to help people who are permanently paralysed. What that something was, both eluded and fascinated him.

Debra handed him a business card. 'In case you still need more proof, this is the doctor that treated me after the accident, Doctor Walter Heinberg. He's here in

Sydney, so—if you like—you can go and see him for yourself . . . Just one thing though, if you do go, don't mention where I am, or anything about my cure. And, obviously, don't mention this place.'

'I understand,' Charlie said as he took the card.

Debra smiled. 'When you're talking with him I think it might be best if you tell him you're there to get a second opinion about your prognosis. I can give you the name of another doctor if you'd rather not mention your own, up to you.'

'I'll have a think about that, but frankly I can't see a problem mentioning who my doctor is.'

'You're probably right; it comes down to asking if your family might become involved, via your doctor, do you see what I mean?'

'Hmmm.'

She studied his features while he had his head turned away. 'You're a handsome man, Charlie Pyrmont, I imagine you might well turn out to be quite dangerous when you get out of that chair.' She kissed him gently on the cheek and he felt a blush rising.

Attractive Debra Rowlands was already *dangerous*.

Debra answered a knock at the door and let in Benjamin Bright.

'Well, how are you two getting along?' he asked entering the room.

Charlie hadn't missed noticing the fond peck on the cheek the director had given Debra earlier when they first arrived, and wondered if they might be an item.

'I'm not going to hold things up,' Bright promised. 'I know you've got to get back to the *smoke*. I just need you to sign this for me.'

Bright handed a form attached to a clipboard for Charlie to read. 'It's nothing sinister, just a disclosure stating you won't repeat anything that you've seen or heard here today.'

Charlie ran a quick eye over the one page disclosure document and signed it with the pen provided.

'All right, I'm out of here,' Bright said holding out his hand. 'Charlie, I hope you decide to join us; Good luck.' After the hand shake Benjamin Bright scooped up the clipboard and left as quickly as he had come in.

Debra raised her eyebrows and said, 'Let's get you back to your wife.'

CHAPTER SIX

Josey studied the vehicle moving away from the colonial homestead through his binoculars. He knew the yellow sports car was carrying the man he had been hired to watch, and the black haired bombshell he had already identified as Debra Rowlands, thanks to a reliable informant at Transport. His primary objective at this point was to remain undetected. With this in mind he put away the glasses and started up his engine in preparation to move off at the right moment. The direction they would be taking back to the city was preordained. He waited until after the security guard had cleared and waved them on toward the iron-gate, then timed his entry onto the bitumen so as to place his vehicle a few car lengths ahead of theirs. He watched in his mirror to make sure they were following; fully expecting this would be a simple jaunt back to the subject's home in time to prevent the good wife from becoming more suspicious than she already was.

The single lane highway prevented Rowlands from passing for the next 20 kilometers, which would allow him to keep them in check without appearing to do so.

'Call Les Pyrmont,' he instructed his sleeping phone.

Les answered after a couple of rings.

'Hi, it's me . . . Right, here's what I've got. He's just spent the last two hours the other side of Katoomba at a place called, Valley Bells. Ever heard of it?'

'No. Is it a town?'

'It's a house—and then some; a colonial mansion more like it. It's laid out on a massive property that appears to run sheep and cattle as far as I can tell.'

'Do you think this place is the University?'

'There are no signs suggesting that, in fact the house itself seems to be operating as a kid's daycare center.'

'That makes no sense.'

'It's like Fort Knox to be honest; the whole joint is surrounded by a solid stone wall laced at the top with razor wire. I had to make my observations from a high point away from guards at the main gate.'

'Sounds like overkill—for a daycare center.'

'I would have thought so.'

'What are the chances of getting in to talk to these people?'

'It may be a wee bit early for that; I did do a little searching on the net though. Apparently it's a family estate that's been operating here since eighteen thirty five. Originally the estate covered one hundred and fifty thousand acres; today it's two hundred hectares with a post office, kindergarten, community hall and a non-denominational church. Not to mention about fifty houses spread out over the whole area.'

'A cult could disappear into a community like that and never be realised.'

'Like I said, it's too early to tell, but be patient, we'll get there.'

'So we're none the wiser at this point.'

'On the contrary, we now know for sure he's not telling the truth about where he goes each day. That's a start.'

Josey decided on mentioning the Lamborghini and the dolled-up woman, but told Ies not to say anything about the driver to Silvia . . . 'The less she knows on that score the better, believe me.'

'Why would they consider using a Lamborghini to carry people around in wheel chairs?'

'Odd I know.'

'It must be a damned tight fit.'

'Well, it fits,' Josey assured him.

'Very strange . . . All right, thanks, Josey. Keep in touch.'

'Will do—Bye.' The line disconnected.

Josey continued to lead the way along the Bells Line of Road to the other side of the mountain range, where link roads took him to the M4, which then provided motorists with a high speed trip the rest of the way to the inner suburbs and the City. Today, Josey's car was an old gray Ford and very forgettable—just the way he liked it. If he had to follow Debra Rowlands again, it would be aboard another equally unmemorable vehicle from his favorite auto pool, *Rent a Bomb*. When his subject's car passed him on the freeway it was a simple matter to keep up with the rest of the traffic, not even sleek sports cars could ignore the revenue-gathering-mobile-cameras that traversed the 30 kilometer stretch.

Just after the toll gates, the detective momentarily lost sight of the car as traffic jockeyed for a position on the narrowing roadway. The red light that then caught him wasn't a real big help in keeping up, but the stark yellow paint job on the sports car was, they were going in the direction expected. A few minutes later he was back on their tail and saw them make a turn he didn't expect.

'What the hell are you up to now, Charlie *Brown*?' he mumbled to himself.

The yellow sports had turned further north, not the way to Beacon Hill. Ten kilometres later his subject's vehicle pulled up outside a two story building set between rows of quaint suburban shops. The driver made no attempt to get out.

As usual, the pillion door gawped opened like a huge metallic mouth, clearing the way for the disabled passenger to alight in his chair without assistance. Charlie turned and waved with a smile at his chauffeur and the car drove away, watched on by several intrigued rubber necks.

'That was a nice friendly smile,' Josey said aloud, talking to himself again; this was something he'd suddenly started doing while on cases unaided—after *Fredie* died.

Fredie was a long-term partner who had been killed on the job. Josey chose to entertain the belief he was talking to his dead partner, and not just himself.

Charlie powered his wheelchair along the pavement for a block before turning left into the next street.

The detective followed in his car, pretending to look for a parking space, thinking he'd take one if it became available.

Charlie was obviously trying to find an address.

Finally, he stopped at an office block; its marble clad entrance supporting a bold silver 46. After Charlie had gone into the building, Josey found parking near to the entrance.

The building had an elevator in the marble clad foyer with companies listed on four floors. Josey scanned the list of names to try and figure out who Charlie might be visiting. There were a couple of GPs, a dentist, and a chiropractor. 'Here we are,' Josey breathed as though finding the final answer on a crossword puzzle.

He called up Charlie's brother. 'Me again; would you happen to know the name of Charlie's Neurologist?' He listened. 'What about a Neurologist by the name of Doctor Walter Heinberg?'

From his flat, Les thought about it for a moment but couldn't recall the name. 'Not as far as I know, I can check with Silvia.'

'That's fine, leave it with me for now; we'll speak again when I know more.'

Charlie waited while the doctor scrolled down Debra Rowlands' file.

'You do realize I can't divulge any part of Debra's medical file,' he said without taking his eyes from the computer. 'I gather you're just after confirmation that I treated her, is that right?'

'If that's okay'

He advanced slowly through a couple of pages as if biding his time . . . 'She suddenly stopped seeing me about six months ago. It was quite strange really; she had an appointment, but just didn't show up. I never heard from her again.'

'Well, she did seem very impressed with the way you looked after her,' Charlie said off the top of his head. 'And, it was her suggestion I come to see you.'

'Did she say anything to you about why she left? Seeing another doctor perhaps?'

'I can't say, I don't really know her all that well actually, we've only just met.' Charlie felt adding a truth to a lie made the lie easier to tell.

Heinberg wanted to find out more about his old patient, Debra, but suddenly refocused on Charlie. 'At the moment you're seeing, Doctor Bramton?'

'Correct.'

'Is there a problem?'

'With the doctor — no, not at all,' Charlie answered truthfully. 'I'm just after a second opinion.'

'Well, Mathew Bramton is an extremely competent Neurologist; I'm probably not able to tell you any more than he has. I have to agree with him, your lower body paralysis seems quite irreversible. Same with Debra as you may already know.'

Charlie had to restrain himself from a strong desire to inform the doctor he was completely wrong, and that Debra Rowlands had in fact been undeniably cured.

Based on the blank expression, the doctor assumed Charlie was having difficulty with acceptance. 'I know someone you can talk to if you like.'

Charlie truly wanted to tell him the whole thing, but knew it wasn't an option without divulging the secret he was asked to keep. With each new revelation that moved him toward entering the University, the trust that they had placed in him became more and more important to nurture. 'I already have a psychiatrist if that's what you mean,' he said doing his best to remove any hint of annoyance.

The doctor seemed to completely lose track of the conversation at that point and began tapping his fingers on the desk. Charlie let it go.

'Excuse me.'

The receptionist looked up to see Cameron Josey standing at the desk. 'Hello, can I help you?'

'Hi, would it be all right if I leave a message for, Charlie Pyrmont.'

She baulked before saying, 'He shouldn't be too long - if you'd like to wait.'

'Actually I'm double parked. After he's done seeing Dr. Heinberg,' he said testing to see if he had the right doctor, 'could you please ask him to wait in the foyer downstairs, I'll meet him after I've parked the car.'

'No problem, I'll tell him.' She dutifully reached for a pen. 'Could I have your name?'

Cameron was already hurrying out the door. He gave the bemused receptionist an apologetic smile.

'Right,' the doctor said closing Debra's file. 'You've seen Debra lately I take it, how is she?'

'She's doing exceptionally well.'

Given that Charlie admitted hardly knowing the girl, his answer was a little brighter than expected, leaving Heinberg wondering why the sudden enthusiasm.

'I'll tell her you asked,' Charlie told him with a hint of smugness.

Dr. Heinberg didn't quite know what to make of Charlie Pyrmont, something in his tone and manner suggested there might be some sort of hidden agenda behind his visit, but he was too busy to ponder it for very long. 'Good luck,' he said standing to usher Charlie from the room.

'There's a message from your driver Mr. Pyrmont,' the receptionist announced as Charlie wheeled toward the desk. 'The man said to wait for him in the main foyer downstairs.'

Charlie was confused. 'Are you sure it was a man?'

The girl's indignant expression suggested she usually had no trouble distinguishing a man from a woman. 'A man, yes - and he left no name.'

Charlie waited in the foyer as he had been asked to do, but soon decided the message must have been a mistake, perhaps meant for someone else. He wheeled around the corner and as expected found the yellow sports car waiting.

Debra stepped out as the door began opening to receive the wheelchair. 'You seem out-of-sorts, did everything go all right?'

Charlie decided not to mention the mysterious *other driver* because he didn't want her thinking he was losing grip on reality, not when he was this close to being accepted into the program. 'Dr. Heinberg sends you his regards,' he decided on saying.

She raised her eyebrows. 'Convinced now?'

Charlie motored into the vehicle, and began locking the chair into place as Debra slid into the driver's seat.

'Well?' she asked, still waiting for an answer.

Charlie's lips slowly curved into a mischievous grin, and he excitedly told her, 'Debra Rowlands, you've won me.'

She appeared to be as pleased for herself as she was for him. 'Great.'

He added, 'The sooner we get started the better I'll like it.'

She started the engine and gave it a rev. 'I know you're excited Charlie, but we still have to take this one step at a time. I'll contact you in a couple of days and explain what happens from here-on-out.'

'I want you to know right now, the money is no object.'

'There are a few other things to discuss before we get down to money. Right now I'd better get you back to the limo.'

The sports car pulled out from the curb and did a U-turn toward the city.

Cameron was on the phone in his car. 'They've just left the surgery.'

Les's voice crackled from the speaker. 'And still with that woman I take it, what's her name?'

'Debra Rowlands.'

'So who is, Debra Rowlands?'

'I assume she works for the University; a bit of a *looker*, like I said'

'It's all very bizarre,' Les admitted with a trace of worry in his voice.

'Let's not get too concerned just yet; the whole thing might have a perfectly simple explanation.'

'I wish I could believe that, for Silvia's sake.'

Josey thought for a moment. Finally he said. 'I hear you. Let's just wait and see what happens.'

'Okay, what's next?'

'I'll run a check on this Dr. Heinberg—make sure he's not part of it—and, I need to find out more about Debra Rowlands. All I want you to do is keep an eye on things at home, find an excuse to stay over and give me a call if he hasn't arrived in an hour.'

'*Righto.*'

'Thank you Les, talk later.' Cameron disconnected the call and made some notes in his little red book. 'Not a bad sort of day, Fredie,' he told his disembodied partner.

CHAPTER SEVEN

The kettle hissed and howled on the stove, summoning Silvia to the kitchen to make the tea. Les appeared at the doorway 'and watched her as she prepared the brew.

'I spoke with Josey, he might be right about there being an explanation for all this,' he suggested.

She handed him his tea. 'Who's paying for all these trips in the limo? No money has come out of our account.'

They walked back into the living room and sat opposite each other at the coffee table.

'Perhaps that comes later.'

She took a sip of tea and he saw her hand was shaking.

'Why is he lying to us?' she asked, at the same time realising her brother-in-law wouldn't have a clue, and accepting his silence . . . 'Can we trust this private detective of yours?' she asked finally.

'He did well by me—you know—with Rebecca and baby Molly.'

Silvia's forehead creased with the memory of Les's divorce from Rebecca, less than a year ago. 'I'll never understand what happened between you two.'

His subdued smile suggested there may be more to the separation from his wife than dare be told; she let the subject slide.

The limousine dropped Charlie off outside his house in Beacon Hill, and he drove his wheelchair up the ramps that wound their way through the well-kept gardens. Les opened the door for him as he reached the top.

'To what do I owe this honor?' Charlie chirped in high spirits.

Les knew it wasn't a visit from his brother that had put him in such a good mood, but rather his little excursion to the mountains with Debra Rowlands. 'You look like you've had a good day.'

'You could say that,' Charlie agreed while making his way into the living room.

Silvia had gone back to the kitchen and was making the mandatory cup of tea for Charlie. He swung into the room and stopped right next to her, trying to evoke a warm welcome. 'How's my girl?'

She didn't make eye contact. 'You're *girl* is fine. Did you have a nice day?'

'Well yes I did,' he said bringing his mood down to meet hers.

Silvia walked toward the living room with the hot cup. 'Come and drink your tea; Les wants to talk to you.'

Charlie wheeled into the living room and sensed the unease. 'This looks ominous,' he observed trying to make light of it. His brother was a complete statue. His wife, sipped at her tea as if in another world. Panning from one to the other he asked, 'Is someone going to talk to me?'

She letup on the tea and put her cup down, meeting his eyes as though trying to read his mind. 'Were you at the stroke club all day today?' she asked afraid of the lie he might tell.

Charlie wondered if they knew what he'd been doing, and about the woman, but decided to test the waters. 'Where else would I be?'

'You were seen at Katoomba around lunchtime,' Les piped up.

Charlie responded with sudden annoyance. 'Excuse me; am I being spied on now . . . What the hell's this got to do with you anyway?'

'Don't get upset Charlie, I'm just trying to help Silvia.'

'What makes you think Silvia needs help?'

'She's worried about you.' Les was doing his best to keep calm.

'Don't try and make out there's some problem here, Les. Silvia and I are just fine, and I'll thank you to keep out of it.'

Les could see his brother was behaving as though trapped in a corner–so he held his tongue.

Charlie wasn't about to let up. 'We're nothing like *you* and your *x-wife* mate. Silvia and I don't play around.'

'Shut-up Charlie,' she snapped.

He came straight back at her on the top of his voice. '*Les-o* here is no, mister innocent.'

Silvia stood up and pushed Charlie's chair aside. 'If you utter one more stupid word about your brother like that, chair or no chair I'll push you on your head.' She quickly ran into the bedroom before the anger could turn to tears.

Les felt awkward and unwelcome under his brother's enraged stare, for Silvia's sake he wasn't about to push the issue any further.

'I'd like you to leave now Les,' he was told with steely calm . . . 'Just keep one thing in mind will you, whatever you *think* might be going on—it's none of your business; it's between Sil and me'

Les desperately wanted to leave, as suggested. *How do I argue with the emotions of a man trapped in a wheel chair?* He got up and walked toward the door.

'Les,' Charlie said in such a controlled voice that it effectively impelled his brother to turn and face him. 'There may come a time when it does become your business, and when and if that time comes - I hope you might watch after her for me.'

Les had no idea what Charlie meant, but there was something in the statement that suggested his brother might indeed be backed into some sort of corner, and—for whatever reason—didn't want his family to worry about it. He opened his mouth to say something, but Charlie held up a hand to prevent it. 'Just leave it like that mate.'

Les could see that there was no point in pursuing the matter. He left the house that night very confused about all that he'd seen and heard during the course of this very strange day.

CHAPTER EIGHT

Charlie continued to attend the meetings at Valley Bells over the next fortnight, learning more about the organisation and what would be expected of him if he were to decide on going ahead. That decision would have to be made soon and he would have lied by denying any concern about the strict conditions. Debra Rowlands was his constant companion at these meetings and he was thankful for her support; just knowing that she had been through all this herself, and knowing that she had been miraculously cured of paralysis, gave him the courage and conviction to get past these first steps. Actually though, Charlie found the meetings to be informal and relaxed anyway, a feeling shared by a dozen other prospective customers who had shown up with varying degrees of disability.

Each newcomer had been assigned with their own individual mentor, people who were probably just like Debra Rowlands. He didn't know too much about their specific circumstances, in fact he'd been asked to respect their privacy by not asking questions. The first thing that the group learned from one of the speakers, who referred to himself as, *The Unit Manager*, was . . .

'These meetings are purely a curtain raiser, a way to make sure each and every one of you understands fully - what you're getting yourself into. If in the end you are accepted—and you do decide to stay—it will not be easy. And, I particularly draw your attention to your families; they may suffer even more than yourselves.'

Charlie decided that the warnings embedded in the induction were centered on early detection of anyone who might be having reservations, even small ones. Each and every person had already signed their affidavits pledging never to divulge anything that was said, seen, or done in relation to The-University-of-the-Next-Life. This particularly applied to those who wouldn't make it through into the program, those who—it would be decided—were too great a risk.

Charlie was surprised at how few misgivings he had, other than the impending separation from his wife. If not for the *Miracle* performed on Debra Rowlands, and presumably the other mentors – it wasn't difficult to understand that the University's claim—to be able to cure-the-incurable—might seem too good to be true.

He imagined the other hopefuls must have all been shown the same undeniable proof of the extraordinary claim; otherwise they wouldn't have remained, and wouldn't be so eagerly awaiting the outcome. It seems they all expected nothing less than an introduction to a technology that would no doubt turn out to be a complete revelation—a revelation that could not be revealed to the outside world — *At least, not yet*.

As far as Charlie could tell, there appeared to be only one room at Valley Bells where these inaugurations took place, and that was in an annex behind the main building. On the mansion's second floor, the University catered for all tastes in food, all paid for by their hosts—for the moment. The newcomers invariably drifted into social groups to discuss what they had been hearing from the various speakers.

Charlie took a particular shine to an unfortunate young man by the name of *Mitchell*, who had fallen from a train and severed his spinal cord. Paralysed from the neck down, the 18-year-old wasn't able to eat without assistance from his mentor, a plump, jolly middle aged woman called, *Cheryl*, who seemed never to stop laughing.

Charlie's mentor, Debra, always dutifully joined this small band at meal time in the restaurant and was thankful for Charlie's good taste in food.

It had been on the second day of the induction that young Mitchell and his bemused mentor had been rescued by Charlie from eating chips and hamburgers. 'Excellent Burgers' Mitchell had told his rescuer at the time. Charlie didn't believe that for a minute. He took them off for a feed of lobster and a glass of wine, where patrons were obliged to pay a percentage of the cost.

That was two weeks ago, and they had now become welcome regulars at Charlie's expense.

'What Religion are you, Charlie?' Mitchell asked over a meal one day.

Cheryl wheezed out a reprimanding chuckle. 'I don't see that's got anything to do with you, you cheeky bugger . . . You know the rules,' she reminded him.

Debra gave Mitchell a look that was completely void of humor, and Charlie felt the need to come to his rescue.

'That's fine,' Charlie assured Cheryl. He sipped his wine and took his time answering Mitchell's question, intrigued by why the boy might need to know . . . 'I'm Catholic,' he said sucking on the wine's aftertaste.

Mitchell swallowed the food Cheryl had just put in his mouth. 'I used to be Catholic.'

Cheryl's face lit up with mirth. 'Is that right, so what are you now?'

Confusion swept onto the kid's face. 'How do you mean?'

She was enjoying herself. 'You're not Catholic you say; . . . what are you?'

With a sheepish grin, he suddenly understood her meaning. 'I'm still Catholic; I just don't go to church.'

Cheryl's bosom bounced up and down as she let out a laugh.

'What made you ask?' Charlie said with due respect, ignoring the funny side.

The kid shrugged.

Charlie eyed him blankly; certain there must be more to it.

'Well, you know,' was the stilted reply after an uncertain pause, 'they tell us people who go to church, if they join the University - that's all over with; right?'

Charlie wondered what answer Debra might have to the kid's question.

She offered a professional reassuring smile. 'We're not saying that . . . If you need to go to church, you can; we have a nondenominational church on the estate and everyone is welcome.'

'What if that's not good enough for say someone like Charlie?'

Debra made eye contact with Pyrmont to see if he appeared to have a better idea where the question was leading, but his eyes were noncommittal, so she said, 'I can't speak for Charlie.'

Charlie knew where the question was leading. 'He means because I'm Catholic.'

'It goes without saying, we have nothing against any religion; we simply cater for *all* with just one church. If you join us, you'll see that we still encourage people to pray. Let's face it, who needs prayer more than you people?'

Charlie lifted his glass in a toast. 'I'll drink to that.'

Debra could see that nothing was going to stand in the way of Charlie Pyrmont.

As usual—after the day's meeting—Debra set out to drive her subject back from the mountains to the Menzies Hotel, where he would connect with the hire car service. Charlie was mulling over all the conditions that he would have to agree to if he was ever to be accepted. He'd already worked out that young Mitchell might be one of those rejected.

'You're very quiet.'

Charlie broke away from his thoughts. 'I was just thinking about that young bloke, Mitchell.'

'You worried about something?'

'It's just that whole thing today about religion. I think he might be the one with the *hang-ups*, he just didn't want to let on.'

'That's very perceptive, Charlie - and your right, but that's not the only reason we're rejecting him.'

Charlie couldn't help wondering if his own niggling concerns for his wife had already been recognised, thereby precluding him from entering the University as well.

'Don't look so worried,' she said as if reading his mind. 'As far as I'm concerned, you're in.'

Charlie tried to forcibly coerce the feeling of relief, but couldn't honestly convince himself that he was.

'We'd really like to help Mitchell, but he's got some really big issues with his family. Plus, we found out he's on probation.'

'*Probation*,' Charlie repeated in surprise. 'Why, what'd he do?'

'Apparently he'd been mixed up with a bad bunch, getting into drugs in a big way - heroin no less. The story goes he trod on some pretty heavy toes and somehow made a target of himself.'

'He didn't just *fall* from that train, right?'

'Right; it seems he pushed someone else first,' she explained with a sigh. 'Then he was pushed himself in retaliation. Mitchell's no angel.'

Charlie couldn't help feeling saddened by the young man's predicament. 'That's very disappointing. I don't know what to say.'

She could see how upset he was. 'We just can't risk bringing anyone in who might attract attention from the law, as you can imagine. I'm afraid he's out . . . I'm sorry, Charlie.'

'It's a hell of a waste,' he said in frustration.

Debra took the car past the turn leading to the hotel and parked at the edge of the harbour. Charlie didn't question this because he knew the need for decisions was getting close and he figured the time had arrived. She slid the hard top down to let in the sounds and smells of the busy quay. A subtle hum drifted in around them on a sweet, salty breeze. The north-side lights danced on the soft black tarmac that held the multitude of ferries and water taxis in buoyancy; their passage traced by dim, foaming trails. This seemed to Charlie like as good a time and place as any to be making life changing decisions.

'We've been very impressed with you, Charlie. I think you must realise we want you to join us. Now, here comes the big question . . . How do you feel about us?'

Charlie had decided from the outset that he wanted this more than anything else in life. The time had come to commit. 'I've told you, Debra, I'm prepared to move forward. I'll do whatever you ask me to do.'

Debra studied his face for any signs of wavering. Although his unyielding expression was one of complete commitment, she still had to test one thing more; something she knew would be hard for him.

'What about divorce?' she asked bluntly.

This new question dragged the growing emptiness over leaving his wife into a chasm of sheer despair. Excluding Silvia from his life was bad enough, but for some reason divorce had not entered his head. On top of everything else, he felt pangs of guilt over what he'd said about his *brother's* divorce.

'I don't understand. Why would you want me to do that?'

Debra knew that this would eat deep into Charlie's soul; all the research had shown he had a very good marriage.

'I left this till last,' she told him sympathetically, 'because I know how much you love Silvia, how hard it'll be for you to leave her. When you think about it though, divorce is the only thing that makes any sense. Once you enter the University, Silvia will effectively be left on her own anyway.

'The day that you don't return home will be the beginning-of-the-end of your marriage. In the years to come she will need to be free of any legal ties with you - perhaps free to even remarry.'

Charlie felt the confidence to-commit drain from his body as though it were his very blood. Debra sat back in her seat and gave him all the time he needed to absorb the final reality of his joining the University. His mind flooded with all the reasons not to accept this latest condition, the good memories of his marriage to Silvia devouring his very being.

Although there was a place inside him where guilt pointed the finger at selfishness, deep down he knew his decision would give his sweet wife the freedom she deserved.

'How long have I got before this needs to happen?' he finally asked.

Debra turned to face him—secretly relieved at the possibility he might be passing over the latest hurdle. 'Not much more than a couple of weeks, Charlie,' she told him as his eyes moistened. 'You'd better be sure, because once you file for divorce - it will be the point at which there is no return.'

Debra understood the emotional tug of war that Charlie was experiencing would continue for a good deal of time to come, but, she and her colleagues had recognised in him the kind of hunger needed to carry him through the entire program to its definitive end, aspects of which were still cloaked in secrecy. Charlie Pyrmont could never have comprehended, or possibly even guessed the University's real agenda, and where the decision to join the University of the Next Life was going to take him.

Cameron Josey sat behind the wheel of his car and fired off a few shots of Debra and Charlie's harbour-side rendezvous.

CHAPTER NINE

Valley Bells basked in the bright Autumn sun, its cold light casting dark shadows into the historic building's innermost crevices. Daycare children ran about the manicured lawns surrounding the colonial mansion under the watchful eye of *Minders*, dotted about like beacons in their bright yellow tops. Still acclimatised to the hot Australian summer months, mums-and-dads, who were engaged in animated conversation, huddled in warmer places away from the chill of a breeze that barely touched 19 degrees Celsius.

On the upstairs verandahs behind the ornate salt white railings, several people bound to wheelchairs gathered as they normally did to collect the warmth. It was Sunday, the traditional day to attend church and *reflect on one's sins*. The pathway that led from the mansion to the little timber church was dotted with able and disabled alike, making their way toward the peel of a bell that sent its invitation out as far away as the distant hills, where cattle ate and ignored the familiar sound. Perhaps these carefree beasts believed the humans were going to this quaint building to be *milked*, after all, it was the sound of a bell that brought them to their own milking sheds.

Charlie sat with the rest of the chair-brigade on the verandah, next to an elderly man who appeared to have no appreciable movement in his body, other than a slight turn of the head—which he strained to make in Charlie's direction.

He spoke loudly, presumably suffering a degree of deafness. 'It was a stroke you say you had—how long ago?'

'Oh, about eight months,' Charlie told him without embellishment.

The old gentleman made a noise that sounded like a grunt, as he painfully relaxed his head back into the chair, whereupon he commenced a lengthy study of the plant-like-moldings in the wrought iron balustrade. Recharged, he spoke again. 'I've never been inside a Church you know . . . I'm what you might call a heathen.' And then he let out a laugh.

Charlie tried to avoid condemnation. 'You obviously don't have a need.'

The man's head turned in his direction again. 'What I *really* need is a *frigin* miracle.'

He waved feebly at the people using the pathway to the Church. 'Don't see myself getting it up there.' He fell quiet, losing himself somewhere in a lifetime of confused thoughts.

'Charlie Pyrmont.' The familiar voice came from the doorway leading into the community room behind him. He swung the chair around to face *Wheelchair Jack*, as he had become known, striding toward him like a footballer entering the field of play. 'It seems you're to meet our *Dr. Gallard* today.'

'I'm game if you are,' he replied as positively as possible.

As the assistant pushed Charlie away in the chair the old guy wheezed out a laugh, amused by some private joke that had suddenly sprung-to-mind.

Jack took Charlie down in the elevator to the ground floor. Debra was there smiling a greeting as the doors parted. 'You ready for this, Charlie?' she asked.

'I better be,'

'Come on—let's get you started.'

Jack and Debra brought Charlie to the tiny waiting area that led into Dr. Gallard's rooms.

'All right thank you, Jack,' she said giving the orderly his leave.

'No problem. See-you, Charlie—good luck.'

He couldn't help watching Jack's springy walk and wished he could emulate it; *perhaps soon,* he thought.

Sitting on one of three other wheelchairs in the room was a man who was reading a magazine, who looked up and gave Ms. Rowlands a knowing smile as she came in. 'Got another victim for the shrink?'

'Charlie, this is Thomas,' she said narrowing her eyes. 'He fancies himself a bit of a comedian.'

Thomas threw down the magazine and wheeled over for a hand shake.

'Be nice,' she warned. 'Don't go scaring off our new customer.'

He gave her a cheeky grin. 'I'll leave that to the *Doc'*.'

Debra bit her tongue and smirked, giving him a shrewd look.

Both men watched her feminine sway as she left the room. 'A hell of a sexy woman our Debra,' Thomas said echoing the thoughts he knew his male friend was having.

Charlie slipped into the mandatory gender repartee. 'No argument from me.'

Thomas was studying Charlie as though trying to make a quick assessment. 'You married?'

A day ago his answer would have been a quick *yes*, but now he had to think about it. 'For the moment it seems.'

'They've already hit you with the *D-word* I see. Don't worry, it's hard at first but time heals all wounds as they say. Occasionally people get cold feet coming here. Some can't go through with it in the end – the ones still in love; they're the people most likely to fail.'

Charlie felt a knot tighten in the pit of his stomach. *That person is me,* he thought to himself.

The man saw the concern. 'But, I've seen it go the other way too; love can bring about sacrifice as well.'

'Is that how it was for you?' Charlie wanted to know. 'Still in love – when you first came in here?'

'I did have a love once, a long time ago – Cathy. She came down with an aggressive breast cancer and passed away just a few months before we planned to marry.'

'I'm very sorry to hear that,' Charlie told him with the utmost sincerity.

'I wasn't in the chair back then.' He slapped his knees to draw attention to the reason he was wheel bound. 'This, I inflicted on myself – I was hitting the grog pretty hard – Crashed my car blind drunk.

Cathy's death was only a month before. Her sudden death really knocked me for a six. I missed her big time – still do. But, the accident was my fault.'

Charlie clung to diplomacy. 'We all contribute to our own demise; one way or another.'

Thomas smiled absently. 'It was a long time ago; yet she never leaves my mind. How do you think *you'll* go?'

'Sorry?'

'Will you get over not seeing your wife again?'

Now understanding, Charlie's worry swelled onto his face.

'I can see it's not going to be easy for you,' Thomas said with a concerned frown.

Charlie hated that his emotions might eventually spoil his chances of being accepted into the program. He reached out for a fundamental lifesaver. 'Like you said, time's the answer.'

'Yes,' Thomas agreed. 'But there's something else they do here that comes completely unexpected, and much more immediate.'

Charlie couldn't fathom what his informant was driving at.

'Have you ever been hypnotised?'

The question came out of the blue and seemed unconnected. 'Why do you ask that?'

'Because that's how they help you get over things.'

'I'm not with you.'

'Dr. Gallard, he uses hypnotism to relax people, get them outside of their own heads.'

Charlie could see how hypnotism might be misused in a place like Valley Bells. He began to wonder if his new found friend might himself already be under the influence of Dr. Gallard's hypnotic powers; perhaps the reason his pain has subsided.

'Don't worry, he won't take your memories away, it's just a way of helping you accept your situation early on. After a while you won't need it.'

'Can I ask you a question?'

'Go ahead.'

'How long have you been here?'

Thomas had been expecting this question, but not so soon. He turned his chair and wheeled to the other side of the room. 'I've got a confession to make,' he told Charlie with his back turned. 'I've been here six years, but not as a patient.'

Charlie watched him push from his wheelchair with ease and turn around to stand as steady as a post.

Another miracle?

'I'm sorry to deceive you like this, but I'm the man you've come to see, Dr. Gallard.'

Charlie couldn't help wondering what sort of game was being played. 'What's this all about?' he asked, his question more of a command than a request.

'Forgive me, it's just a little trick I use to relax people into our first meeting, I hope I haven't upset you.'

Charlie wanted to shake the suspicion that perhaps Gallard had already begun his hypnotic work . . . 'No, that's fine,' Charlie said awkwardly, still a little rattled by the deliberate deceit.

'Are you happy to continue then?'

'I've come this far.'

Dr. Gallard smiled and led Charlie out of the waiting room. 'You know, Charlie, I think you've got what it takes to make it through this.'

They entered a large room that was more like the private library of an eminent university professor than a doctor's surgery. The walls were covered from floor to ceiling in dark timber shelves loaded with volumes of thick technical books. A mahogany desk sat at one end in front of a large window that took in a view across the back of the estate. At the other end of the room a large screen hung from the ceiling awaiting images that might spit from a suspended projector a short distance in front of it. The chairs around the desk were in deep red leather—obviously the room invited people other than those in wheelchairs.

Dr. Gallard wheeled Charlie beyond the desk and out through a wide doorway leading onto a private deck overlooking rolling grasslands. Beyond this undulating green carpet, the Great Dividing Mountain Range was cloaked by the blue veil of eucalyptus oil and distance.

'Quite an office you've got,' Charlie observed.

The doctor stepped back inside, leaving Charlie to take in the view. His voice took on an echo. 'I like to call it my studio - I'm ordering coffee, would you like something?'

'Coffee, black; thanks.'

Charlie's eyes wandered over the countryside as the voice behind him summoned the kitchen staff to bring up the hot drinks.

With the morning tea ordered, his host came back outside and sat on a woven cane chair next to Charlie. He rubbed his chin thoughtfully, a gesture that seemed designed to cushion him into a beginning . . .

'You might have guessed we ask a lot of questions,' he suggested with a warm smirk. 'We do this because we need to understand where our patients are coming from. Debra tells me your mind is made up.' He raised his thumb. 'That's good for me.'

Charlie looked away.

Gallard seized the opportunity to study Charlie's strong young features, a complete contrast to the prison the rest of his body was in. *A good subject*, he immediately decided. 'What would you say if I told you some of what you will hear from me, over the next few months, will not always be exactly the truth?'

Charlie was genuinely alarmed by the suggestion of further deceit, but he was also surprised Gallard would voluntarily draw attention to it. 'I'd say it doesn't seem like a real good way to convince me to stay.'

'And you're probably wondering why I'm throwing up a negative so early.'

'You could say that - Why are you?'

'Trust me when I tell you this deliberate ploy is all part of the wonderful journey you're about to go on. To make you understand nothing is what it seems'

Charlie swallowed hard on a dry throat. 'Is your car accident not what it seems?'

'No, that story is true. I was cured, just like Debra. My cure led to my staying here to work. Don't let the studio fool you—actually I could make a lot more money on the outside—this whole place is owned by, Bright.'

'Did he get his money from people like me?' Charlie asked bluntly.

'Actually he puts his money *into* people like you.' He turned toward the grass covered hills. 'The Bright family go back a very long way on this place, their considerable fortune was amassed in agriculture and cattle; and surprisingly, in vineyards. Old man Bright died just last year, leaving Benjamin, his only offspring, to carry on the business.'

'How did he die?'

Gallard turned and faced him. 'He died of too-many-years,' he said pleased with his own turn of phrase, 'a hundred and six of them.'

Impressed, Charlie blew out a gentle whistle . . . 'A good innings.'

'*Good innings* is the best we could do for the old guy,' Gallard told him, seizing on the sentiment. 'But I'll tell you more about that later.'

Charlie was certainly hoping a good innings was something they could achieve for him; an innings that would be spent as an able-bodied man.

Gallard stood and moved to the balustrade. He clasped the iron rail, leaning his weight against it with his back turned to Charlie. 'Let's start with death,' he said finally. 'What are your thoughts?'

Charlie wondered how the question was relevant. 'You mean, do I believe in life after death?'

'That's one aspect, yes.'

Charlie thought for a moment. 'I definitely think there is a type of creator involved in us being here. Not a person or anything like that, something much more akin to nature. I think the supernatural and the physical are connected.'

Gallard turned and leant back against the rail facing Charlie. 'Quantum Physics?' he offered.

'Could be, but I don't think quantum physics has found the supernatural yet. When it does, I think it will be sort of, godlike, in the sense that conscious energies will be captured there without need of the physical world.'

'Do you mean like a soul?'

'That's probably the closest analogy.'

'Do you believe a soul can be lost?'

'I don't believe in hell. I do believe a soul can be lost in the sense that it won't go on after death.'

'You mean it will just disappear from the universe.'

'That's one thought.'

'Why do you think the Creator—whatever that might be—would seek to destroy certain *souls*?'

Charlie grinned. 'These questions are becoming a little odd.'

'None more so than your answers; you don't have to answer them, but humour me, keep on taking a stab, for fun.'

'All right,' he said resignedly. 'Tarnished energies might upset the balance of creation – how's that?'

'Pretty deep.'

'Well you said take a stab.'

Gallard laughed . . . 'I see. Can I take your comments to mean, if you could be proven wrong, about any of them, it wouldn't particularly faze you?'

'You can take it that way if you like. But if life-after-death were proven to be a complete fantasy, I think I'd be pretty disappointed.'

The doctor laughed again. 'There's hope there.'

'More than a *bit*.'

'Expanding on your theory; do you mind if I call it a theory?'

'It's a theory, that's fine.'

'In your *theory* then, how do you suspect the creator communicates – if that's what you're saying – with the physical universe?'

93

'I have no idea, but I can take another stab if you wish.' Charlie was beginning to enjoy the game.

'Please.'

'Well, for arguments sake, it might be the same as the way our brains communicate, or make a connection with every cell in our bodies. It's a force of nature.'

'Your comments don't really differ then from your catholic upbringing. Both ideas have elements of what some could say is science fiction; would you agree with that?'

'I wouldn't disagree,' Charlie admitted.

'Do you think *your* life's energy will survive death?'

'It might be too arrogant for me to say.'

Gallard smiled. 'Let's leave death. Let me ask you this . . . Are you prejudicial?'

'Religious prejudice?'

'Any sort of prejudice.'

'I think I could be accused of it, but I don't believe I am.'

'Can you give me an example . . . of being wrongly accused of prejudice?'

Charlie searched his memory in order to give as accurate an answer as possible . . . 'An example might be say, if someone uses the traits of a particular race or religion to explain the actions of another person. I'll make the subject Catholic; that way—if I offend—then I offend myself as well . . . Someone could say to a Catholic man, who has committed a murder, *You think you can get away with murder because you just go to confession and all is forgiven*. A comment like that is really a slam at a person's attitude to having killed someone, and yet it can sound like a prejudice toward Catholics.'

'Did you feel you had to give an example from a Catholic point of view? I mean, do you think there is a way to give an example using another religion without sounding prejudicial?'

Charlie couldn't give an immediate answer. 'I think there are occasions when you can't.'

'What would you do in those cases?'

'I'd say nothing.'

Gallard showed the slightest hint of a smile. He moved off the subject once again . . .

'Do you think Aliens have this life-energy that you talk about?'

Charlie wasn't sure what he meant by aliens. 'Are we talking ET's?'

'Yes, ET's; do you think they have souls?'

'If they have consciousness, than I believe they have souls, yes.'

'Does that mean you believe in other living creatures in the Universe?'

'I believe it is impossible for there not to be.'

'What about animals. Do dogs and cats have souls?'

'Why not; it might be a lower form, but yes.'

The doctor gave a broad grin. 'I hope your right on that one.'

Charlie suspected Gallard might lean toward a belief in life-after-death himself, and perhaps be an animal lover to boot.

'I saw my brother's ghost the day after he died,' the doctor said, confirming Charlie's first suspicion. 'Do *you* believe dead people can revisit the earth like that?'

'I've never seen a ghost,' Charlie confessed. 'But I believe you did if you tell me you did . . . My brother claimed to have seen our Dad after his death . . . The closest I've ever come is a vivid dream of my dead folks being together, very young, and very happy.'

'Do you think that was a dream you needed to have?'

'Possibly; my grandfather died the day I turned ten. Mum packed me off to an aunt's place to shield me from the funeral. All my life I knew that I hadn't cried about his death—but I accepted it—because of my age I guess . . .'

Tears flowed as his voice failed. Charlie broke down, much to his embarrassment — and *astonishment*.

'Charlie, listen to me.' Gallard had knelt beside the wheelchair. 'You've been hypnotised. I apologise for not telling you I was going to do that. Can you forgive me?'

Charlie couldn't speak.

'I discovered you had been holding the grief inside for thirteen years.'

Charlie wiped away the tears with his fists and swallowed the golf ball lodged in his throat . . . 'When?'

'You won't remember, but after you told me about your grandfather I put you under, and — well I think you see the result.

Charlie could see the hypnotism had heightened the doctor's interest in him, and he thought he knew why. 'This makes me the perfect candidate.'

'Yes it does,' he told him. 'People quite often release pent up anxieties under hypnosis. Which brings me to my next question; now that you've had this experience, how will you feel about the hypnotism being part of your program here?'

'It worked for me once; my only criticism is that I had no idea until a few minutes ago that it happened.

In future, when you hypnotise me, all I ask is that you tell me about it beforehand.'

'My apologies again, I'll make sure you're informed. You still won't remember what happens, but all the sessions are recorded, and you can view the vision later.'

'Can I ask what future hypnotisms will entail?'

The doctor studied his hands for a moment before answering. 'Remember I said there would be things that wouldn't exactly be true. If I were to tell you the real reason for the hypnotic sessions, you'd probably walk away now. Having said that, when you're able to see all this in hindsight, you'll be able to understand why we had to be so secretive.'

'But I'll be able to view the sessions, right?'

Gallard explored his hands again. 'Not straight away, no.'

Charlie was feeling uncomfortable again; he was beginning to wonder at what stage he'd be taken into their confidence.

'Are you concerned about the secrecy?'

'I'd be lying to you if I said no,' Charlie admitted, concerned he may again be jeopardising his chances. 'But, as I've told Debra, I'm in, where ever it takes me.'

'I'll let you in on a little secret; you've already made the grade as far as we're concerned. These questions are more to do with where and how we move forward.'

He had no idea what the doctor meant by moving forward. 'I can't say I'm not puzzled,' he breathed.

'That's common at this stage, and I won't kid you, a lot of people leave us because of it. The negatives I've thrown at you are to test your resolve; you've really got to want to do this, or you'll never make it to the end. We have to know that you can leave your old life behind. Your new life will include nothing of your past. What's revealed to you in the end will surpass any preconceived notions you might have about where you're going. The best advice I can give you is, be ready for surprises—as I said, nothing is what it seems.

'You and I will see a lot of each other over the next few months. In that time, you will develop a trust in me that will be quite overpowering and in all honesty I have to tell you, part of that trust will be derived from hypnotic suggestion . . . When you get to see your sessions—inside of the next nine months—you will see the truth of what has happened, and; dare I say, you will accept what has happened because, by then, you will know where the program is taking you. I know how committed you are to this, so I have every confidence you'll make it to that day.'

Gallard placed his hand on Charlie's shoulder. 'This journey is yours, Charlie. Only you can put a stop to it.'

Charlie Pyrmont had no intention of putting *a stop to it*. Any concerns he had were buried completely by the weight of his disability. Even the prospect of death seemed a welcome escape.

As Debra was helping Charlie into her car, Benjamin motioned her back to the steps at the main entrance. She could see that he was worried about something. 'What's the matter?'

'Don't turn around,' he told her. 'Someone is on the road taking pictures.'

'Who do you think he's watching?'

'It could be Charlie, so keep an eye out.'

Through his telephoto lens, Josey watched the two people in conversation, wishing he'd learnt to lip read.

Debra moved out of the frame toward the car, but he kept the camera trained on Benjamin Bright, capturing his image into memory. Instinct told him he was going to need that memory.

'Time to move Fredie,' he said to the heavens.

CHAPTER TEN

Cameron Josey sat beside Dr. Heinberg's desk on the pretense that he was there as a new patient, at least that's what he'd told the receptionist.

Heinberg busied himself checking through the details received from the front desk.

'Hmmm, I see you were referred to us by Debra Rowlands,' he said without taking his eyes away from the computer.

'That's true,' Josey agreed. 'However I have a bit of a confession to make.'

The doctor looked across at him with such suspicion that Cameron found himself hesitating—

'I'm afraid I'm not here as a patient.'

'Then what?' he asked flatly, returning his attention to the computer.

'Fact is I'm concerned for Debra's wellbeing.'

This time the doctor leant back in his seat and swung his chair to face Josey directly.

'Strange, this is the third time in as many months someone's mentioned her name to me. Has something happened?'

'The thing is, we don't know where she is.'

'Can I ask what your connection is?'

The detective shifted his weight in the seat and studied his hands. 'It's complicated . . . A friend of a friend asked me to find her.'

Heinberg became suspicious again, sitting up straight as though he was about to ask his inquirer to leave. 'You're an investigator are you?'

Josey looked up from his hands and realising he needed to come to the point—took his *ID*-wallet from an inside coat pocket and flipped it opened. 'My friends believe she may have come to some sort of harm,' he continued to lie. 'I apologise for the slight deception, but my clients are at their wits end.'

The doctor relaxed a little at the sight of the private detective's registration and pushed out a deep sigh. 'I understand; . . . it's bad enough when someone's missing, but when they're disabled. . .'

His voice trailed off and Josey mustered all his professionalism to hide the surprise at learning Debra Rowlands had been handicapped. He wanted to ask about the details, but couldn't reveal his real reason for the interest in her.

'So, obviously you haven't heard from Debra?' Josey asked.

'No. It was very odd the way she just suddenly stopped coming. She gave no clue that anything was wrong. Actually I remember she seemed in particularly good spirits the last time I saw her. For a long time she was extremely depressed at the prospect of being in a wheelchair—it's for the rest of her life you realise—and of course, there's the loss of a promising career in swimming. I tried to convince Debra the accident wasn't her fault, but she'd decided otherwise.'

Josey had mixed feelings about the information he was getting and in spite of the excitement he always felt when he'd unearthed something out of the ordinary like this, it didn't show on his face. A really observant body-linguist might have been able to detect a slight involuntary tilt of an eyebrow.

Knowing privacy laws wouldn't allow him to ask *what sort of accident* she'd had, he was confident the rest of the information could be found amongst public records.

'I'm sorry I can't help,' the doctor said as he stood from his chair and extended his hand to Josey.

'No, that's fine.' They shook hands and Detective Josey gave him a business card. 'If you hear from her, give me a call if that's okay.'

'Likewise,' Heinberg countered.

Dr. Heinberg could have mentioned the visit from Charlie Pyrmont, but decided to adhere to the same privacy laws that had concerned his latest visitor. He couldn't help wondering though, how Mr. Pyrmont could have seen Debra Rowlands lately, if she was in fact *missing*—as the detective had claimed.

At the public Library, Josey panned the microfiche in search of Rowlands' name and found it within ten minutes. - *On the 19th of February*, the paper reported, *Debra Rowlands, a promising athlete, sustained serious spinal injuries in a car crash.*

'Well look at that,' Josey breathed as he studied an accompanying photo of the horrific crash.

Les Pyrmont answered his mobile from his unit in Drummoyne, straight away recognising from the detective's tone that he was onto something.

'This, you are not going to believe my friend,' came Josey's wave of excitement. 'I've just read through a recent newspaper story about Charlie's new girlfriend. Just over a year ago she was involved in a serious car accident. She was badly injured. Turns out; right now she should be sitting in a wheelchair - do you see what I'm saying?'—

Les had walked out onto his 11th floor balcony and stood blindly considering the distant monoliths of the city.

'Are you suggesting she's been cured?'

'Well, I can promise you that right now she appears to have no disability.'

'There has to be another explanation. People bound to wheelchairs don't just suddenly get up and walk.'

'Logic tells me you're right, but at this point in time an explanation escapes me.'

'What should I say to Silvia?'

'Just tell her what I've found out.' Josey advised. 'No reason not to anymore.'

'This whole thing is just getting crazier and crazier.'

'Anyway, Heinberg seems to be on the level, I don't think he knows about the so called University. It was interesting though, apparently according to him a few people have been asking after our little Ms. Debra Rowlands recently.'

'What do you make of that?'

'One of them was Charlie, which we know.'

'So . . . what's next?'

'I'll have a think about that. You fill in Silvia. I'll call you later to find out how she took it.'

'Right; talk to you then.' After disconnecting, Les stood taking in his distant view of the inner suburbs and wondered if other people's lives were quite as complicated as theirs.

Charlie had spent another day at Valley Bells, and now—back at home—was going through the motions of domestic life. Silvia hadn't said a word to him since he'd entered the house and that should have annoyed him immensely. But he seemed quite happy to accept her silence, almost as though it were a relief not to have to respond.

Les's visit earlier in the afternoon had pushed her to the point where she could no longer hold her tongue. 'Charlie,' she finally said with desperation in her voice. 'I need to understand what is happening to you.'

Charlie continued sifting through a pile of magazines on a small table at the side of his wheelchair, as though he hadn't heard her speak.

It would have been easier for Silvia to continue the silence, but it was the not-knowing that drove her to persevere. She bent onto her haunches beside the table, making it impossible for him to ignore her, 'Why all this secrecy, Charlie?'

He lifted his eyes and she saw in him a deep sadness that frightened her.

'Do you know how much my life has changed?' he asked in a whisper.

Her frown revealed the fear.

'I'm sorry that it has to be like this.'

His comment sounded completely cryptic.

'Like what? I don't understand.'

'Come on Silvia, sitting in this chair is no sort of life. If it was you, wouldn't you want to fix it given the chance?'

Tears pooled into her eyes and moistened her cheeks. He gently wiped them away with his thumb. 'I do love you, you know.'

Silvia brushed her nose with the back of her hand. She was trembling. 'Then tell me what you're doing, - going to this, *Valley Bells* - or whatever you call it.'

'It's a chance, Silvia.'

'A chance to do what?'

'To get back my life.'

He had spoken with such a low voice that Silvia wondered if he believed it. She desperately wanted to wave a magic wand and rewind the clock to a time before Charlie's illness.

She lifted herself from the floor and sat on a lounge facing the view across the reserve. She was hesitant in telling him what she knew, but it needed to be said. 'When Les told me the story about Debra Rowlands, I couldn't believe it. I immediately saw how easy it'd be to get roped in by their promises.'

Charlie was more than a little annoyed that his wife and brother had discovered the name of his contact at the University — and profoundly surprised. 'I see,' he said controlling his tone. 'How much more have you two learnt—from your spying?'

Her expression hardened. 'Probably no more than you, I'd say.'

'Oh yes, and what's that supposed to mean?'

'It means you need to be careful, Charlie.'

Charlie pondered over the extent of their meddling. 'Not sure who else is helping you with this, but don't assume you've got the full story.'

'That's something you might consider yourself,' she said with total conviction, her voice raised.

There was a strength in Silvia he'd never seen be-fore; a resolve that he *welcomed*. Her newly acquired steadfastness would be needed, and very soon, it was almost time to drop the bombshell that would change their lives irreversibly. He desperately wanted to hug and make love to her, but knew all that was in the past.

'Face it, Silvia, life together is over for us.'

'Shut up, Charlie!' she shouted, 'I'm not going to listen to this.'

He decided it was time to close her out—to present her with the beginning of the end. 'Then don't . . . Either way it's over,' he concluded.

It was the performance of his life.

Silvia couldn't comprehend the finality in his voice. This was not her husband talking. She opened her mouth to try and speak, but failed to find the words.

Charlie couldn't bear to watch his wife in such torment. He wheeled out of the room, locking himself in the study with the lights doused. Perhaps the darkness would hide his anguish.

CHAPTER ELEVEN

When Josey answered the phone in his car two days later, he immediately picked up on the distress in his clients voice.

'We've got a major problem,' Les told him. 'Silvia tells me he didn't come home last night.'

'Yeah, I know,' the detective answered flatly. 'He's at the Menzies Hotel. When they got back from the mountains, they both booked in. I had someone stay there all night and they didn't leave.'

'What the hell's he playing at? Silvia's having a complete breakdown.'

'Hearing *this* won't help,' Josey suggested.

'I'm not telling her another thing until we know more.'

'You'll have to tell her something, tell her he stayed at the hotel by himself.'

'The state she's in—she'll work out their together.'

'We don't know that ourselves yet. He's in the hotel and that's *all* we know. Tell her I saw Rowlands *leave* if you must. Tell her not to even think about coming over here, my cover may be blown already.'

Debra was pacing back and forth in front of Charlie's chair, plainly ticked off with the turn of events. 'Things are definitely not going well for you, Charlie,' she assured him. 'I'm extremely disappointed.'

Charlie felt glum and just as disappointed with himself. He could find nothing to say in his own defense . . .

'A week ago I was convinced you'd get past this. Now I'm not so sure. The longer we stay in the open the bigger the chance you'll become a risk.'

Debra dropped herself onto the edge of the bed, and swung her feet up to lie down.

She was extremely beautiful lying there on her back, and here he was, geographically in the perfect place to show his appreciation. But in fact, he was emotionally and physically in the worst possible place.

With eyes closed and hands beneath her head, she appeared to be some artist's depiction of a sleeping angel. Her silky-soft skirt clung to her like cling-wrap.

'What happens now?' Charlie mumbled, done with voyeurism.

She opened her eyes and saw him slouching in his chair at the foot of the bed.

'We wait,' she explained ahead of closing her eyes again. 'Benjamin will make a decision - and then, we see.'

God she's beautiful, he thought – *it's hard to believe she was badly injured just a year ago* . . .

He desperately wanted what she had regained so magnificently, a healthy, perfect body.

He imagined—given his *own* physical rebirth—she might even invite him to lie beside her.

A subtle head-shake betrayed his innermost thoughts, heralding a return to reality. 'What chance do you think I have, really?'

She opened her eyes, sat up and slid across to the end of the bed, positioning herself directly in front of his chair. 'Honestly, I think you still have a good chance, but, only if you do this thing with Silvia. Do you think you can, Charlie?'

Despair gripped him. 'I don't really see that I have a choice.'

She left the bed and moved to the mini bar to pour herself a straight brandy . . . 'Charlie, do you know anyone by the name, Cameron Josey?'

'No,' he answered truthfully.

'He's a private detective,' she told him in a matter of fact way, holding up her glass to offer him a drink.

He shook his head—far too depressed for alcohol.

Rowlands made her way back to the edge of the bed and sat there sipping her brandy thoughtfully. 'He's been following you.'

Realisation crept across Charlie's face.

'You suspected that didn't you,' she guessed.

Charlie was embarrassed more than anything. He suddenly felt his chance of being accepted had been irrefutably spoilt by his family's interference, also by making things worse with his own failure to mention his suspicions.

Debra had moved to a bedside table and taken a photograph from her purse. 'I want you to keep this with you,' she told him as she brought it over.

The photograph was of Josey.

'This's him?'

'It is. Memorise his face and let me know if you see him again.'

'You said you think I still have a chance,' Charlie said doubtfully. 'I would have thought something like this would cruel the whole thing.'

'Almost, but, as yet we are safe to proceed; on the condition you sever all ties with your past, and soon; by the end of the week in fact. It's time to accept that your old life can no longer continue.'

Charlie felt glum.

'You're not on your own with this, Charlie; I'm here to help you. That's why we're here in this hotel—just the two of us, alone.'

'I don't understand,' he admitted.

'Detective Josey has worked out we're onto him, he's put someone into the hotel to keep watch. We plan to allow that person to see the two of us together,' she added with a smirk. 'When this gets back to your wife, your impending divorce will become mandatory.'

A knot twisted in Charlie's stomach. He understood that the time had come to bite the bullet, but hurting Silvia was still something that greatly troubled him. 'I think you know my resolve,' he told her.

She felt genuinely sorry for Charlie, and clearly wanted to console him . . .

'We've all gone through this,' she confided. 'In my particular case, my life was in *WA* before I accepted the University's terms. I left a fiancé following the accident, even though he desperately tried to convince me he would take care of me the rest of his life. I could see how unfair that would have been on him. The last thing I wanted was to get down the track and have him resent me. I still love him. I would happily go back—if I could.'

'Why can't you?'

'It's because, like Silvia, he was reluctant to accept what he considered was the university's interference.'

'That's the tough part,' Charlie agreed, 'I don't see why our partners can't be involved, swear to the same secrecy?'

She gently touched the side of his face. 'You know that can never happen,' she reminded him. 'So long as our partners present a risk it just has to be this way. We know your wife is against us. Bringing her in would never work.'

She leant forward and kissed him on the cheek, her soft tantalizing lips then moved to pause near his. He felt her sweet breath washing across his mouth for a moment before they touched. He responded to her kiss and felt the elation of desire, and of being desired. *She's right*, he thought, *if I ever get back my manhood, I'll be dangerous*.

Charlie's emotional response was exactly what was needed right then to move the plan forward.

In the hotel lobby the following morning, Maxine Priest raised her eyes from her laptop to see Debra and Charlie leave the elevator. The couple went right past where she was sitting and continued on into breakfast at the *Wynyard Cafe*. Maxine opened her email server and typed in a message;

Josey@joseyinvestigations.com.au
They've just shown up for a late breakfast together. Keep you posted. Maxine.

Cameron Josey liked using Maxine for this kind of operation because of her modern gothic guise. Most people would take one look at her dark ominous eye-shadows and black fingernails and not suspect what she was really up to.

People did tend to gawk at her though; she was an odd cross between a trendsetter and a young executive. In all the years of working for the detective agency, she prided herself in never having blown her cover. That is until now . . .

A business card speared onto her keyboard from over her shoulder. She turned to find Charlie's companion standing right behind her.

Instinctively, Maxine slammed down the lid of the computer to hide the screen and its contents, obviously too late.

'Give that to your boss, sweet-cheeks,' Debra told the shocked girl. 'Tell him he's wasting his time. Tell him, Charlie is here of his own accord.'

Rowlands turned and walked back toward the dining room.

'Oh, and one more thing,' she said stopping to face the girl again. 'Pass on to his wife that he's after a divorce.'

She gave the young snoop a smug wave and returned to Charlie.

Maxine opened the laptop, retrieved the impromptu business card and read it.

University of the Next Life
DEBRA ROWLANDS
Consultant

'Holy shit,' she let out under her breath as she pocketed the card.

'Who was that?' Charlie inquired as Debra returned to the table.

'That,' she told him smugly, 'is the detective's little messenger.' She picked up the pot of Earl Grey. 'Tea, Charlie?'

As Charlie nodded, her eyes went straight past him to Maxine darting into a cab outside the hotel and talking excitedly into her mobile; presumably the *message* was already on its way.

The distraction caused her to overflow the tea into Charlie's saucer. She laughed softly at her clumsiness, but to her alarm Charlie wasn't responding.

'Are you all right?' she asked while cleaning up the mess

'There's one thing we need to get very straight,' he clarified, his eyes holding a cold warning. 'Dealing with Silvia is my concern, not yours. I'll have no interference on that score. And, I'll say it again—as difficult as it is—I will see this thing through.' He leant across the table and touched her hand. 'I don't need you seducing me.'

Debra placed her other hand over his and gave him her best smile. 'That's not what this is about, Charlie, believe me.'

Charlie felt his heart leap inside his chest. This beautiful woman was undoubtedly seducing him.

CHAPTER TWELVE

The untimely collapse of Josey's scouting had brought about a desperate meeting at the Pyrmont house. They no longer needed to worry about Charlie walking in on them it seemed, as he hadn't been back to the house in just over a week. Silvia was doing her best to remain strong in the light of what seemed like an UN-savable situation. Josey ran his eye over the divorce papers Silvia had handed him, while Les sat studying his clasped hands, conjecturing on what to suggest.

'I have no intention of signing it,' she told them.

Les agreed quickly. 'No, of course not.'

'What *will* you do?' Josey asked as he passed the papers back. 'If you don't mind me saying, it seems he means business—'

She waved the documents in their faces 'I don't care how it seems, *this* is not Charlie.'

She was as wild as hell and holding up much better than both men expected. Josey had seen this scenario a million times, *the vilified wife unable to believe her husband could be so extraordinarily callous, believing it has to be the other woman—the hussy who has taken her man away on a sea of sexual fantasy.*

'This supposed bloody cure of *Debra Rowlands*,' she continued with eyes popping, 'you don't believe it do you, Detective?'

Josey shifted in his seat.

'I believe—if she *was* cured—it's not at the hands of the Valley Bells Brethren.'

Silvia nodded, feeling her point had been vindicated.

'But,' Josey concluded referring to the papers in her shaking hand, 'they've convinced Charlie enough to give you those.'

Les cleared a dry throat. 'Sil, maybe you have to accept that Charlie's just as much to blame here as Rowlands is.'

Silvia's lips thinned with determination. 'Listen to me. Charlie's not doing what you think.'

Josey checked Les to see if he understood Silvia's point.

'Don't look at him,' she said firmly. 'He has no idea what I'm saying.'

It was true, Les was clueless.

Tears spilled from her eyes. 'Charlie is trying to give me my freedom.' She ran her hand across the smeared mascara under her eyes. 'It's the only thing that makes any sense.'

Josey reached into his pocket and handed her a folded handkerchief to pat her cheeks. She sniffled hesitantly into the hankie. 'He's doing this because he's concerned I'll ruin the rest of my life caring for a cripple.'

Josey thought, *she could be right. Or, she could be in denial.*

'This has nothing to do with sex,' she demanded as though it were a scolding for even thinking such a thing.

Although Charlie couldn't feel hands touching his legs, he could plainly see his masseuse in the wall mirror. He had been placed face down on the bed with his head turned on the side, a hotel towel across his midsection.

'You have nice skin, Charlie,' Debra whispered.

Stripped to her underwear, she sat straddled across the saddle of his naked back massaging his calves, her buttocks rising and lowering steadily as slender fingers kneaded frozen tissue. This mirrored image provided him with a sense of intimacy he hadn't felt in quite some time.

'Right, let's get you rolled over shall we.'

Her reflection swung away when he was rolled onto his back, her leaning torso rising into view above him as she lifted to straddle his pelvis once more, the hotel towel and her thin panties all that separated their sex.

'I think it's time you gave *me* a little massage,' she suggested removing her top.

Her round perky breasts were exposed to him for the first time. She brought his good hand there to feel his touch, for him to feel her.

Charlie's eyes were wide with lust as he swam in the gifts before him.

Eyes shut, head arched, she appeared to be enjoying the sensation he was providing.

He fantasised. The gift of satisfaction was something he desperately wanted, not only to receive, but to give.

She could be with any man she wanted, he thought, *yet here she is with me.*

Debra leant and gently kissed him while his hand fell beneath her, poised to show his appreciation, to show her what his good hand was still capable of—

As Silvia cried into Les's handkerchief, the phone in Josey's coat pocket vibrated. He discretely accepted the call and gave the interface a quick glance before dropping it back into his pocket.

The damning text message from Maxine had shown that, although it was unknown if Charlie had indulged in sexual activity with Debra Rowlands, he was clearly interested in doing so.

Josey made eye-contact with Les to encourage him to take the divorce papers back from his sister-in-law. He was thinking that—if she had no intention of signing them—it would be best to have them removed from the house and taken back to her solicitor — for the time being anyway.

At this point, Josey and Les had no idea about the affidavits. 'All right, I guess there's more to this than meets the eye,' Les told Silvia. 'I think it's time you had it out with him. You're the only one who can do that.'

Her resolve faded.

He took her hand. 'If Mohammed won't come to the mountain, we'll go to Mohammed. I'll try and set up a meeting.'

Silvia was suddenly frightened. 'What am I going to say to him?'

'Tell him how you feel. Ask him to come home?'

Les noticed the restless way Josey was edging out of his seat and thought for a moment the detective might be opting out of a situation too difficult. Josey gave him a look that said otherwise.

Silvia suspected the detective's edginess might be about payment. She leant across and touched him on the arm. 'I think you know I'm not short on funds.'

Having read the conditions of settlement in the divorce papers, Josey considered Silvia's comment a complete understatement, half of six million dollars, a house and a late model Mercedes Benz definitely did not suggest a *shortage-of-funds*.

'This isn't about money, Silvia,' Josey assured her in all seriousness. 'I need to talk to Les and plan our next move. Try and relax while we work it out. Once we set up a meeting, we'll need you to be in a nice strong state.'

'I'm not sure how much strength I have left,' she admitted.

He patted her hand. 'You'll be fine.'

As Josey made his way to the door, Silvia couldn't dispel a distinct feeling his departure had been unusually sudden.

Les kissed her and said, 'Try not to worry.'

'I'll try.' Her answer sounded a whole lot less than convincing.

In the drive way of the house, Les was trying to keep up with Josey's walk. 'Where's the fire?'

'*Where*, is a good question,' the detective answered cryptically as he got into the car.

Silvia watched from an upstairs window as the car drove away, still trying to fathom why Josey had seemed in such a hurry to leave.

'They've just left the hotel,' Josey told Les as he pushed the car away from the house, 'Checked-out according to Maxine.'

'Did she say where they went?'

'She lost them. For all we know they could be coming here, but I doubt it, they left in the Lamborghini, not the limo.'

'So, what do you think?'

'I think they could be on their way to the infamous Valley Bells, maybe for good, which means we need to bring the meeting forward.'

Josey took the car out onto the Western Freeway in the hope he could get to the location before Debra and her passenger made it to the gate. He was concerned she may already be on the freeway ahead of him. If she was, there was little chance of catching up.

He needn't have worried. By the time they made it onto the Bells Line of Road, they saw the yellow sports car parked outside a roadside pub.

'I'm not in the mood to have a race with that thing,' Josey said, referring to the Lamborghini's obvious grunt. He pushed down on the accelerator figuring a few extra kilometres over the speed limit would get them to Valley Bells first.

'What the Hell's this!' Debra moaned as she slowed the car's approach to the University's security gate an hour later.

Josey had his car parked across the driveway leading into the entrance, blocking any possible passage. The Lamborghini pulled up inches from the obstruction.

She couldn't see who the owner of the car was because he had his back turned, and Les was sitting inside out of sight . . .

'Haul your bloody backside!' Debra commanded with considerable annoyance, her unexpected brash tone giving Charlie in particular a bit of a start.

Josey was leaning against the side of his car under the glare of the security guard, who was opting to stay within the property behind the safety of the gate's steel bars. The clear visibility of Josey's gun holster under his coat might have influenced his decision.

It was evident to Debra her demand was falling on deaf ears, so she sprang out of the *Lam* ready for a confrontation. 'Call Benjamin!' she told the security guard. 'Get some backup.'

Josey turned to face her as she rounded his car.

'Oh, it's you,' she said with frustration.

'Do you know this guy, Ms. Rowlands?' the guard asked, holding off on her order to call for help.

She decided the last thing she wanted was a scene. 'It's all right. Forget the call John, he'll be leaving soon. I think he just wants a little talk with my client. That right, Detective Josey?'

Up close, he could easily see why Charlie was in knots over Debra Rowlands. 'Not me,' he clarified pointing at Les. 'It's his brother *wants a word.*'

Without waiting for an invitation, Les made his way out of Josey's Ford and over to the sports car to crouch down to Charlie's window.

'What's all this, Les?' Charlie asked without facing him.

'I might ask you the same question.'

Debra started to move off to interrupt the discussion, but Josey grabbed her by the arm.

'Why don't you let them talk,' he told her.

She glanced down disapprovingly at his hold on her, which he obligingly released.

'Look at it this way,' he explained, 'either he has this family powwow here, or I make a nice friendly call to my copper mates in Windsor.'

Debra's phone buzzed and she accepted the call with force.

'Benjamin,' she said, recognising the caller ID. 'It's nothing. We'll be down in a minute.'

Josey tracked her with his eyes as she strolled back to the driver's door of the Lam. He imagined, from Les and Charlie's viewpoint, her overly accentuated hips would be framed by the opposite window. *Perhaps her intention*, he thought.

'This,' Les said referring to the framed hips, 'is a short term thing, Charlie. Have you thought about what it's doing to Silvia?'

The question ate into his soul, emotion pervading his answer. 'I know it's hard for you to understand, Les, but I'm doing this for her.'

'Funny that. She said the exact same thing. But you know what; I don't buy that for a goddamned second.'

'You don't need to buy it. If Silvia's thinking that way, than that's the best possible outcome I can hope for . . . So why don't you take your detective buddy over there and clear off.'

'Charlie,' he pleaded, 'Silvia is broken hearted. Why don't you come home; forget all this nonsense.'

Charlie submerged into deliberation, sifting through his options just one last time . . .

But, the inevitable answer swelled to the surface once again, unadorned by alternatives. 'I'm sorry Les,' he said finally. 'Tell Silvia I love her; and that I always will. Tell her, it has to be this way.'

Debra, having waited impatiently, allowing the brothers their moment, bent into view at the driver's window, questioning Charlie's intentions with an arched brow.

His countenance, feeble as it was, assured her this conversation was over.

'If it's any consolation,' Charlie offered turning back to his brother. 'Tell Silvia, there'll come a time when she will understand.' Charlie held out his hand to Les in a final gesture. 'Goodbye, Les, promise me you'll look after her.' He turned to his waiting driver with steely determination. 'Let's go, Debra.'

Debra snapped the door open and gave Josey a *shove-off* wave, instructing him to move his car from the driveway. Les stepped back as she fired up the Lamborghini, which she followed up with a long horn blast intended to embolden Josey back into his car - to reverse it out of the way. He abided, resignedly; there was no point in prolonging the inevitable.

The two men watched as the big gate slid open, leaving the way clear for the Lamborghini to carry Charlie away into who knows what. Les's heart sank with the knowledge that he had failed in his mission to bring his brother home to his distraught wife.

'That's the last we'll ever see of Charlie,' Les said as the car made its way into the distance.

'Not if I've anything to do with it,' Josey promised.

Les hoped with all his heart that Detective Cameron Josey wasn't just all hot air.

CHAPTER THIRTEEN

A month later, Josey hadn't given up the idea of finding out what was going on at Valley Bells, in spite of having been taken off the payroll. Charlie's brother Les had informed him that Silvia had decided to drop the case, and that she was giving Charlie what he wanted. Josey's final assignment was to deliver the divorce papers to Charlie in the mountains. He was expected at the security gate, and allowed to enter without fuss.

He drove down the tree lined driveway toward the house, his nose for something wrong twitching like never before. The sight of kids playing, and their parents sipping coffees in the sun, seemed all too perfect. Why would such an innocent, serene place need such elaborate security as razor wire and guards with vicious hounds on leashes? Several of these burly Gestapo types scrutinized his progress toward the house, schmoozing covertly into their communication devices as he passed.

He was met at the front door by no less than Debra herself, a far cry from the threatening appearance of the macho *A-Team* positioned the length of the driveway. Rowlands was all smiles now that she was getting what she wanted, but Josey's main problem was why she wanted it, why she and the University wanted Charlie's divorce so badly.

He showed her a full set of teeth, at the same time thinking, *Sooner or later I'll figure out what you're up to.*

'My-my; you're quite the messenger boy aren't you,' she told him with a sweet smugness.

'I might bring something for *you* one day if you're a good girl,' he responded banning her from getting the better of him.

'I look forward to it.'

Debra led him into the foyer where several happy groups were standing around chatting. Some not so fortunate people sat in wheel chairs, but none the less cheery. Debra seemed aware of the detective's disquiet at seeing such a completely normal, happy scene.

She ushered him to Benjamin Bright's office and tapped lightly on the door.

Entering without waiting for a reply, they found her boss at his desk, head down in concentration. When he finally looked up, Josey was struck by his professional yet immediately likable persona. He seemed genuinely happy making this new acquaintance. Perhaps it was the divorce papers under Josey's arm that had him feeling so amiable. Or, *Bright by name and bright by nature,* he thought.

'Detective,' came the smiling welcome, 'nice to meet you at last. Please, have a seat.'

Josey obeyed and squeaked into a plush leather chair, maintaining a firm-hold on the documents, which he placed on his lap with a possessive pat.

'You know, you could have sent those by post,' Bright said, 'No need to have trundled all the way up here.'

'*Trundling's* no problem,' Josey informed him with matching professional sarcasm. 'I'm a helpful *kinda* guy.'

Bright gave a sick smirk. 'Bit unusual you'd have to agree, hiring a private eye to deliver divorce papers.'

'Oh, I'm not hired,' he informed him with relish. 'I just wanted to see the sort of people who have Charlie so enticed.' He gave Debra a *look*, as if to say, I think I get the reason.

Bright lost none of his calm. 'Enticed is not quite the right word.'

'No? What would you call it then?' Josey was blunt and not *really* asking a question.

Benjamin Bright furrowed his brow as if hurt. 'The way you say that . . . I mean, it's like you suspect us of something.'

Bright was now fully on stage.

'My mind is open,' Josey told his smug opponent. 'I'm just not sure Charlie's is.'

The managing director seemed a little lost for words after that, clearly wanting to terminate the conversation.

So soon?

Debra slid forward on her seat and took over. 'What is it you think we're up to, Detective?'

'If I had to guess, I'd say it has something to do with—money maybe?' . . . definite question this time.

126

'We do get paid,' she admitted. 'Our clients are well aware there is a fee and happy to pay for the service we provide.'

Josey had to smile at the connotations of the word *service*, but maybe he was being too cynical. 'Now there's the thing,' he said pushing on, 'exactly what sort of service *do* you provide?'

'Respite,' Benjamin answered quickly.

'Respite you call it. When a guy has to leave his wife to get it—while all the time believing your about to make him walk again . . . I call that a great big scam.'

The company director was visibly beginning to show his dislike for the nosy, outspoken detective. 'Let's get one thing perfectly clear, Mr. Josey,' he said while focusing on Debra. 'It has never been suggested, by any of us, that he must leave his wife.'

Josey knew, based on Debra's performance at the hotel in telling Max, *Charlie's wife wanted a divorce*, and Silvia's observation that the divorce idea wasn't coming from Charlie, Bright was lying through his teeth.

But, Josey noticed Debra had taken on an unexpected expression of guilt.

'That's my fault,' she confessed with expert sincerity. 'I happen to have fallen in love with Charlie.'

Josey had to strain every muscle in his face to avoid snapping his mouth open. Her acting was okay he thought, but decided that's all it was. Benjamin Bright was doing his best to convince Josey her admission was some sort of revelation.

'Give me a break,' Josey chimed with a chuckle. 'You two are absolutely priceless, do you know that.'

'She's telling the truth detective,' Charlie's voice came from behind.

Josey turned to find Charlie had entered the office and was now wheeling his way across to the desk. Josey had spent months watching Charlie, and this was only their second official meeting. Would it be the last?

He came to a stop beside Debra's chair and swung around to face Cameron. 'You must believe, nothing sinister is going on, I'm here because I want to be . . . I love this woman.'

'And what of all the other wheelchair cases,' Josey pointed out with sarcasm. 'Who do they love?'

'That's very funny, Detective,' Rowlands quipped.

Bright came in at this point. 'Every disabled person here has their own story as to why they've decided to stay. Each and every one of them is free to leave at any time.'

Josey considered Charlie's demeanour for any sign of entrapment—there was none, but he asked the question anyway. 'Is that true, Charlie?'

'I'm perfectly at peace. I'm not in any danger. None of us are.'

Clearly nothing further could be achieved at this point, and good old fashioned detective work would have to be incorporated if he was ever to get to the real truth. He decided to take his leave and fight another day.

'There you go,' he said to Charlie, handing him the envelope of documents. 'Your release forms.'

Josey walked to the door without ceremony and just a touch of attitude, he wanted them to believe he wasn't done, and to make sure Charlie grasped that he didn't have his approval. 'There's one thing I really don't get, Charlie,' he added turning to face him from the doorway. 'How do you get off saying this's some sort of sacrifice for Silvia's sake?'

If Charlie was harbouring words in his own defense, he didn't let on.

Josey swung his way out the door and closed it.

His visit to Valley Bells left a bad taste in his mouth. He hated it when something was wrong and his hands were tied against finding it. For now, all he could do was drive back to the city and get a good night's sleep.

'Tomorrow's another day Fredie,' he said out loud to his dead partner. It wasn't the first time Cameron Josey chose to believe his old friend was helping him - and it wouldn't be the last. The work-alone detective realised he was playing both parts, but it didn't matter; it was comforting—and actually less argumentative than when Fredie was alive.

CHAPTER FOURTEEN

Josey's visit to Valley Bells, which was to have been his last, only inspired him to continue the investigation, *without pay* he reminded himself.

He entered Dr. Heinberg's surgery the following morning and found the doctor sitting in an arm chair near the window instead of the usual place at his desk.

'I must say, I wasn't sure if this was a consultation or an investigation,' he explained to his visitor.

'You're in the right seat, *Doc*',' Josey replied fitting in with the medico's rhetoric.

'I thought I might be.'

The detective stood waiting in the middle of the room for an invitation to sit, which he got with a wave toward the patients chair. He wasn't sure what to make of the doctor's amiable demeanor. It was as if he already knew the exact reason for the second visit.

'I need your help,' Josey revealed testing the waters.

'If you're wondering if anyone else's been in asking after Debra Rowlands, the answer's yes, last week - a new patient.'

Heinberg waited for the detective's response, he knew he was telling him what he wanted to hear.

'Can I ask who?'

He grinned. 'I'll tell you what *I* know—if you tell me what *you* know.'

This condition made the investigator hesitate. One of his golden rules was never to give out information about a case; that is, unless absolutely necessary. He decided this was . . . 'I don't have a problem with that,' he agreed reluctantly.

The doctor was leading up to something—like a bad gambler about to turn over a trump card. 'Have you found Debra?'

'Actually, I have, yes,' Josey admitted instinctively deciding on honesty.

'And . . .?'

He could see the doctor wanted, or perhaps already knew the full story . . . 'And, she's no longer in a wheel chair.'

'I know,' Heinberg huffed, releasing his trump.

Josey came to realize why the doctor was being so incredibly cooperative, so very interested. 'You've seen her!'

'Not that she knows it, but yes I have. I saw her with my new patient, and I'm telling you, Detective, I could not believe what my eyes were seeing. How she could possibly be walking is beyond me . . . Can you shed any light?'

'I was hoping you could. Or, maybe your new-patient could.'

'Good luck with that, she was fairly reticent when I spoke to her. A bit like yourself the first time you came in.'

Josey absorbed the doctor's intentional dig and moved on. 'Is she disabled?'

Heinberg knew exactly why he was asking. 'Yes, but I must point out that any approach will have to take place away from the surgery; I'm assuming that's what you want - to meet her.'

Josey nodded. 'It is.'

'All right . . . She's coming in on Thursday. Her name is, Joan Crestling.' The doctor felt guilty; he was breaking a cardinal rule, but he wanted to know how Rowlands had gotten up and walked as much as the detective did. 'I reiterate,' he continued, 'by all means identify her from the waiting room, but take the investigation outside. And—you didn't hear that from me.'

'Hear what?'

He showed his appreciation with a grin. 'I'd better hunt you out of here. Keep in touch if you wouldn't mind, under the circumstances I think I've a right to know how this turns out.'

'You do, and I will.' Josey stood to leave. 'But can I ask, is there any chance at all Rowlands was faking her disability?'

'None,' the doctor divulged without hesitation. 'I'll stake my license on it. That woman was crippled for life; anything else is completely impossible.'

The idea Debra Rowlands somehow deceived the specialist was now skating on extremely thin ice, but that just heightened Josey's resolve to find a practical solution to the riddle. 'In my business, impossible can suddenly turn into possible,' he assured the doctor.

Josey left the surgery feeling he was armed with information that would transport the case forward. The Rowland's miracle cure didn't faze him in the least, *well; maybe a little*.

Heinberg had prodded him for more information, but he'd stayed off giving him anything on the University, for now . . .

The purr of the engines made Charlie feel lethargic. Below, he saw the endless desert rolling away like an untouchable tapestry of rich earthy colors. They had been flying for three and a half hours at thirty six thousand feet in Benjamin Bright's private Jet, on their way to a secret location in the center of Australia.

Debra opened her eyes and checked her watch. She leaned past Charlie and tried to get her bearings outside the window. The sun was setting somewhere to the front of the aircraft, casting long shadows into the valleys.

'We should be able to see the launch site pretty soon,' she told him.

'Unbelievable. I had no idea this sort of thing was a reality.'

'You're going to love weightlessness, Charlie; it'll make you feel whole again.'

This is obviously why the University of the Next Life is so shrouded in secrecy, taking people into space has to be illegal, and dangerous.

How can they keep a clandestine event like this from the authorities?

Debra had told him Governments believed the University was conducting unmanned research flights to compete with Branson.

Yes, this has to be the reason for all the secrecy; the affidavit—the divorce.

His heart and mind thought of Silvia.

'There it is,' Charlie told Debra, pressing his face against the window for a better view.

The giant rocket was waiting on its launch pad streaked with the late golden light from the sinking sun. Soon he would be in orbit and floating free of the gravity that held him prisoner. The next best thing to walking—perhaps the first *step* . . .

When Thursday came around, the detective sat in Heinberg's waiting room ready to make a visual ID on the patient, Joan Crestling. The receptionist had been told the truth, and knew what Josey was doing there.

Crestling wasn't the only woman in a wheelchair that day, but he had no trouble recognising her from the description he'd been given. After she'd come out from her appointment and wheeled her way to the front desk, Josey made his way down to the foyer and waited for her to leave the only way she could.

She traveled the expected couple of blocks before meeting up with the yellow sports car. The Doll of Valley Bells sat beaming behind the wheel with her usual professional smile. He assumed seduction would not be part of Debra's plan with Joan Crestling, unless of course young Debra was multitasking in more than one genre. Josey also figured that it was early days for the new candidate and therefore she probably wouldn't be staying at Valley Bells overnight.

With this in mind he made no attempt to stay close to the Lamborghini on the way up the mountain, he was more interested in when-and-if the visitor left the property following her visit.

After arriving at the University's location, he parked his car on a small rise, slightly more concealed than when he came to watch Charlie.

From there, a kilometer away, he would be able to plainly see the distinctive yellow car leaving via the security gate - on its way back to the city.

'Now we sit and wait, Fredie.' . . .

An immense, deafening shudder ate its way through the entire vehicle, migrating into Charlie's body and blurring his vision.

Debra sat beside him, similarly strapped in for the launch. Ahead, through his helmet visor, all he could see were two other people in space suits, sitting beside the pilot, beyond them a deep blue sky was just visible through tiny windows at the front of the cockpit.

He was having trouble remembering how he got there. After landing and transferring from the jet to a bus, recollection of events leading up to his boarding the space ship were immensely unclear.

There was however vague ideas seeping from his subconscious, presenting the notion some unknown person had taken blood.

Even with the noise and confusion of the fiery blast off, he was more-and-more certain that a blood sample had been drawn from his arm using a hypodermic; yet, he had no idea why anyone would want to do this without warning him.

With ten times the force of gravity, his frail body was sucked back into his seat, drawn there by some magic magnet. His face slumped inward, forming a grotesque, unrecognisable mask.

The relentless pressure propagated intolerably, pushing his brain to the back of his skull. For a few second he imagined being able to feel his lifeless legs in the form of pins-and-needles. Then, as instantly as a switch imbibes light from a room, Charlie was blind.

In this deep darkness he slipped slowly into unconsciousness

Following sunset, the Lamborghini left Valley Bells heading for town. This time, Josey would have to keep the subject in view. He let a couple of cars overtake to create a safe distance, than settled in for the long drive.

An hour later, he was watching the Lamborghini pull up outside a house in Double Bay, a well-to-do suburb nestled on the harbor at the edge of the C.B.D. The wheelchair access yawned open, allowing the disabled passenger to alight onto the sidewalk. As Crestling made her way along the ramps leading to the large Edwardian house, the car restored its sleek shape and drove off smartly.

Josey had been a block away, waiting for the coast to clear before rolling down to park at the front of the residence. He wrote in his little note book and tore out the page.

Checking that there was no obvious observation from the house before moving from the car, he delivered his message to the mailbox. Now it was wait and see if Joan Crestling responded to his request to meet.

Judging by her house, there was one thing he could be certain of, she had lots of equity and probably lots of money—just like Charlie.

The following morning was a beautiful autumn day, peaceful and safe. Josey had chosen an equally safe location to meet, an open plaza surrounded by people browsing through the boutique shops. He wasn't sure if, or even how she would show up, trusting it wouldn't be in the Lamborghini.

As Josey sipped on his coffee, a modified cab with Crestling on-board pulled into a disabled parking bay right nearby. Her arrival gave him renewed hope of progressing with the case. As the tailgate opened to remove the wheelchair, Josey went to the *Cabbie* standing at the back of the vehicle and paid him the fare.

'You didn't need to do that,' she told the detective while trying to turn her head as the driver wheeled her backwards.

This was the first time Josey had clearly heard her speak other than recently on the phone when she called him about the note he'd left in her mailbox. Her voice sounded cultured. He first noticed her attractiveness at the surgery. Although looking thirty-something, he noted she was well groomed for that age group. Her black leather jacket furnished her with quite a trendy appearance, contrasting with her model-like features.

At the base of the exit ramp the disabled passenger pivoted the chair to face her new acquaintance, making her own instant assessment of Cameron Josey. He was slightly older than she'd thought on the phone, about forty, but she felt he had quite good character in his face. The graying temples, the well-defined lines either side of his friendly mouth and the sleepy eyes gave him a calmness that she immediately liked.

'Nice to meet you,' she said with a kindly smile sounding like she genuinely meant it.

He invited her to accept his handshake, which she did. 'Thanks for coming. I wasn't sure you would.'

'Perhaps when you've heard what I have to say, you'll understand why you needn't have worried.'

Her straight to the point assurance lifted his hopes even further, something told him this meeting would amount to something worthwhile.

A waiter noticed them and came across as Josey helped her manoeuvre the chair into the table.

'Can I get you guys something?' the waiter chimed cheerfully.

'Yes, thank you; I'll have a long black,' she informed the helpful sounding young fellow.

He grinned, taking a tad too long pulling his eyes away. The wink she gave Josey put the waiter's overly keen attitude on hold. He left with the order.

'I'll bet you get that a lot,' Cameron suggested.

'I get *that* a lot too.'

Josey wasn't sure if his cheeks had reddened with embarrassment—but it felt like it—he clearly saw she considered her good-looks secondary. This lady had business in mind, possibly wanting to talk about the University just as urgently as he did.

'So, Mr. Josey-the-detective, what makes you think I may be in danger?'

Josey recognised there was no point in pussyfooting, *she* definitely wasn't. 'It's connected with a case I'm working on. One of my clients is very concerned about her husband's immersion into the so-called *University* you're attending at Valley Bells.'

'How do you know I am?'

'You just told me.'

She gave a light chuckle. 'So I did.'

'I must apologise for following you around. I hope I didn't freak you out.'

'You didn't freak-me-out. I thoroughly checked you weren't with *them* before I came here.' Her efforts sounded mandatory.

Josey smiled.

'Would I be right in saying your client was asked to give her husband a divorce?'

He nodded, her reaction telling him she had been expecting the answer.

'Funny that,' she mused. 'Richard, my husband, left me the same way. They sucked him in with some incredible promises before I had a chance to stop it. Do you know the story?' The last thing she wanted was to repeat details he might already have.

'About the cure you mean?'

'Mmmm . . . do you believe any of it?' She swept her head from side to side indicating she didn't believe it herself.

'Given the evidence I probably should.'

'But you don't?'

'*But I don't,*' he confirmed.

'There you go,' the waiter said as he returned, placing the coffees on the table. Preoccupied, she ignored him and he quickly left.

'What do you make of it?' she asked the detective absently peering into the black brew.

'Personally, I think it's all about money. Beyond that, I'm at a bit of a loss.'

Crestling raised her eyebrows in agreement and took a cautious sip of the hot coffee. 'You haven't asked why I became involved,' she said finally.

'I'd say you have the same interest as me. You're obviously not the type to believe in miracle cures.'

Her smile confirmed he was right. 'What's his name; the woman's husband?'

'Charlie Pyrmont,' Josey said. 'Have you come across him?'

'No they didn't really give me time to meet anyone. I didn't lay eyes on Richard either.'

Alarm bells screamed inside Josey's head. 'I take it they don't know you're Richard's wife.'

'No way; I told them my name is, *Marcella Simons*. It wasn't easy pulling that one off I can assure you.'

'I believe it—I also believe it's a hell of a risk you're taking.'

'I honestly don't care about the risk; I just need to know Richard is safe.'

'In that respect you and I are practically on the same mission. I'm a bit surprised they didn't pick up on your connection,' Josey pointed out. 'Usually they watch their candidates like hawks.'

'They wouldn't have seen us together. Richard and I are living apart, which I won't go into. But I can promise you, until little *Miss* Debra Rowlands came along—there was no talk of divorce.'

Josey decided it was time to mention Charlie's infatuation, and Debra's performance in Benjamin Bright's office, plus—how indefensibly obvious it was that the whole thing was a complete charade.

'If it's any consolation, she pulled the same stunt with Richard.'

'It doesn't surprise me.'

Crestling was staring into her coffee cup again. When she lifted her eyes she discovered the detective was off with the fairies himself. 'I know you want me to help you with this,' she told him with a quirky grin.

Josey smiled, feeling like giving her a kiss for more than just the sheer appreciation of the help she was offering.

'If you weren't already so committed, I could never ask you to get involved. I don't trust these people any more than you do.'

'With what my husband and I have been through I don't find this particularly daunting.'

Her large dark eyes expressed honesty and sincerity, a woman easy to like.

'Have the both of you always had your disabilities?'

'I was already in the chair when Richard and I met. Ironically six months ago—a year into our marriage—he was paralysed after falling from a ladder. Even though we started living in different houses, we were fine until the University came into our lives.'

She sipped on her coffee thoughtfully, memories of better times with her husband flooding her mind with unreachable desires.

'Apart from finding your husband missing; what else have you learnt out at, Valley Bells?'

'Well, apparently they're allowing me to move onto the first stage.'

'Do you know what that entails?'

'Not sure, but tomorrow I have to meet with some, *psychiatrist*, who'll give me my first glimpse of the *program.*' She'd drawn inverted-commas in the air, to highlight her attitude. 'By tomorrow I should be able to tell you a lot more.'

Josey leant back in his chair and let out a loud sigh. Joan Crestling's positive attitude made it easy to forget the desperate situation she was in.

'Have they asked you for money?'

'Not yet, but they will. I'm sworn to secrecy as you possibly know. Theoretically, talking to you could land me in a lot of legal hot water.'

'I wouldn't worry about that; they'll be in a lot more legal *hot-water* if any of this ever comes out. There's plenty kinds-of-other-trouble though, so I suggest you keep your wits about you.'

'I plan to.'

Josey felt slightly uncomfortable about a woman in a wheelchair putting herself in such potential danger to help him solve a case, but she had her own reasons for wanting to help and he wasn't about to stand in her way. Josey recalled his promise to Heinberg - not to break his confidence - but he was convinced talking to Joan Crestling would be kept between them.

'Your visits to Heinberg obviously didn't convince you of Rowland's recovery,' he suggested.

A light bulb lit up inside her head. 'Ah, that's how you found me . . .'

As he expected, she skipped over the Heinberg connection and continued with her answer.

' . . . No, I just found the whole thing baffling. I'm still not sure she was disabled in the first place.'

'Apparently she was,' Josey told her, wishing he could say otherwise.

'I take it you've seen the news reel of her accident then,' Crestling assumed.

'No, but I have seen newspaper reports.'

'Anyway, I don't really care,' she told the detective with determination. 'Perhaps she just got better on her own, it happens. My only concern is finding Richard.'

The detective could see that Joan Crestling—like him—wasn't particularly captured by the proof of Debra's miracle cure. He had to admit though; said-cure definitely had him thinking . . .

Charlie awoke to the soft sound of gentle wavelike music. He felt so incredibly light . . . *floating*.

He opened his eyes to learn that he was indeed buoyant, without weight. The room in which he drifted like an autumn leaf was spherical in shape and heavily padded. His body brushed its silky smooth walls, sending him tumbling freely with no sensation of up or down. Approaching the opposing wall he held his legs outstretched in preparation to spring effortlessly into flight once more. This was the first time since his stroke that his lower limbs had experienced mobility.

Although he couldn't have felt happier in this serene place, he was once again struggling to understand how he'd got there.

His mind overflowed with questions.

Why am I here?

Will my legs still work when I leave?

What is making them work now?

He had no answers.

Just as before, none of the previous events appeared to be linked, except that they were chronological — a fight to the launch pad — a blast into space - and now this, floating in weightlessness. What was outside of this room? He had no idea. Was the spaceship in orbit? It didn't matter—he felt completely safe.

'Are you enjoying yourself, Charlie?'

Debra's voice startled him at first. He turned to see her floating nearby, he was sure she hadn't been there a moment ago. *She was even more beautiful in space,* he thought; her long hair was swaying like sea grass beneath an ocean swell.

'Look behind you,' she advised.

Turning wasn't so easy in zero gravity, but Charlie managed, doing as she instructed. Nothing could have prepared him for what he saw . . . a giant window had opened up, affording him a spectacular view of space. He realised with fascination that they were not orbiting Earth as he imagined they aught to be, the elapsed time between blastoff and now was far too little to have travelled such a vast distance; to have reached *the moon* and fallen into orbit around it—

My God, where are they taking me?

CHAPTER FIFTEEN

The following day, Valley bells was bathed in an Autumn warmth that brought early risers to the well-worn track leading from the estate house to the quaint stone church. Another Sunday of prayer and devotion from people whose only hope until now, had been faith in a Miracle. There were those on the path who would claim miracles came to the believers here by simple request, rather than by faith alone. The first timers would be wheeled to this place with hope in their hearts. At first there was very little else.

Benjamin Bright seemed only too happy to bring the newly initiated to the hill for their weekly dose of devotion and to partake of Christianity's most sacred sacrament. Marcella Simons was his latest member to join the fold. He pushed her the half kilometer to the tiny archway that led inside to a kaleidoscope of color, provided there by half a dozen traditional stain glass windows.

A middle aged woman in a motorised chair came through the archway independently of helpers and locked her attention on Marcella. 'Benjamin,' she called cheerfully. 'Who's the new girl?'

Benjamin turned to the familiar voice and flashed his pearly whites. 'Bernice, this is Marcella.' He maneuvered the chair to one side to allow the two women to come side by side.

'Hello, Marcella,' Bernice said with a sort of unconditional friendliness. 'Welcome to our little church.'

Joan felt extremely uncomfortable thanking her, not to mention responding to a nom de plume name. Getting introduced to someone so soon in strange new surroundings was unsettling; she would rather have remained unnoticed.

The congregation consisted of about twenty five people seated in chairs, half of whom had chaperones assisting them.

Having brought the two ladies together, Benjamin Bright seized the opportunity to escape. 'Would you girls like to sit together during the service?'

Bernice took an enthusiastic breath. 'What a great idea—do you mind?'

'Wonderful.' Joan answered, surprised by her own wave of sudden confidence. 'You can show me what to do.'

Benjamin straightened; somewhat relieved.

The church had no pews other than a few stools along the walls for able bodied people. Those in chairs made up their own rows, leaving enough space for the minister to move through to administer the sacraments. A small man came onto the altar from a side door and bowed reverently with his back to the congregation.

He wore no robes—gray trousers and an open neck white shirt were unadorned by religious emblems. Benjamin took his leave of the ladies and met with the celebrant inside the area set aside for the ministerial altar.

The atmosphere was relaxed, everyone engaging in unrestrained dialogue with each other. Bernice was no exception. Joan mostly listened, and watched.

She noticed Benjamin and the minister were facing in her direction as they engaged in a discussion with each other, and she thought maybe she might be the subject of their conversation. Her stomach rolled.

Hopefully they're not planning to draw special attention to me during the service.

She needed to observe—rather than be observed.

A half hour into the service, melodic tones of nondescript religious songs floated across the fields in comforting waves of optimism. At the conclusion of a song that had the congregation completely captivated, the minister raised the familiar chalice, the symbol of Christ's death and resurrection.

A new thought occurred to Joan, *Is being Christian a condition of entering the University?*

The man offered a chant toward the upheld cup, signaling the arrival of the spirit that was to enter the hearts and minds of the faithful.

The summoning complete, he moved with the cup to the first row of wheelchairs and began offering the wine to the willing. Bernice drank from the cup and reverently handed it on to Joan, not expecting that her new found friend would try passing it on to the young man next in line. The minister gently pushed the goblet back, his body language suggesting she should drink.

'We all partake of the Sacrament,' the man told her with a kind smile.

The statement was so benign that she couldn't help feeling foolish for not joining in. The attention she was getting was the very thing she wanted to avoid, so she accepted the drink and handed it on. The minister smiled with approval and Bernice squeezed Joan's hand in support.

Following Communion, Joan felt that the voices of the congregation had lifted to greater heights, certainly greater volume. She even joined in herself. The singing became almost party like as people began to loosen up. She sensed the unmistakable feeling of euphoria.

The rest of the day was spent relaxing around the grounds of the estate and the many communal areas inside the house, making new acquaintances. One new acquaintance was a handsome young man who had kept his distance while he watched and waited for Joan Crestling to be sitting by herself. That moment came late in the afternoon on the Verandah of the mansion, just as she'd felt the need to close her eyes and rest.

'I saw you in church today, Marcella,' he told her as he moved in and parked his chair. 'What did you think?'

She responded without annoyance at the unexpected approach.

'*What did I think*,' she repeated. 'How do you mean?'

'I mean, did you like it?'

Part of the reason Joan had taken time out to rest her eyes was because she was having head spins following the service. She was certain the wine had been heavily spiked. It was difficult to know if her young friend was just making small talk, or perhaps interrogating her.

'What about you?' she asked.

He laughed . . . 'The wine was good,'

His comment hit her like an ice breaker—if the wine *had* been altered, he obviously had no problem talking about it.

'The name's Phillip, I'm at the final stage.'

She wondered what *final Stage* meant.

'All signed up,' he told her enthusiastically.

Joan wondered if Richard may have already reached that stage, and then moved on to where ever patients go when that happens. If her husband *was* signed up and he had paid out money, she wouldn't know about it because their financial affairs were kept separate.

'I know who you are,' he suddenly divulged with complete abandonment.

Joan had no idea where this was heading. Was he speaking metaphorically?

'I know your name is Joan, not Marcella.'

He saw the alarm spreading across her face and quickly wanted to assure her the secret was safe with him. 'I won't tell if you don't,' he offered.

She noticed he was holding a mobile phone cupped in his palms—hiding it from view.

'I was told I couldn't have one of those in here.'

He turned the phone toward her, allowing her to see the photograph that he had brought to the screen.

'Do you know this guy?' he asked, confident that she did.

Joan was amazed to see a picture of her husband and another man talking with Dr. Gallard.

'Richard and I became good friends . . . talked about you a lot. He was convinced you would eventually come looking for him, so he made me promise I'd talk to you—put your mind at rest—let you know he was safe.'

Her eyes were as wide as saucers. 'And *is* he?'

'He is, absolutely.'

'So, where is he now?'

Phillip turned off the phone and put it away. 'He said to tell you, the only way of ever seeing him again is to go through the program. Find out for yourself what it's all about—not to be scared—what they're offering is totally real. It's just not legal, which I'm sure you've heard a thousand times.'

The feeling that the young man was somehow working for the University returned to Joan like a storm cloud. Josey's warning—*that her mission would be dangerous*—seeped to the forefront of her mind.

'I saw you snooping on the third floor,' he told her bluntly.

Here it comes. He's about to march me off to Benjamin Bright's office and I'll be asked to leave—or worse.

'Snoopers on the third floor are picked up by the security cameras.'

She felt fear grip her stomach. 'Does this mean I'm in trouble?'

'No, I don't think so. Snooping is just part of what newcomers do, they expect it. The important thing is, they mustn't find out you're *not* who you say you are. But again, your secret's safe with me . . . I ask that you give me the same courtesy.'

'Yes, of course,' she assured him reservedly.

The chat with Phillip on the Verandah had lifted her spirits. She was really beginning to believe nothing particularly sinister was going on, in spite of the fact her husband was nowhere to be seen.

People were certainly friendly enough, and on the main, most appeared to be relaxed. This new found optimism vanished immediately when Jack appeared in the communal area on the second floor—to take her to Benjamin Bright's office.

CHAPTER SIXTEEN

Josey could not believe what he was hearing. 'This might well be the last time we see each other,' Joan informed him as they sat at the bow of the Harbor Ferry.

'I don't understand, I thought we were in this for the-long-haul.'

'Things have changed.'

Cameron Josey couldn't hide his disappointment; he had felt certain—as a team—they could uncover what was really going on at the University. 'Can you tell me what happened to change your mind?'

Forcing herself to meet his eyes, she presented him with the honest truth. 'They let me talk with Richard.'

Cameron couldn't deny he was surprised. 'Really, what about Charlie, did you see *Charlie*?'

Pangs of guilt squeezed in on her chest, and she felt the need to apologise for being selfish.

He thought he saw something else, raising hope. 'You did?'

... 'No. I'm really sorry, Cam.'

No more than me, he thought ... 'So, what are you planning to do?'

She began a study of the distant sailing craft, taking her eyes away from his. 'I've decided to join the program.'

It was obvious to the detective that Joan had made this extraordinary decision under some sort of duress, and he believed he knew what it was. 'Let me guess, if you don't—you'll never see Richard again, am I right?'

Her expression was a mixture of confirmation and denial. 'He spoke to me. It's what he wants me to do.'

He spoke to me. Cameron mulled over those exact words, suddenly realising Joan hadn't actually seen her husband in the flesh. 'He wasn't in the room, was he!'

Not a question.

There was no denial in her expression this time. 'No. He wasn't. But our conversation was live. I was seeing him being streamed on a computer screen.'

Josey drifted into thought. *What can I possibly say to this woman to change her mind*? He gave it another try. 'You told me they're openly using hypnotism, as part of their, - healing process, right?'

'Yes,' she answered guardedly.

'How do you know he wasn't brainwashed under hypnosis.'

Joan didn't want to accept the detective might be right, or that she had the very same doubts. In the end, she had convinced herself joining the University was her only option if she were to ever see her husband again. 'I don't really care where this takes me; I just need to be with him, to know he's all right.'

Josey could see her mind was made up, but he wasn't about to give up so easily. 'Just hold off on your decision for a few days, that's all I ask. I'm making progress, and I truly believe you don't have to do this. You will see your husband again, I promise.' Cameron was clutching at straws, he knew he had nothing to back up his promise, but without her help he had even less hope of helping Silvia and Charlie.

They sat in uncomfortable silence until the ferry reached the quay. As he was wheeling her down onto the floating wharf, his cell rang and he took the call, it was Maxine.

'High Max, what's up?'

He stopped walking and Joan turned her chair around to wait.

His face had lit up. 'Wait for us; we'll be there in fifteen. Great work, Maxi.'

Joan wanted to know what had got him so excited, but he was like a cat-on-a-hot-tin-roof. He hailed down a special-vehicle-cab and instructed the driver to take them uptown to the office.

As the cab wound through traffic, Joan was insistent on knowing what was said on the phone. 'Are you going to tell me the reason for all this excitement?'

He refused to give her any specifics, other than to say, 'I'm about to give you a reason to change your mind.'

Joan hadn't been to the detective's office before, and noticed it was neat and conservative like the man himself. Maxine stood-out like a sore thumb, but it didn't take long to realise she was a very nice person, and underneath quite conservative herself. She handed her boss an envelope while focusing back on Joan. 'What can I get you - coffee, tea?'

Cameron had removed several photographs from the envelope and was studying them. 'Forget the tea-and-coffee, Max - break out the Champagne.'

'*Champagne*? This *must* be good,' Joan chortled.

She wheeled herself around to his side of the desk. 'Can I see?'

He held the photographs out for her to take. 'Oh yes indeed, I think you'll see this is *definitely* good.'

A glance told her the enormity of what Cameron Josey's assistant Maxine had found. 'Who would have guessed this,' she breathed in surprise.

'I think this changes a few things, Joan,' Cameron urged, winking at Max as she lay out the champagne glasses.

Joan was in a state of disbelief. 'How'd you find this out?'

'Full marks to Max, she got the evidence.'

'You worked it out, boss.' Maxine said throwing the compliment back at him.

'Holly shit,' Joan breathed as she studied the pictures of Debra Rowlands and her seriously identical twin sister, identical except for the fact that one was in a wheelchair.

This was making Josey's day. 'I think it's time the real Debra Rowlands stood up, don't you?'

'Somehow I don't think she can,' Joan quipped as she considered the real Debra, sitting, bound to her chair. 'All this time we've been dealing with her twin sister.'

'*Lisa* Rowlands,' Maxine volunteered as she brought over the champagne bottle and filled the glasses.

Cameron raised his glass in a toast. 'Here's to better days - and, truth at last.'

'I don't know how to thank you both,' Joan told them from the heart.

'Here's to *truth*.' Cameron took a hearty mouthful of champagne, enjoying the fizz all the more for the breakthrough it represented.

Noticing Joan wasn't drinking; Maxine caught Cameron's attention and flicked her eyes in their client's direction. The smile on Joan's face from a moment ago had been replaced by dark clouds of worry.

He knew that expression, this was a woman trapped in some strange way. He put his glass down on his desk and quickly moved out of party-mode. 'There's more isn't there,' he suggested patiently.

She finally did take a drink, a long one. 'I've already signed up to join them,' she revealed with the courage the champagne provided.

Cameron was utterly lost for words, a phenomenon Maxine rarely ever saw, his face was asking *why*, but his mouth remained open as though he had lost the ability to speak.

Max spoke for him. 'Why would you do that?' the young girl asked with waning respect for their client's feelings.

Joan was alarmed by her tone, and thought, *she's angry, after all the effort put into exposing Debra Rowlands.*

Tears threatened to spill.

'I'm sorry; . . . I know you've worked hard on this.'

'You think?' Max put forward.

Cameron closed his mouth and hurriedly rejoined the conversation, anxious to prevent Maxine from saying something she'd later regret. 'Please, don't apologise,' Josey told Joan. 'We're still all in this together. Just tell us exactly what you mean by, *signed up*.'

Joan fiddled with the arm of her chair. 'I've paid them thirty thousand dollars.'

'What?' Maxine squealed in protest.

Josey reprimanded her with his eyes before calmly returning his attention to Joan. 'No big deal, we sort of knew this was coming.'

Maxine gulped down her champagne and retreated to the sink to wash the glass, feeling she had nothing left to contribute.

Cam sat on the floor beside Joan's chair. 'I said from the outset that the decision to help us was yours alone. Nothing's changed, except these photographs suggest the Valley Bells Brethren may be more dangerous than we thought—the further in you go, the more dangerous it will become.'

Strangely, Joan appeared more ready to take that risk than before. 'You're right about one thing, Detective, these photographs change everything, and yet nothing. I need to get him out of there.'

'You need to be careful,' he insisted.

'That's another thing that hasn't changed.'

Maxine recognised the woman had strength, and guilt forced her to begin saying, 'Mrs. Crestling, I was way out of line, I'—

'No, please. I understand . . . now it's my turn.'

The resigned exchange between Maxine and Josey confirmed there was no point in arguing with her.

Josey placed his hand over hers and said, 'Promise me you'll keep in touch with us . . .'

Her worry lines deepened. 'That might be difficult. I'm to meet Debra; sorry, I mean—what's her name, *Lisa* Rowlands, at the international airport first thing in the morning.'

Maxine swung round from over at the sink. 'That's not good.'

Cameron raised his hand to pause her. 'Max has a point,' he told Joan. 'After what we've just shown you, do you think it's wise to leave Australia with these people?'

'No,' Joan freely admitted. 'But if it takes me to Richard—'

'Joan, listen to me. What you're doing is not safe. My advice, we take this straight to the police.'

'No,' Joan begged urgently. She knew Cameron was serious about going to the authorities, and it's the last thing she wanted, but not for the reason Josey thought. 'You said yourself; we need to help each other.'

Maxine was as worried as Josey. 'Maybe you should listen to my boss; he's got a good nose for this sort of thing.'

'I'm certain he has, but my mind is made up. I'm going wherever this takes me.'

Let her do it, Chief, Maxine thought, *we need her.*

Cameron wasn't happy with the risk involved. 'Joan, I don't think you should go—not a good idea.'

She smiled. 'You scared?'

'For you, yes.'

'You're a detective,' she countered. 'Surely you can follow me.'

Crestling had him there. If he couldn't successfully tail her, he probably should throw his credentials in a deep-dark-draw and go fishing.

'I need to find Richard—you need to find Charlie . . . but if it's a question of money'—

'It's not the money; while there's a chance of finding Charlie I'm fairly sure my client will cover me.'

'I can't expect that,' she said. 'Have a talk with your client and let me know how I can contribute.'

Cameron caught Maxine's eye and she nodded her approval with a satisfied smile, *my work has not been wasted.*

Josey came across to Joan's way of thinking. 'I'm assuming you don't know where they're taking you.'

She shrugged her shoulders with no idea.

As soon as Joan left the office, and figuring Silvia wouldn't want to talk business, Josey placed a call to Les Pyrmont. He agreed to come up with the necessary funds to allow the investigation to continue—at least until Charlie was found—or couldn't be.

CHAPTER SEVENTEEN

Patsy Bova's beady eyes worked overtime, studying the crowds milling into the departure lounge of the International Airport. Her main focus was females in wheelchairs. Although she had *Lisa* Rowlands' personal appearance memorised, every time she caught sight of a possible double for *the black haired bombshell*—as Cameron called her—chair or no chair, she'd check the photo on the face of her cell phone. Different clothes and hairdo can change a woman's appearance dramatically. She was also conscious of the fact the two subjects might not yet be together, and she wasn't taking any chances of not identifying either of them.

In the absence of Maxine—who could very easily be recognised by Rowlands—Patsy was an equally good choice for this kind of work. She was your typical middle aged *Sticky Beak*, the kind of person to look-people-up-and-down just out of pure interest.

Her observational post was the window of the news agency, directly facing the people herding toward the departure gates. She wouldn't have been able to position herself for this job if Joan Crestling hadn't been told which airline she would be flying with, now it was a matter of finding out which flight, and where to. But first things first . . .

Here they come . . . traversing the moving foot-way.

Patsy left the news agency to follow them. Mingling in amongst the crowd, she was every bit the happy traveler. Patsy carried those few pounds that creep up on you with a little age—she was pushing fifty-five—she could have given the bombshell a run-for-her-money back in the day.

Rowlands' perfect posterior was casting its spell on every red blooded gentleman that had the good fortune to end up walking behind her, *unavoidably* taking in the delights of her tight red dress.

Male magnet!

She wheeled Joan off the foot-way at gate eight and took a seat beside the wheelchair.

For Patsy, now came the tricky part. She needed to make contact without appearing suspicious. Waddling nonchalantly past her subjects, she went over to the handsome attendant waiting to collect boarding passes.

'Excuse me,' she said sounding confused, 'what is this flight number?'

The young guy stopped what he was doing and saw she wasn't holding a boarding pass. 'Where are you traveling to?' he asked dutifully.

She hated when people answered a question with a question. Of course she knew the answer; all this was just a ruse in lead up to what came next. Her answer was on the departure screen - *Flight 155 to Hong Kong, gate 8, Boarding 8.30am.*

'Hong Kong,' she announced.

He smiled. 'You're in the right place.'

Patsy started rummaging in her handbag, continuing the subterfuge. 'Shit.'

Her expletive came slightly unexpected. 'Sorry?' the attendant queried with a frown.

'I'm sorry for swearing . . . I don't seem to be able to find my boarding pass.'

'I can organize another one for you if you like.'

Having wasted enough time talking to the attendant, it was time to move on to step two.

'That's fine. I'll just take a seat and find it. Once I get past the kitchen sink in here—I'm sure it must be in here somewhere—thank you.'

'Good luck,' he offered as she turned to walk back toward the seats.

Continuing to fluster over searching for her boarding pass she sat directly opposite Joan and her chaperone. Aware they were watching her antics; Patsy looked up to Joan and pulled off the perfect embarrassed smile. 'I wanted to change my seat,' she lied, 'they've put me near a window. I've got this terrible fear of flying.'

Rowlands stared at her blankly, without a hint of interest, or suspicion.

'I am the worlds-worst,' Patsy sighed as she kept rummaging. 'Do you like flying?' she rattled, giving Joan her cue.

'This is my first time,' Joan told her politely, hoping Debra wouldn't recognise the mechanical sound in her voice. *Do you like flying*, had been prearranged to allow Joan to recognize Maxine's stand-in.

Joan's boarding pass was already in her hand ready for the next move. She let the ticket drop to the floor—and as planned—Patsy retrieved it and handed it back, taking a quick peek at the seat number.

'Thank you so much,' Joan told her with a smile.

Patsy returned the smile. Her job done, she returned to rummaging in her handbag, faking frustration. 'Now I can't find my damn boarding pass; I think I might have done the same thing you just did.'

Confirming her disinterest, Rowlands turned away long enough for Patsy to give Joan a wink. 'I might have dropped it at the news agency,' she concluded for Lisa Rowlands' benefit.

Patsy darted off to complete her mission.

Away from gate eight Patsy pressed her cell phone against her ear, and spoke in hushed tones. 'I've got what you need,' she breathed sounding like there was never any doubt. 'They're in first class.'

Cameron listened to Patsy as he sat in the Qantas CEO's office. 'First class - good,' he reiterated into the phone as he caught the CEO's eye, 'that makes life a bit easier.'

The CEO was already studying his computer screen, aware of the urgency.

'I'll need a *second class* ticket,' Cameron told Patsy and the CEO at the same time. 'Thanks again *Pat*, I'll bring you back an Oscar. Get yourself some breakfast. Bye.'

The call for passengers to board flight 155 for Hong Kong was already echoing throughout the airport.

'You can be lucky,' the CEO told him, proud he was able to find a seat at such late notice. He pressed a few keys and a boarding pass started printing.

'Thanks again, Thomas,' Cameron offered.

Thomas handed his friend the boarding pass. 'Enjoy traveling with Qantas.'

'Nice,' Josey told him with a wry grin, 'no wonder you made, CEO.'

Josey rushed toward the gate, anxious not to have his name announced over the PA. At least he now knew Lisa wouldn't be on the flight, thanks once again to, Thomas. There was one more friend he would need to rely on for help. He dialed a number into his cell and kept striding in and around people as he waited for the connection . . .

'Lou, Cameron Josey,' he announced breathlessly. 'I'm coming into Hong Kong this afternoon and I may need to get into China in a hurry, can you fix it up?' The receiver of his call answered quickly. 'Thanks - you're a gem. See you soon.'

Cameron had no sooner pocketed his cell phone when he saw Lisa Rowlands walking toward him. He pulled out his phone again and turned his back on her as she passed. He was pretty sure she hadn't seen him, and it was good to know she wouldn't be on the plane. He waited until she was out of sight, and then jogged to the departure lounge.

The attendant checked Cameron's boarding pass and closed off his computer, satisfied the detective was the last passenger to board.

CHAPTER EIGHTEEN

In the arrival lounge at Cheklapkok Airport, Lee Sung was stationed with Joan Crestling's name scribbled across a card for her to see. She had no idea what her expected visitor looked like, only that she was a European woman in a wheelchair. Josey stood among the crowd that had located themselves around the baggage carousel and watched the woman as she waited for her contact to approach and identify herself. Even though Joan had sat alone throughout the flight, he couldn't be sure other people connected with the University weren't watching her every move. For now he'd keep his distance. Although there was no concrete evidence that Joan's life was in any sort of danger, back in Sydney he had made sure she knew not to acknowledge him, not even with the slightest glance.

'Where was Joan Crestling being taken, and what would happen when she got there'? - He would have been happy to follow this question even without pay.

He allowed himself to enjoy the moment; indulging in the euphoria he got from trying to uncover a mystery.

Joan was impressed by how modern and huge the airport terminal was. Descending onto the new tarmac on Lantau Island had been spectacular in itself. Everything about this place was so clean and fresh, it made her feel she was right to come here. The feeling grew when she caught sight of the smiling young woman holding her name.

'Hello,' Lee Sung chimed in perfect English as she moved forward to take the chair. 'You are Mrs. Joan Creastling?'

'Yes, and you are, Lee Sung,' Joan confirmed.

Josey watched the two ladies becoming acquainted as they made their way toward the baggage collection. He mingled and waited for his bag to slide into view. *The next phase might be tricky,* he thought. There was no way he could know their travel arrangements, but he figured the first leg of their journey should take them on the ferry to the T.S.T district on the Hong Kong waterfront. From there it might be a Red Cab to a hotel. Or, a special hire-car perhaps; he hoped not, because that could take them any place. Without knowing if they'd already organised a visa for Joan, he couldn't determine if she might even be taken *directly* somewhere else in China. If that happened—with a bit of luck—Chen would, hopefully, have a visa waiting if Josey needed it. There was also the possibility they'd take the high speed train.

There was another option he hadn't even considered, because of Crestling's disability.

With bags in tow, they went to a courtesy bus, one capable of taking a wheelchair. It wasn't the bus that he hadn't considered; it was where the bus was taking her. An insignia on the side of the vehicle made its destination perfectly clear - *Lantau Link Helicopters*. What wasn't clear was where the helicopter would be taking them. Josey had carefully studied the half dozen other people who had boarded the bus and decided there was only one person who could identify him, and that was Joan Crestling. Of course the Chinese lady might have been given Josey's description, but that was a stretch. With little choice, he decided it was time to take the risk of becoming a passenger. As he entered the bus and passed where the ladies were seated, Joan turned to the activity outside the bus, relieved that the detective was still with her.

The helicopter lifted above the tarmac and stretched away from Lantau Island. Below, streams of crawling vehicles traveling along Route-8 made their way toward Hong Kong City. Running parallel with the cars, the M.T.R express train was barely matching speed with the chopper.

The spectacular Tingkau bridge slid beneath them and a minute later they were setting down on the rooftop pad of the Peninsula Hotel, right on the waterfront in the Tsimshatsui District.

The Peninsula, with its old-world charm, attracted the kind of patrons who had no need to squabble over money. Most people who checked in here were either loaded, or had someone else paying. Josey had the Pyrmont-expense-account to cover his stay. People no longer worried about their personal appearance when visiting classy places like this—not like they used to. This suited Josey's casual style nicely, the last thing he wanted was to stand out. As Joan and her Chinese companion checked in, he deliberately stood close to eavesdrop on the details of their stay.

'Lee Sung, your penthouse apartment is on floor thirty five,' the desk clerk said, sounding like she was talking to the Chinese Emperor himself.

'No,' Joan piped up decisively. 'I want a room to myself.'

'It is an apartment, Joan,' Lee assured her. 'You have your own bedroom.'

'Please, I need to be by myself.'

Lee and the girl behind the counter glanced at each other as if Joan had invented a brand new problem, one never before encountered by them.

'I have two adjoining rooms on the penthouse level,' the girl volunteered hopefully.

Lee thought about it for a moment and decided it would be okay. 'Thank you; that will be fine.'

The girl gave the computer the changes and handed over the new keys.

'Rooms number three-five-zero-eight and three-five-zero-nine, with a very good view of the Space Museum and Salisbury Gardens; I think you will both find them very satisfactory. Room three-five-zero-eight is for Mrs. Crestling.'

'Thank you,' Lee said again, taking the keys.

As they left the desk and moved toward the lift, Josey was satisfied he didn't need to follow; he now had the chaperon's name, and Joan Crestling's room number.

An hour later, relaxing at the bar, he rang through to her room.

'If you're not alone—just say, no I didn't order any champagne.'

'I *am* alone, and *no I haven't ordered champagne*,' Joan answered in high spirits. 'But if you're buying.'

'I certainly am,' he told her without hesitation. 'I'll send something up.'

She understood that to mean he wouldn't be coming. 'Oh, right.'

'Love to join you, but best I stay out of sight for now.'

'Right.'

'Any clue as to where your next stop is?'

'No. I asked her, but she's obviously been told to keep it to herself.' Joan sounded nervous.

'Hmmm, well, I guess there's nothing we can do until morning. They may have an open account, so I'll watch she doesn't take you straight to the car park.'

'How will you know?'

'I've organised a little help from a friend,' he assured her. Joan's silence convinced him she was beginning to feel the pressure. 'Try not to worry, my friend is very influential.'

'I'm so glad you're here. I don't know how to thank you.'

'I'll think of something,' he joked.

Joan released an exhausted laugh, accepting his joke graciously.

'One thing Joan,' Josey warned, 'if you don't lay eyes on me in the morning, promise you'll refuse to go with these people.'

Joan was silent again.

'Joan?' . . .

'You have my word,' she finally agreed.

'All right; get some rest. I'll see you in the morning.'

'Yes you will,' Joan confirmed.

Josey closed off the call, finished his drink and headed off to order Joan's champagne.

While waiting for help at the front desk he dialed a local number into his cell. 'Lou, it's me,' he announced after a second or two, 'As expected, I need your help.'

Lou Chen arrived in the hotel foyer and flashed his badge at the male receptionist and spoke in Chinese. 'Detective Sergeant Chen. I'd like a word with the hotel manager.'

Josey watched from a comfortable lounge nearby, the worried manager arrived to find out what the police detective wanted, listened, nodded and moved to a computer terminal.

Casually, Chen looked around the foyer until his eyes fell on Josey.

There was no sign of recognition between the two men.

Chen responded to the manager as he returned to the desk. A few words were spoken, and the policeman handed the man his card. He then walked toward the exit without giving Josey a second glance.

Outside the hotel, Chen got into the passenger's seat of a police car and placed a call.

Back in the hotel lounge, Josey answered. 'Hi.'

'A hire car is picking them up at eight thirty in the morning,' Chen's voice told him. 'I will have an unmarked car here to pick you up at eight.'

'Many thanks Lou; I'll be ready.'

At 8.30am, Josey and Chen watched from an unmarked car as Joan and Lee were picked up outside the hotel by a special purpose vehicle.

The last person on Josey's mind at that moment was hidden from view inside the lobby.

Benjamin Bright watched the black limousine pull away from the valet driveway and enter traffic. He turned his attention to the unmarked police car that followed and spoke softly into his cell phone. 'They're following. You know what to do.'

The driver of the limo carrying Joan knew very well what to do. He panned to the rearview mirror to get visual confirmation and to note the make and model of the car following. 'Right,' he said simply, aware not to alarm his passenger. Lee Sung caught the driver's eye in the mirror. She knew instantly what was happening and lost the practiced smile she'd been wearing while in Joan's company.

Leaving the hotel, Bright made another call and waited for a response. 'There's been a hitch,' he told the person on the other end of the line. 'The subject may be late.'

The limo took several strange turns within the city, making Chen suspicious. 'This driver is either new to Hong Kong, or he is onto us.'

A knot gripped Josey's stomach. 'We can't lose her Lou,' he pleaded. 'I promised Joan she'd be safe.'

'Don't worry. There's no way he can get out of the city without detection, I'll call in backup if necessary.'

The words had hardly left Chen's lips when the limo lurched to the left into a narrow lane way and increased speed. 'Time to call in those troops,' Josey suggested urgently. Chen pushed his car toward the lane, but got held up by pedestrians. He set-off the siren to disperse the hapless group and called for backup.

'What's happening?' Crestling screamed as the limo squeezed its way down the narrow lane at high speed.

'Nothing is wrong Joan,' Lee told her calmly. 'We must hurry to make our connection.'

Crestling wasn't convinced by her explanation. Unless things were different in China, drivers trained to transport the disabled never put their passengers at risk by speeding—not for any reason. 'I want you to slow down right now!' she demanded on top of her voice.

The crazy chauffeur suddenly appeared to over react by screeching to a halt and leaning on the horn. A man came running out of a building in response and entered into excited dialogue with him.

'What the hell is going on?' Crestling screamed with agitation. The man outside gave her a glance as he waved the limousine on.

In a rear facing mirror provided for wheelchair occupants, she was able to watch behind as the man on the street and a select group of his friends began blocking the road with barrows and anything else they could lay their hands on. She barely saw the car carrying Josey come to a smoky stop the other side of the hasty obstruction, hardly heard the siren wailing in annoyance. An immense fear gripped her—she was on her own.

At the makeshift roadblock, with the getaway vehicle already receding from sight, Chen jumped from his stationary police car and pointed a revolver at the men and women responsible for the barricade. He shouted at them in Chinese ahead of a shot into the air. They began shifting the mess as clumsily as they could.

Fed up with the lackadaisical response, Josey slid into the driver's seat and created a path by plowing the remaining mess out of the way, along with the idlers who suddenly found the energy to move.

'Get in!' he yelled back to his friend when he came to a stop. Chen didn't argue.

The limo had gone out of sight by the time Lou made it into the passenger seat, encouraging Josey to pour on the power, narrowly avoiding running down remaining loafers.

'This is a police vehicle,' Chen reminded him with exaggerated calm. 'My helping you did *not* include you driving it.'

Josey wasn't listening; they were losing their grip on the situation, losing sight of the limo, the tight lanes contributing to placing his client's life at risk.

She's living her worst nightmare right now, he thought as they rounded a bend.

His guilt swelled to despair as he brought the police car to a sudden halt - behind the stationary limo—

Abandoned!

Chen checked inside the cabin—she wasn't there, which meant she was either, still alive and living the nightmare, or . . .

He didn't want to think about it.

Josey checked the empty vehicle for clues while Chen pushed and pulled at doors of nearby buildings calling out her name—thinking she may have been taken into one of them.

Finding nothing inside the car, Josey diverted his attention to the immediate surrounds. 'Chen; take a look!'

Chen saw Josey staring at the roadway. He was studying thick black tire marks that had been traced into the bitumen.

'She's been transferred,' he told the cop.

The alternate vehicle had sped away to god-knows where.

Josey paced like a lion lamenting lost prey.

Chen barked orders into the police radio in an attempt to find out who owned the limousine that had been left behind. He glanced at his friend and read his mind—he was blaming himself . . .

At police headquarters, Josey continued his pacing in Chen's office as he put through a call to Australia. Maxine answered. 'Max, there's a real problem. I'm afraid I've lost the tail on, Joan.'

She heard the stress in his voice. 'Oh, no — where are you?'

'Still in Hong Kong; I'm with Inspector Chen.'

'Can't he do something?'

Chen was sitting at the other side of the desk with a glum face. 'Not that simple,' Josey told Max, 'the hire car we were following was down from Nanjing; rented out by *T-S-Tours*—who just happen to not exist.'

'What happened?'

'They got onto us and switched cars.'

'I guess this means we can be certain they're up to no good.'

'Not that there was ever any doubt . . .'

Maxine had seldom heard her boss sounding so depressed. 'Got some news that might cheer you up,' she told him with a lift in her voice.

'I could do with a little cheering right now.'

'Good, because you're going to love this; I did a little digging, found out she can't have children'

Josey's brows collided, forming a furrow. 'Who?'

'Joan — she *can't have children*?'

'What does that have to do with anything?'

'Perhaps everything.'

'I sense you're itching to explain, so how about you get on with it.'

Maxine laughed . . .

'So, Silvia rings me, right, out-of-the-blue like. Says she wants to talk. We meet, have coffee, we talk. First, she talks about Les, about how he admits to reinstating you. She's pretty negative about that—so, I begin to think, it's just a *whinge-fest*. But then, she just comes right out and tells me, *Charlie has lost interest in sex*.'

Maxine couldn't see his impatience but could hear it in his voice. '*Max*—'

'I'm getting to it . . . So, when I get back to the office, I start thinking, maybe that's what they've *all* got in common.'

'They've all *lost interest in sex?*' Josey asked losing sight of her point.

'No—I mean, they all can't have children.'

'You've lost me.'

'Joan is sterile. And, Charlie is impotent. I did a little delving—off the books—hope you don't mind.'

Maxine finally had Josey's undivided interest, and understanding. 'And I'm betting Silvia doesn't know about Charlie's impotency?'

'From the way she spoke, not a chance - she just thinks he's lost the plot—'

'Do me a favor; try finding out the *stats'* on Joan's husband, Richard. Also, check out how many tickets to Hong Kong have been booked by Valley Bells and how often.'

'On it,' she agreed enthusiastically.

'Good. Let me know how you get on.'

'Will do—'

'Good work Maxine. Please call me when you've got something . . . Right, bye.'

Josey pocketed his phone and stared at Chen blankly, his mind still on Max's conversation.

The Inspector didn't look happy. 'Joan has been issued with a visa; she is now able to go anywhere in China.'

'Great,' Josey expressed with aggravation.

'It will be very hard to find her.'

'Not your fault Lou. Anyway, we're not done yet. I may still need your help once Maxine gets back to me.'

'No problem,' he offered defensively, 'so long as it doesn't involve you driving one of my police cars or car chases throughout our city.'

Josey managed a weak smile.

Josey stood at the window of his hotel room taking in the grandeur of the bustling harbor. Max's call finally came through an hour after speaking to her in Lou's office . . .

'There have been twenty three bookings in as many weeks,' she told him. 'The next one is in three days; a man by the name of Francis Dainry.'

'Max, you're a Gem.'

'I know,' she joked. 'Hey, hope this helps.'

'You and me both, let Silvia and Les know what's going on, but make sure they stay put until I know more. I don't want them running up here just yet.'

'Understood.'

'Thank you Max, send through what you've got on this guy and we'll talk later.'

'Done.'

Josey finished the call and poured himself a stiff drink. He now had a potential chance to pick up the trail on Joan Crestling, but this time he'd have to be smarter about keeping it. He knew someone had to have been watching him, but had no idea who. Benjamin Bright hadn't entered his head.

CHAPTER NINETEEN

With eyes closed, Charlie Pyrmont felt the warmth of the sun across his entire body and allowed imagination to present the tropical scene to his mind's eye.

He saw the crystal clear turquoise water and the palm trees that hung like whispering umbrellas over the pure white sand that he lay on. The sound of birds flying overhead and the gentle waves slapping against the beach completed the picture.

The air, fresh with salt and sun-lotion, brought a new smell.

Footsteps squeaking toward him in the sand raised his expectations. He smiled with eyes closed. Sprinkles of water, transported from the ocean by her lovely body, created cool freckles on his skin.

'Are you going to lie there all day?' she inquired.

He opened his eyes to the shapely silhouette and the glare of the sun's aura that encircled her.

'Well?' she persisted.

He rose to his feet sharply . . . 'Race you in.'

Charlie leaped into the lead, pushing Rowlands onto the sand to get an early advantage.

She regained composure and caught up as he carved a path into deeper water, lunging forward with arms outstretched to create the biggest title wave he could muster. She leaped onto his back and gripped his shoulders for a journey toward the projected mosaic patterns on the pure white sand twenty feet below. Their movements were slow and sluggish in syrup like water, conjoined; they employed a combined effort to remain submerged.

After great exertion they reached the sand. Staying there became a new and greater challenge. Charlie wrapped an arm around her waist and dislodged a loose rock to use as an anchor. Her legs drifted toward the surface and she clutched his hands to prevent from floating away. Swaying like sea grass in the currents, she pulled herself down to meet his lips, whereupon they continued to breathe, drawing air from each other.

They remained in this embrace without fear. Seconds turned to minutes, attracting the curiosity of schools of tropical marine life.

A hammerhead shark swam near enough for them to reach out and touch its smooth body.

A sea snake coiled around Debra's torso, lifting her away toward the rolling surface. Charlie released his makeshift anchor and ascended through the thick salty water in pursuit. Twenty feet above, her entwined companion released its hold and swam away as she broke the surface. He lifted with such speed that he jettisoned beside her like a whale breaching - bobbed in the water like a float - and settled knee deep with her. He marveled at his freedom of movement and the mysterious buoyancy that they were achieving without effort, conjoined seaworthy buoys swaying together in a tight embraced.

'Would you like to make love?' she breathed with their lips touching. Charlie answered by leading her toward the shore, knee deep—suspended above the sand—until their feet touched bottom. A small fish darted from beneath for fear of being trampled.

Hand in hand up the beach, Charlie somehow knew none of this was real, but he didn't care.

Just being able to move was all that he craved.

As before—when he had experienced weightlessness in space—the memory of how he got to this paradise was vague.

If this is not real, then it sure feels like it, he thought.

One thought skipped to another, again without any form of connectivity.

. . . Now, in the shade of the beach palms, they sealed their passion, caterpillars wrapped in infinite ecstasy.

They levitated, as before . . .

Where gravity should rule, they floated, tall grass swaying beneath them, sliding away with increasing speed, with increasing excitement . . . unified release manifesting a staggering, unbearable *throbbing* inside his head—

A merciful blackness ended it—

'Charlie, are you awake?' He heard Doctor Gillard asking . . .

Director Benjamin Bright was his usual bubbly self as he entertained his newly arrived guest. His office here in paradise was very unlike that of his Valley Bells office, reflecting the resort-like appearance of the rest of the establishment. Floral shirts, shorts and sandals were the order of the day, even for newcomers like Joan Crestling.

Joan seemed to have overcome the trauma of the odd way she had been brought to the island, helped by the fact she was again in the company of her husband.

Looking the quintessential resort director, smiling Benjamin sat opposite them in a comfortable wicker chair laden with colorful floral cushions that reflected the tropical environment.

'I'm really very sorry for alarming you, Joan,' Benjamin told her with sincerity. 'I trust you're feeling better now.'

Joan turned to her husband and reached out to hold his hand. 'I'm with Richard, that's all that matters.'

'I hope you understand why we can't just invite people into our trust without the strictest secrecy. We've made a big concession in your case, mainly because, to be frank, we had no choice.'

Joan wondered what would have happened to her if a choice had in fact been presented to them. 'I won't pretend I'm impressed by the way you people work, but I can assure you I am not a threat to you.'

'Nor we to you,' Benjamin told her with his most professional smile.

CHAPTER TWENTY

Cameron Josey rushed into a cab outside his hotel and instructed the driver to hurry to, *Jetty Wharf,* on Canton road . . .

As the taxi arrived outside the wharf's entrance, Josey saw the police vehicle pulling up next to the *No Stopping* sign and instructed the Cabbie to do the same, which he did with a degree of uncertainty.

Inspector Chen and Josey met up and without so much as an *'Hello'*, hurried into the Xiangzhou ferry terminal accompanied by two police officers.

'According to Immigration,' the Inspector forced from breathless lungs, excitedly bringing his friend up to speed, 'Joan Crestling has only a *one-day-pass* on the mainland, but this does give her multiple entries once she reaches any island outside of a sixty mile radius.'

'How many islands are we talking about?'

'Not many; . . . fifty!'

Josey elevated his eyebrows. *Not many* seemed a complete understatement.

'Don't look so worried,' Lou told him. 'We know exactly where she has been taken.'

Josey thought there would have been less stress on his heart if he'd have said *that* first.

They reached the gates and made it onto a harbor ferry, which was already fired up to leave.

'We followed Mr. Francis Dainry to the island of Dawanshan,' Chen told Josey as they traveled away from the mainland. 'With any sort of luck, we will find your other friends there as well. Officially though, the Hong Kong Police are only concentrating in whoever has abducted Joan Crestling.' The inspector had doubt written all over his face. 'If in fact; she has been.'

'I appreciate this, Lou.'

Chen gave him a knowing squint. 'You can thank me after we successfully leave the island without being arrested ourselves.'

Josey fully understood.

The ferry berthed at the tiny island of *Dawanshan*, where they were greeted by the island's one and only police officer - complete with a rusty no-name vehicle that may have reached its used-by-date sometime in the sixties. Although the officer had probably spent a bit too much time in the saddle, he obviously knew his way around, taking them directly to their destination, *Greener Pastures Resort.*

The police and Josey stepped from the old copper's vehicle at the entrance to the resort's main building.

The two police waited outside while Josey and the inspector made their way up a wide wooden ramp, which led to a massive open doorway that a train could fit through.

The foyer opened into a rustic replica of a *House Tamberan*, reminiscent of those in Papua. It was also laden with Polynesian and various other South Sea island Artifacts—to the point of congestion.

Except for the anxious little Caucasian man rushing toward them, the area was void of people.

'Forgive me,' he breathed with an outstretched hand, 'this morning has just been absolutely crazy. I'm Murray Carmichael, Director, Bright asked me to look after you.'

Chen reached for his hand and introduced the others dutifully. No one noticed Josey's reaction to hearing Benjamin Bright's name because he hid his surprise.

'If you would like to wait here,' Carmichael told his temporary guests. 'I will bring Mrs. Crestling to you.' He spun away like a ballerina to leave the foyer.

'We'll come with you,' Josey quipped, stopping him in his tracks.

The man appeared positively dismayed.

Josey ignored whatever it was that was putting his nose-out-of-joint, remaining steely faced. 'We'd like to see her husband as well.'

The man flicked his eyes across the faces of his visitors, one to the other as if to sum up who was boss. 'I'm afraid that's not possible,' he finally said. 'I'll get her for you.'

Josey went to say something, but the inspector jumped in. 'That will be fine Mr. Carmichael. We will wait here.'

Josey wasn't impressed.

Once Carmichael was out of earshot, Lou thought a diplomacy lesson might benefit his gung-ho friend. 'At the moment they do not seem too hard to get along with. We should try and keep it that way.'

'I'll let you do the talking,' Josey said giving in far too easily.

Joan appeared a couple of minutes later accompanied by the indignant Murray Carmichael.

'You may be seated here,' he told them pointing toward a low solid table surrounded by equally low wicker chairs. As he proceeded to join them, Josey *bailed* him up a second time. 'We'd like to talk to the lady in private—do you mind.'

The man was beginning to understand who the boss was and that his comment wasn't a request. He was much quicker to assess his position this time. 'Fine,' he said, and pivoted away.

Lou gave Josey a sharp glare, but eased back when he noticed Crestling was actually enjoying the brash approach. He decided to let his friend take the lead in talking to her.

'Are you really okay, Joan?'

She smiled comfortably. 'I can see why you might doubt that, given the circumstances. Believe me; I am completely happy and safe.'

For Josey, this was beginning to sound like a cracked record. 'You were kidnaped, brought here against your will, and you're happy with that? I don't get it.' He studied her for any sign she was under any sort of duress. He had to admit she seemed relaxed—but he wasn't done. 'So, I gather you've seen, Richard.'

'Yes,' she admitted without hesitation, 'and he's fine too.'

Josey unnerved her with a blank stare, and then leaned back into his seat like the whole thing was suddenly unimportant to him. 'Well, I guess that's it then.'

She felt he was playacting, not buying any of it.

'What about Charlie?' he asked automatically.

'I haven't seen him.'

'Do you know if he's here?'

She hesitated, but only for a second . . . 'I'm sorry, I don't know.'

Josey checked to see if the inspector had any alarm bells ringing; it was hard to tell with Lou, because until he was absolutely certain of a misdemeanor, his poker face remained completely noncommittal. But then, like someone snapping out of a trance, he had his say. 'I appreciate that you say you feel safe, but in spite of your assurances, Mrs. Crestling, the Department will have to interview those in charge here over the manner in which you were brought to this place. And then there is the matter of trying to evade police in Hong Kong. That may carry a jail sentence.'

Joan showed panic. 'My God no, they will throw me out of here for all the trouble I'm causing.'

'It gets worse,' he told her with seemingly complete indifference. 'By your own words, it appears you came here willingly. That could make you an accessory to the fact.'

Josey thought, *he's bullshitting her*.

Joan searched for understanding—for Josey's help.

He recognised Lou was testing her resolve to stay at the resort and—for the moment—played along; telling her, 'It's a police matter now. Not much I can do.'

Desperate to neutralise the situation her demeanor changed, telling Josey, 'I'm still your best chance of finding out if something bad is happening here—'

'And how is that exactly, Mrs. Crestling?' Chen said weighing back in.

'She means she'll continue spying for me, that's the reason she came here in the first place.'

A light comes on in Lou's head. 'Am I wasting my time here, Detective? Did you, or did you not, lead me to understand this was about making sure Mrs. Cresting was safe, and about finding her husband; why all the pretense?'

'No pretense, Inspector,' Josey explained in a serious tone, keeping his eyes on Joan. 'I was against Mrs. Crestling spying in the first place. I haven't changed my mind.'

The two men sank away from the conversation as Carmichael returned. 'Mrs. Crestling has a therapy session in ten minutes,' he told them with a renewed sense of power. 'Can you gentlemen finish up soon?'

'We're done here,' Joan volunteered.

'One thing Joan,' Josey said putting a hold on her departure. 'May we see Richard before we go?'

He switched his eyes to study Carmichael's expression for any sign of alarm. He saw a slight glimmer of disquiet, but nothing definitive.

'I've already told the police that won't be possible,' Carmichael answered. 'You only applied for clearance to see Mrs. Crestling.' His eyes had rested on Lou.

'Is there a problem?' Josey wanted to know.

187

'No. No problem,' Carmichael told him with a snooty tone, dismissing the request . . .

He wheeled Crestling away, gawping back at the visitors as he left. 'I trust you gentlemen can find your own way out.'

Josey felt completely uncomfortable leaving without Joan.

Chen was simply confused about the whole meeting. 'Please tell me *you* understand what that woman is thinking by staying in this place?'

They began making their way toward the exit.

'Tell you what I *do* understand,' Josey said. 'She's in danger whether she knows it or not, and we need to get her out of here.'

As they descended the stairs toward the island taxi, Chen told him, 'Forget the, *we*. You do get that I was bluffing. Officially there is nothing I can do, not without proof she is being held against her will.'

'Then I guess I'll have to find you some.'

'Right,' Lou expressed nervously. 'Why does that thought scare the living crap out of me?'

'I don't know Lou; maybe coppers are just naturally nervous.'

The old police-taxi-driver was waiting at the curb, awake. He started the engine as they opened the back door to get in.

'Maybe it is people like you who make us nervous,' Lou told Josey as they settled in, 'just don't tell me what it is you are planning.'

The taxi moved off with the door open, which then slammed, almost catching Chen's foot. 'The sooner we get off this island the better,' he grumbled.

The expression on Josey's face indicated he didn't share the sentiment.

'Whatever it is you are thinking my friend, I don't want to know.'

Josey pressed his lips together and grinned at the disgruntled cop knowingly . . .

When they alighted from the island's transport at the wharf, Chen was careful not to notice Josey wandering away, deliberately avoiding drawing attention from his two officers, who had been patiently waiting for their chief's return.

He covertly watched Josey make his way deeper into the jungle, along the road that led back to the Greener Pastures Resort.

Under cover of darkness, he had little trouble gaining access via an unlocked door that led into a downstairs kitchen that was finished for the night. From there he found his way onto a narrow fire escape that took him to the second floor. From its balcony he got in through an open window that faced a wide empty corridor with a dozen closed doors. At the end of the corridor, one side of a double-swinging-door opened and a woman in a neat white uniform came out. She entered one of the other rooms paying him no attention. He walked toward the swing doors, careful to appear relaxed just in case there were hidden security cameras.

When he gently pushed the door in, he saw a dozen or so occupants in wheelchairs facing him, transfixed by a flickering light. They were watching a movie. Their attention captured, they paid him no heed, and he was able to advance into the room unnoticed. Even as he passed the rows of chairs no one turned to look at him.

He could now see what they were watching. Projected onto a large screen was a scene inside a laboratory, with people in white coats moving about among what appeared to be other patients — some in chairs, some standing—

A door swung open at the back of the room and Josey plopped into a vacant wheelchair.

A man in the same sort of white uniform that the woman in the corridor had been wearing made his way between the chairs and stopped beside Josey. He'd seen Josey come in and automatically believing him to be a patient placed a blanket over his knees and left via the double doors.

On the movie screen, the laboratory scene had given way to a shot of a young man and woman running between beds of flowers in a field, accompanied by rousing, romantic music. They fall to the ground in slow motion and kiss.

Applause and raucous approval rose from the appreciative audience. Josey moved his attention to a chair moving out toward the swinging doors. As the dark figure was then illuminated by light from the corridor, Josey recognised it was Charlie. Remaining in the wheelchair, he followed; keeping a safe distance to avoid the probability Charlie would make a fuss and draw attention.

As Charlie reached the lift, Josey was prevented from following by the arrival of a couple of the staff entering the corridor. As they passed, he turned his back on them and took a drink from a water fountain that was mounted low on the wall for people in chairs.

While he drank, he noted that the elevator could only go to the third floor.

The moment the staff members moved from sight; Josey chanced being spotted by running up the stairs carrying his chair to the third floor.

He sat at the elevator doors and waited for Charlie's arrival. The doors slid open and Charlie immediately recognised him from the couple of meetings they'd already had in Australia, not to mention the photo that he still carried.

'Hello,' Josey said with an impish grin.

Charlie brought his chair to a stop outside the lift. 'You don't give up, do you?'

'I try not to.'

'How the hell did you get in here?'

'Can we talk,' Josey requested in the hope Charlie wouldn't create a scene, 'in private.'

Charlie was extremely put-out by Josey's unsolicited and unexpected presence in his most secret of secret places, but thought accepting a quiet talk might be in both their interests.

'Follow me,' he said as he wheeled away.

Josey did so, remaining in the chair, and hoping he wasn't being marched into custody.

CHAPTER TWENTY ONE

Charlie had a private room to himself, comfortable and spacious, boasting a king size bed positioned under a generous window and with a living room that could have held a party of fifty. It had its own kitchen, itself a generous size. Complete with an oven, island bench, refrigerator and all the accessories one expects to see in a modern, up-market home, it also came with some necessary modifications to cater for people in wheelchairs.

Josey relaxed on the maroon leather sofa while Charlie prepared cups of instant coffee, a one-handed-task that he had become adept at.

'If you keep this up, you could really jeopardise my position here,' Charlie reasoned as he made the brew with hot water on tap. 'But I suppose you don't really care about that.'

'Maybe it's you who should show *care* . . . Care about Silvia—she loves you, you know.'

Charlie opted to say nothing in immediate response. He rested Josey's coffee on the arm of the wheelchair and brought it over.

'I don't need you to tell me who I should care for,' he said as he handed the coffee across. He wheeled back to the bench and collected his own cup, returning to position himself between the door and the kitchen.

Josey noticed there was an intercom within arm's reach from where Charlie sat.

'My being here is my business,' he told the detective with contempt, 'and my business alone.'

'Level with me, Charlie, do you really believe these people can offer you a cure?'

He looked Josey in the eye. 'Yes I do; that—and *immortality.*'

Josey was gobsmacked, responding with a sort of negative wonder . . . 'Really - and I'm betting you're not allowed to tell me how that's done.'

'I'll say one thing chum, you're a cheeky bugger.' He reached up to the intercom button. 'You know what - I don't much like your attitude.'

Josey slid his pistol out and pointed it. 'I'd prefer you didn't do that.'

Charlie wasn't expecting the gun—any more than Josey expected to resort to it. He had no intention of firing it, not even Chen could save him from prison if he pulled the trigger.

'We can do this easy, or hard. Either way you're going to hear what I have to say.'

'About what?' Charlie asked as he relaxed his hand into his lap.

'About this place being an illegal con; hence the secrecy.'

'You know, I can't imagine you know something that I don't. In fact I'd be prepared to place a bet on it.'

Josey kept the gun on him. 'What would you say if I told you I can *prove* this whole thing is one great big scam?'

Charlie let out an unrestrained laugh. 'If you're talking about the twin sisters I already know about them.' Charlie leaned forward in his chair to amplify an additional point. 'It makes no bloody difference,' he said defiantly.

Josey's priceless expression pleased Charlie no end. 'What else you got - *Detective?*'

The wind was undeniably taken from Josey's sails. 'If you already know it's a scam, what the hell are you still doing here? I don't get it.'

'And you never will *get it*, because—as you quite rightly point out—what they do here *is* top secret - and very-very illegal. And just to be sure you've got it straight - you didn't hear that from me.'

'If I had to guess again,' Josey added, 'I'd say you know what their secret is - otherwise you wouldn't still *be* here. Is that how it is?'

'Bingo,' Charlie agreed, awarding him ahead of another heartfelt laugh.

'Let me ask you this then,' Josey continued, drawing new energy from a change of tack. 'Why is it you can't include Silvia in this wonderful and *illegal* promise of immortality?'

Charlie wasn't expecting him to mention his wife. 'I just can't,' he said bluntly.

Keeping Charlie on the ropes, he asked. 'Can it possibly have something to do with your impotency?'

Charlie couldn't hide his surprise at the detective's Intel, a smirk dissolving from his face. 'Not even my wife or brother knows about that,' he confessed.

'I won't ask why you think she doesn't - your sex life doesn't interest me. But, *she knows all right*,' Josey lied. 'You can take my word for it.'

Finally, he had said something that truly rattled Charlie. He pushed on. 'So, tell me; how does the impotency tie in?'

'I'm not saying it does.'

'You're not saying it doesn't either,' Josey pointed out.

Angered by Josey's line of questioning, Charlie hit the button on the wall. 'This conversation is over.'

Josey put his gun away and took hold of Charlie's chair. 'Thing is, Charlie, I'm hired to get you out of here; whether you like it or not.'

Charlie tried holding the wheels from turning as he was being pushed toward the door, but Josey was far too strong.

'Why not just tell your goddamn wife what's going on,' he said as he brought the chair into the corridor.

The situation had Josey a little rattled—weighing up *why Charlie seemed so determined to stay*, against *questioning his own involvement in trying to make him leave*.

'This is not your business, you bastard! Leave me be!' With Charlie making such a noise there was little chance of reaching the main exit without detection. But, it was too late to turn back—the elevator had already announced its arrival on the floor, presumably with someone about to alight. Josey started toward the stairs, but noticed a ramp at the last moment and wheeled onto it.

Charlie continued protesting on-top-of-his-voice, his cries attracting the attention of the orderly that had stepped from the elevator. The man rushed to the top of the ramp and saw what the ruckus was all about. Astounded at seeing someone taking an occupied chair down the spiral-ramp at running speed—he took chase.

With the orderly almost on top of him, Josey made the kneejerk decision to remove Charlie from the chair and carry him the rest of the way, throwing him over his shoulder. The abandoned chair fell into the path of his pursuer, ending his pursuit.

Charlie was still screaming-blue-murder when they made the main lobby, attracting the attention of two burley security guards with pistols on their hips. They drew the weapons and trained them on Josey.

'Stop!' one of them shouted taking on a targeting stance, one that he probably learnt at some obscure academy.

There wasn't much Josey could do other than as directed. One thing was certain, Charlie was getting heavy and he needed to be put down—a three seated lounge was the closest and softest place to roll Charlie onto. It didn't stop Charlie projecting invectives over his less than dignified treatment, the offensive rave encouraging an orderly to rush in and attend to extraditing such unfamiliar language in the vicinity of the resort lobby.

The guards maintained combat poses, holding Josey at gunpoint.

'I'm not here for a shoot-out,' Josey told them with his coat open to expose his holster. 'Can we put the guns away, guys?'

One armed guard moved in and gingerly attained the pistol. The other advanced in cautionary steps with his weapon held at arm's length.

Josey raised his hands in the air in the vain hope that the guards might see him as no threat, but, following protocol, together they wrestled their perpetrator to the floor and held him there with combined encumbrance- by sitting on him.

Charlie had finally been convinced to stop swearing, but could not dispel mixed feelings of anger and fear. His *fear* was a consequence of Silvia's stress, so great it seems, she had felt the need to send her detective to bring him back. An even greater fear was that he might give in to her and return home.

The mollified orderly that Josey had left on the ramp, limped into the foyer with the abandoned chair just as Josey was being ushered away by the two guards.

'Tell Silvia to forgive me!' Charlie called out to Josey as he was being marched away.

'Tell her yourself!' he retorted. 'She'll be coming to see you!'

Josey had no idea if that would ever happen, or for that matter if the University of the Next Life would ever *let* it happen, but he still felt the urge to stir the pot. He still wanted to know *exactly* what it was that was being promised to Charlie and all the other individuals who had fallen-prey, and to understand what was keeping them from leaving.

The notion of *Immortality* was just too ridiculous, though he couldn't deny, Charlie's knowing about the twins had placed a serious chink in his armor of open-minded-deduction.

Flanked by the two security guards, Josey was ushered out of the lobby onto the covered landing just outside the massive entrance. At the base of the timber ramp, the old island copper sat sleeping in his beat up police car—

'Please, can I have a word with Detective Josey before he goes?' The woman's pleading voice brought Josey's marching orders to an uncertain pause.

The trio turned to Joan Crestling, her chair backed up against the outside wall.

A carefully considered nod from a guard offered Josey a moment to talk with her.

Taking up a bench seat next to where she had parked her chair he sincerely hoped she would finally tell him something he wanted to hear. It wasn't to be.

'Are you going to be all right?' she whispered sadly, genuinely worried over Josey's predicament, although clearly of fixed mind.

Nothing had changed.

He really didn't need any more belts over the head; Joan had made herself perfectly clear. There wasn't a thing left he could think to say or do to persuade her to leave, but given how far he'd put himself out for this confusing case, he believed he deserved something of an explanation. 'Tell me, Joan,' he said in a relaxed tone, 'did you mean what you said in front of the police officer, or was it just about being with Richard?'

She glanced away for a moment and he could see a film of tears glistening.

'I hope you don't believe these people can offer immortality?'

Joan gave him a light smile and lowered her voice. 'Honestly, about the *immortality thing*, I don't. But, Richard does. So, I tell them *I do*; and that lets me stay with him.'

'And the spying?'

'I'm sorry, I didn't want to go to gaol.'

Josey digested her reasoning, and then said, 'Lou was bluffing in case you haven't worked that out.'

Her expression gave away nothing.

He decided he wasn't quite done. 'You know, if you'd rather leave here, with Richard, I can still make that happen; no matter what he believes.'

'Josey, please let me put your mind at rest,' she said pleading for understanding. 'I've made these people promise me you'll be able to reach us at any time - well into the future. You can call and see that we're safe.'

Reasonable promise, but only if true, Josey thought.

'I gather you believe them.'

'Contact me in a month, a year, whatever. If I'm not okay you'll soon know. If necessary you can bring your policeman friend to the rescue and close this joint down.'

Joan had struck the final blow to any argument Josey had. He was feeling a little foolish for continuing to debate the point. 'I wish you luck then Joan,' he told her. 'I just hope you know what you're doing.'

'I'll look forward to hearing from you,' she offered with a comfortable smile, forcing Josey to return the gesture.

'A month, a year, and so on,' he agreed.

She laughed and held her arms out to invite his embrace, which he welcomed by giving her a heartfelt hug, thinking, *what a lucky man Richard is*. He couldn't help wishing Silvia had Joan's strength.

He eased away and straight into the arms of the guards, who then walked him to the waiting police car.

'My gun,' Josey requested.

The security guard removed the bullets, pocketed them and handed Josey his weapon.

As he and one of the guards settled into the back seat, the other guard reached through the sleeping driver's open window and tapped him on the shoulder to gain his attention, pointing to his passengers in the back.

Still groggy, the elderly fellow lifted his head and straightened up his policeman's cap. 'Where we go?' he asked in stilted English. The security guard rolled his eyes, the resort only had one destination possible—the ferry wharf.

As the car jerked away, Josey kept his eye on Joan until she was out of sight. He wasn't to know her distant wave was the last he would see of her in a very long time.

Leaning back into his seat, Josey studied the windows of the three story building as they slid by, wondering how many takers were in those rooms receiving their indoctrination into the University of the Next Life. He didn't have to wonder who was behind the last window on the west wall of the third floor, the one with the light still on. That was Charlie's room. Out of curiosity he kept his eye on it as they drew closer, wondering if Charlie might have been returned there to settle down for the night. He was about to wonder no more—

When very nearly adjacent, he saw something that made him shift to the edge of his seat for a clearer view . . . 'Stop the car!' he demanded.

The driver slammed on the brakes thinking he may have hit something.

The guard leant across Josey to see what he was looking up at; he saw what it was and wondered why he was so interested in the people who were standing in the back-lit window. He decided he didn't care and barked angrily at the driver in Chinese. Josey told him to *calm his bowels*, which he didn't appreciate, so he shouted at the driver again, presumably reiterating the order to move on.

Nothing was going to take Josey's eyes away from what he was seeing, as strange as it was. He jumped from the car before the driver could respond to the order to drive.

With his pride in tatters the security guard leaped out on his side and rounded the vehicle drawing his gun.

Josey ignored *him*, and the gun that was pointed at his head, his attention was fixed on the scene that was playing out in the window above . . .

Crippled Charlie Pyrmont was there, framed against the light of the room — looking down — smiling with contempt, and by all accounts—*standing*.

If this wasn't enough to blow Josey's mind, a woman came into view carrying a very small baby. There was no mistaking—the woman was Charlie's impervious mentor, Lisa Rowlands, Debra Rowlands' able-bodied twin sister. She rested close at his side like a proud new mum bringing bub to daddy.

If there was any doubt Charlie was standing as firmly as she, it was dispelled the moment he turned and took hold of the baby, cradling and kissing the infant.

The image of Charlie nursing a baby, *and standing*, was utterly surreal—impossible to believe.

Josey thought, *if there is any truth at all in what I'm seeing, why the con-job with the twins?*

Needless to say, Josey wasn't sold.

Lisa turned and looked down at the car as if she'd been aware the whole time that Josey was watching, evidenced by the fact she made no attempt to close the blind.

He watched the endearing trio in *disbelief* - trusting his eyes, but not what he was seeing, because what he was seeing made no sense . . .

Why the charade in the wheelchair if he's able to stand?

With all the disabled evidence that he had just seen inside, seeing Charlie upright flew completely in the face of logic.

Why have him standing in the window like that? To make sure I see him?

The guard decided his aimed pistol wasn't working so he housed it and opted to use physical force. Josey saved him the trouble by getting into the car before he could lay hands. The driver watched in the rear-mirror as the frustrated guard swept around behind the trunk and got in next to his enslaved passenger—one angry bark and the old copper dropped the clutch, catapulting the car forward.

Josey couldn't have been less focused on the antics of the driver, or the cantankerous security guard, who had taken to resting his pistol on his lap. He was more interested in the window and the fantasy within it, but the car's progress was beginning to leave the bizarre charade behind. He craned his neck, holding onto the image for as long as possible. Once it had left his line of sight, the memory of Charlie and the baby remained, playing over-and-over indelibly in his mind.

He thought, the possibility that the University had somehow provided Charlie with the power to stand, contradicted their inability to do the same for Debra, Lisa's crippled twin.

Logic refused to leave him.

Why go to such extraordinary lengths of deceit, if they could more easily have selected other successful candidates from their ranks, people who had been legitimately cured?

The more he thought about it, the more the whole thing began to once again, *stink*.

He decided he'd go with that thought.

Every bone in his body expressed the absolute need to continue doing his job, to figure out what was really going on inside those walls; but now of course—he had the added mystery of the baby to deal with. What possible connection could the baby have to what's going on?

Josey decided it wouldn't be a conundrum if they hadn't deliberately chosen to present him with such obvious inconsistencies. He also decided that this was undoubtedly the most interesting case he had ever been involved in. The prospect of getting to the bottom of it excited him.

'This is a good one Fredie,' he told his dead partner.

CHAPTER TWENTY TWO

Josey had plenty of time on his journey back to the mainland to think about his next move. He knew there was nothing he could do on his own; he would certainly need Chen's help; how to get it was the problem.

It was nearly midnight when the ferry reached the Canton Road terminal and what he really needed more than anything right then was sleep. He made the five minute walk back to his hotel and placed a quick call to Maxine in Australia, instructing her to book flights for Silvia and Charlie's brother Les to come to Hong Kong as soon as possible. He informed his assistant that he would contact them in the morning and explain things when he was feeling a little clearer in the head.

A couple of days later, Josey, Silvia and Les sat in Lou Chen's Hong Kong office listening to his reasons for not being able to include the police force in extracting Charlie from the Greener Pastures resort.

'You're beginning to sound like a copper, Lou. Why in hell can't you forget protocol and get a thorough investigation going.'

'You know very well why, clearly I cannot - on such hearsay. I need evidence, of impropriety. And even if I had it, it would take time to instigate. Your actions at the so called university have not helped the situation.'

Josey visibly slumped, amplifying his frustration. 'Lou please; there must be something you can do to help these people.'

Chen met Silvia's sad eyes with an apology written across his face. 'Can you understand, Mrs. Pyrmont, my position?'

'From what Josey has told me I only understand one thing, Inspector, my husband has been brainwashed into believing he can be cured; not only cured, but made to live—*forever*? . . . What sort of *shit* is that?'

'I agree with you,' Chen confessed, 'but my problem is this, none of those people have made an official complaint.'

'That's because they believe a miracle is about to happen,' Silvia pointed out. 'They're not likely to be *complaining*.'

'Then maybe it is not a policeman they need,' Chen suggested. 'Perhaps they would be better to solicit the help of a psychiatrist.'

'That's cute Lou,' Josey told him flatly.

Chen turned to Les and found him studying the floor. 'You've been very quiet Mr. Pyrmont; what do you think of all this?'

Les lifted his head, his eyes full of reluctance. 'If I had my way, Inspector, we wouldn't be here. I think we're flogging a dead horse.'

'We're here now Les, so let's make the best of it,' Silvia snapped.

Josey jumped in with support. 'I agree.'

Les gave Josey such a sour stare, the air could have been sliced with a knife. 'You can agree all you like, but I'm close to pulling out. And that means no more money.'

Josey stood and walked to the back of the room knowing full well he had contributed to Les's attitude, him being the only one he had told part of the story to, it was time to tell the others; and to fill Les in on the rest.

Turning back around, he found all eyes were resting on him. 'I was about to throw the towel in myself,' he admitted, 'but then, something happened that surprised even me.'

Noticing apprehension creeping onto Silvia's face, Josey knew he'd have to explain things to her gently. 'I wasn't planning to mention this until after you'd had time to settle in, but things have changed.'

Silvia shifted forward on her seat, deep fear taking hold . . . 'Go on.'

'When I was being escorted from the premises, I saw something that seemed to destroy everything I believed was going on out there.'

'Oh, God, can this possibly get worse?'

Josey returned to his chair, taking his time to ease into the story.

'You hired me to get to the truth about these people,' he reminded her, 'and, to bring Charlie home. Thing is, once I latch onto something, I'm like a dog with a bone, I tend not to let go while the bone is still juicy. And I can assure you; this bloody bone is definitely juicy. What I saw convinced me—without a shadow of a doubt—that, yes, the University is operating an incredible scam; that much we all believe. However, the scam is not at all what it seems.'

'What did you see?' Silvia asked with trepidation.

'Silvia,' Josey warned, 'I don't want you to get yourself upset, or be confused by what I tell you, because I promise there will be a plausible explanation in the end.' He scanned the faces, all anxious bar Les, who was clearly pouting. 'As I was leaving the resort, I saw Charlie standing at his window.'

Silvia's eyes lit with surprise. 'What do you mean, *standing*?'

Even Chen was leaning forward now, surprised that Josey hadn't mentioned this to him earlier.

'They were letting me see what they wanted me to see.'

No one was keen to buy into Josey's suggestion, but Chen finally did. 'Why would they do that?'

'To make sure I never came back.'

'Are you saying it was some sort of trick?' Les asked.

'It was a trick all right.'

Chen queried this, 'Exactly how do you suppose they performed this, *trick*?'

'I was only able to see Charlie from the waist up, he could have been held there by some sort of frame—an apparatus.'

Silvia wasn't sold. 'Couldn't he have been sitting on a tall stool or something?'

'Someone was right beside him. Their stance was clearly upright.'

The worry on Silvia's face was a good reason not to mention Lisa Rowlands or the baby just then, but Les's next question made him feel he aught not to conceal what he was hiding, his question seemed to demand it. 'Who was the other person?'

'No idea,' Josey lied, *shut-up, Les - please*.

Josey's description of what he had seen opened up a smorgasbord of scenarios, with everyone's imaginations adding to their own take on what was happening at the University's resort. The meeting went on for another half hour before Chen was forced to hunt them out so that he could get on with more pressing police business.

'Friend or no friend, your policeman buddy isn't going to be much help,' Les told Josey as they waited in the station's outer office for Silvia to return from the bathroom.

'He comes-*good* when least expected,' Josey warned. 'If anyone else in his department were handling this case right now, I'd be behind bars. Don't count him out just yet.'

Les glanced toward the ladies powder room, and then said, 'Why'd you hold back on telling the others about Rowlands and the baby?'

'In Silvia's case, better she's told in private. I've only told you to gage your reaction to telling her at all. My advice is to wait till we know more.'

'Knowing Silvia the way I do, she'd put two-and-two together . . . It's been nine months, right. She'll immediately assume Charlie's been having it off with Rowlands.'

'That's what I thought you'd say. However, there's more to the story.'

Les was reluctant to hear it, but appeared ready to listen anyway.

'She could be right in thinking the baby's Lisa's, but imagining the baby is Charlie's would be wrong.'

Les's furrowed brow requested clarification.

'Charlie's been impotent since he had his stroke,' Josey revealed.

'And you know that, do you?'

Josey ignored his skepticism. 'I do. I also know Silvia doesn't.'

Les glanced and saw that she was exiting the ladies. 'A small blessing I suppose. Will you tell her?'

'Not me,' Josey told him outright. 'I'll leave that to you when the time feels right, which isn't now.'

As she drew up next to them, Les offered comfort by taking her arm. 'Ready?'

She nodded despondently and the trio left the police station to make their way back to the hotel.

CHAPTER TWENTY THREE

Josey awoke with a start to the sound of gunshots, *no, not gun shots*, someone pounding on the door. He sat up and looked at the bedside clock—unsure if he was still dreaming—it was three in the morning.

The pounding continued, becoming gradually more real. He dragged himself from the bed and put on a robe. 'All right, I'm coming! . . .'

Josey's mouth felt dry, and his head felt thick with uncompleted-sleep . . .

He peeked through the peephole and saw it was Les making all the fuss, the distress on his late-night visitor's face encouraged him to quickly remove the latch.

Les pushed on the door as it began parting, almost hitting Josey in the face. 'Steady on,' he protested.

'She's gone!' Les told him without apology.

'What do you mean, *gone*.'

'She's left the hotel.'

Josey of course knew he was referring to Silvia. Her leaving in the middle of the night was undeniably unusual, but he would have preferred being fully awake with time to think straight - a chance to bring her actions into proper focus.

'Wait,' Josey said, trying to rein in the situation. 'How do you know she's not gone *walkabout* in the hotel. Did you check the Lobby?'

'The night clerk says he saw her leave with her handbag. She didn't check out apparently. Or maybe she's left that to us.'

'Did she give any signals this might happen?'

Les appeared a little off colour.

Josey figured he knew why. 'You told her, didn't you?'

'What,' he said, trying to focus on the meaning of the question?

'About the baby; you told her—'

'I had no choice. Like I said, she guessed you were holding something back.'

Josey doubted that. 'How would she?'

'I don't know, maybe when I quizzed you about the other person in the window.'

Annoyed, Josey told him, 'This is why I wanted to wait.'

'I've known for a while she's not a lady you can hold things back from. Somehow she senses when you try. My sister-in-law hasn't been dealing with Charlie's leaving. She's extremely suspicious of everybody and everything. If you must know, I've been worried she might harm herself' . . . Emotion surged, 'I've done the best I can.'

He was beginning to see Les's reason for panic. 'I get that,' Josey said finally giving him some slack. 'Let me get dressed - I think she's gone to the island.'

He left him standing at the door with mixed feelings about her safety . . .

. . . Just as Josey suspected, Silvia had made her way to the harbor side only to find the ferry services had ceased for the night. Her heart was pounding with the fear of being alone in a strange country in which she spoke not a word of the local language.

In spite of potential danger, she finally plucked up the courage to approach a Chinese man who appeared to be living on his boat, and in the hope he spoke English asked for passage to *Dawanshan Island*. The man knew enough words to understand what she wanted, but seemed a little bemused by a woman alone in the wee hours of the morning. He could see though, she was not someone likely to take the risk of running away without paying him for his trouble, and judging by her appearance, probably handsomely. He helped her on-board, fiddled with the motor for a while, then out into the harbour. *Hopefully,* Silvia thought, *to the intended destination'*.

When the boat pulled into the wharf normally used by the ferries and Silvia saw the large sign confirming the boatman had brought her to the right place, she released a discrete sigh of relief. During the journey she had shifted the majority of her money into a concealed part of her purse leaving just enough notes visible to offer the man. As she paid him, she made sure that he could see the purse was void of further money.

He gratefully accepted the money she gave him and helped her onto the wharf.

'Which way?' she asked as the man began powering his boat away.

'Hill,' he said waving his arm, presumably in the direction of the resort.

Silvia looked, but could see only jungle, and a road leading into it. She turned back to the man, whose boat was receding into the dark, barely visible, still waving his assurance toward the jungle road.

Once the boat was out of sight, she waited until the beat of its motor could no longer be heard, hesitant about entering the jungle . . .

A deathly silence brought about a loud ringing in her ears.

When the boat owner completed his journey back to the Canton Street Wharf, he couldn't have been more surprised to find two more prospective passengers.

Les asked him. 'You see a woman here?'

He nodded expectantly. 'You want, go?'

'To Dawanshan Island?' Josey asked.

The man grinned happily and gestured for them to board his boat. They jumped aboard without further invitation and Les handed the man some money, which he gladly pocketed before powering the boat away from the wharf. This skipper was having a really good night.

Moving across the harbor, Les sat quietly watching the black water as the boat's wake slid to the stern. His silence was stemming from much more than Silvia running about in the middle of the night by herself. Here was a man who was worried about what his distraught sister-in-law might do. He wasn't the only one.

They sat in mutual silence for the whole trip.

Nestled among the surrounding jungle, the Greener Pastures Resort building appeared dark and ominous. Silvia's heightened imagination summoned a fantasy that somewhere inside of its walls her husband was having sex with Lisa Rowlands. The insidious hatred that was devouring Silvia's heart frightened her more than the task that lay ahead.

She moved cautiously toward a ground floor window, wondering if she was perhaps being watched at that very moment. Josey had relayed how he'd gotten into a downstairs kitchen, but she couldn't find it. From Josey's story of how he'd seen Charlie, she was fairly certain she knew which window was his. If she had it right, it should be three windows up, directly above the one she was approaching at the edge of the building.

The upstairs window she assumed was Charlie's was open, but all she could do was stare and wish she could fly. If only she could get in through the bottom window, it shouldn't be too difficult then to find her way to Charlie's room. But how would she manage breaking in through a closed window without making a noise. She picked up a garden rock, but then abandoned the idea.

Maybe the window isn't locked, she thought, *what if there's someone inside unable to sleep—already aware she is lurking outside—and just waiting for her to break in to hit her over the head.*

Her imagination was running wild.

She drew a deep breath and tried sliding the window up; it wouldn't budge. Reaching to her backpack she retrieved a sizable flashlight and held it against the glass, taking the risk of illuminating the room . . .

In the middle of the floor there was an elderly man soundly sleeping in a reclined wheelchair . . .

To one side of the window she noticed a metal frame with leather straps . . .

This must have been what Charlie was standing in when Cameron saw him.

Spurred on, she hatched her next move. This would be even riskier. She rapped on the glass, leaving the torch shining into the room.

The man awoke, saw the light at the window, and as expected couldn't see past its glare. At first he wasn't sure what to do, but then he righted his chair and wheeled apprehensively toward the mysterious orb.

Silvia switched off the torch and ducked down out of sight as the man grew near. As she hoped, the window opened. It opened so smoothly that she deduced it was electrically driven. The man's chair reached the wall preventing him from extending far enough to lean out the window. He couldn't know that Silvia was hiding in the garden below.

Gripping the solid flashlight nervously, she waited for the man to give up his search.

Moments later, the low hum of the automatic mechanism became her que; she reached up and placed the handle of the flashlight on the sill, causing a safety device to automatically reopen the window when it hit the obstruction.

It wasn't what she expected to happen, she would have been satisfied with an achieved five centimetre gap, enough to allow her to prize her way in once the man had fallen back to sleep. She removed the torch from the sill and waited to see if the man noticed the window was open, but after a minute or two realized he hadn't, or perhaps was happy to leave it. Perhaps he was hard of hearing.

Silvia waited in the hope the man would go back to sleep quickly. He began snoring so fast that she felt a touch of envy.

Once again she shone the light in, saw he was sound asleep, and then climbed silently into the room . . .

Charlie's wife couldn't have been further from his mind at that moment; Rowlands was straddled on top of him doing the work, but then without a hint of paralysis he rolled her over and took up the task as their lips met . . .

Silvia made it all the way to the second floor without detection. She traversed the lengthy corridor counting the doors until she reached the one where she believed she would find Charlie. The torch she had used at the window had weight to it, enough of a weapon if she needed to protect herself, held like that, it was ready.

The sound of Charlie's voice suddenly crying out held her back, an unmistakable expression of passion; a sound she was unprepared for.

In spite of her fantasies, it was a sound she didn't want to hear, a sound that froze her heart instantly.

Fighting through the shock she reached for the door handle and gently applied pressure — it began turning. When it had rotated fully, and she had dealt with the surprise it was unlocked, reluctantly, to see what was behind the door, she mustered the emotional strength to thrust it open—

She was presented with the sight of her husband and Lisa Rowlands on the bed together - exactly the way she had imagined — or was it?

Lisa swung round, shaken to see Charlie's wife at the open door.

What Silvia saw in that room shocked her, *yes*, but confused her much more.

Rowlands was fully clothed, and Charlie, fast asleep. This was *not-the-picture* she had built in her mind.

Charlie released another cry of sexual passion while Lisa slithered from the bed, more from embarrassment than anything else. She started to speak in her defense, but was cut short by Silvia charging at her with the torch. Too startled to move she took an unrestrained blow to the head, enough to make her stagger . . . She didn't pass out, yet appeared close to doing so. With blood pouring into her eyes she barely saw the torch raise again, ready to strike—

'Wait, you're making a mistake!'

The desperate voice had come from behind, startling her into abandoning the attack. The torch shook in her hand, as if it were a strong force mercifully bracing her wrist. She spun and saw the identical twin sister bound to a wheelchair, trying to make sense of what she was seeing.

'He's in a hypnotic state!' Debra pleaded from the chair. 'If you kill my sister, I promise he will never come out of it!'

The look-alike sitting in the chair *may-or-may-not be telling the truth* she thought, but given that all the shouting hadn't awakened him, Charlie certainly did seem to be in some sort of deep sleep, *perhaps under the influence of a drug?* 'What in God's name are you-people doing to him?' she whimpered in despair.

'If you've a mind to drop that torch,' a stern male voice offered from the shadows in a corner of the room. 'I will tell you when Lisa recovers from the injury you've inflicted on her . . . I'm Doctor Gallard and I have your husband in a deep state of hypnosis.'

Silvia was lost for words, and had no idea who Gallard was. She knew nothing of the hypnotisms, and was at a complete loss to understand what Charlie had become mixed up in.

She let the bloodied torch fall from her hand and went to the bedside where Charlie lay in a lather of sweat. She wiped his forehead with her hand and kissed him gently on the lips.

He began uttering words that were unrecognisable.

Lisa was sitting on the edge of a divan and holding a doily against the side of her head to stem blood flow, outwardly calm but feeling ready to have a stroke of her own – for real this time.

Dr. Gallard and the twins were less than settled by Silvia's sudden and unexpected arrival, and extremely stressed about what her presence might lead to.

Josey and Les looked up with bewilderment as a police helicopter raced in the direction of Dawanshan. It was now five o'clock and the sun's early rays were licking at the island's high ground.

'I don't have a good feeling about this,' Josey confessed as he watched the chopper recede.

Les let out a nervous breath. 'Can I take that to mean you didn't know your copper mate was coming?'

Les had learnt, the presence of a worried expression on Josey's face wasn't a common sight and marked cause for alarm.

In five minutes they were setting foot on the wharf. Les gave the skipper additional money and motioned for him to standby for their return. 'Okay?' he asked searching for the man's understanding. 'We come back. You stay for us.'

Money being the international language, the man smiled and nodded agreement.

They made their way off the wharf and started to jog along the jungle road that led up to the resort. After a twenty minute struggle up the steep climb, they came within sight of the resort's roof line. They heard the chopper firing up, presumably to leave. Even with their exhaustion, they managed to pick up the pace, arriving a minute later at the edge of the grassed area in front of the resort's main entrance.

The helicopter was there creating an increasing gale as they made their approach. Beyond the machine they could see Silvia had been handcuffed and was being led out of the building by police.

'Jesus,' Les breathed, 'what's she done?'

Josey wasn't waiting to find out; he rounded the spinning blades and made his way up to the entourage to ask that very question. Silvia couldn't believe her eyes when she saw Josey approaching with Les close behind. She couldn't fathom how they'd figured out where she was, or how they had got there so quickly.

Lou Chen was wondering the same thing as he stepped in front of Josey to stop him coming any closer. 'Don't even think about getting involved in this, Cameron!' he demanded above the noise. 'I swear if you make trouble here I'll arrest you and her brother-in-law as well!'

'I'm not stupid Lou!' Josey told him with a little anger of his own.

'Given your recent history, my friend, that's debatable.'

Josey brushed past him, striding toward Silvia and the two cops that were escorting her.

'Stay out of it, Detective Josey!' the inspector warned as he tried to keep up.

'What's she being charged with?'

'Not that it's your concern, - but *break and enter* and *aggravated assault*!' Chen stopped walking, drew his gun and pointed it at Josey. 'Stop; or I'll shoot!'

Josey never thought he'd hear those words from his good friend *Lou*. It was the surprise and not the threat that made him stop and turn. 'You're kidding, right!' he suggested.

'I am not kidding! Trust me! Move away!'

Josey noted that Lou's eyes seemed to be constantly darting away to his left. He turned in the direction of Chen's nervous glances, and saw Benjamin Bright. A realisation surfaced. 'Oh, I get it!' Josey said relaxing a little. He moved in close to the barrel of Chen's gun. 'Not here, not now. Is that how it is, Lou?'

Chen softened in recognition Josey had finally tuned in to the situation. 'Maybe *stupid* was a little harsh.'

'To prove it, if you take the gun off me I promise to behave.'

'What's happening over there?' Bright wanted to know from the steps of the resort. 'Doing a little deal with your buddy, Inspector?'

Josey was seething, but kept his back turned so that Bright couldn't see it. 'How serious are the charges,' he asked Chen.

'She hit Lisa Rowlands over the head with a torch.'

'That's it?'

'It's enough when the ass-hole making the charge is Benjamin Bright.'

'I hear you,' Josey agreed. He stepped backward, away from the policeman, visibly signifying defeat and indicating to Les to do the same.

'I'd like to talk to Silvia now,' Les demanded.

'Later,' Josey insisted. 'For the moment Lou's hands are tied.'

Chen signaled Silvia's escorts, commanding them to get aboard the helicopter with the prisoner. Feeling helpless, Les watched on as his sister-in-law was taken into custody. Chen gave Benjamin Bright a mandatory salute and joined the others in the Chopper.

The rotors roared to full speed, lifting the machine from the wind swept grass and away from the island toward the mainland.

Josey and Les agreed there was no sign of Charlie, or Joan, which was curious in the light of the noise and excitement. They saw Benjamin Bright looking pretty happy with himself, projecting a sickening grin as he marched in their direction.

'Let's leave before I break my promise,' Josey told Les.

Bright slowed his pace when he saw them walk away—heading across the grassed area and out of sight into the jungle. His disappointment at losing his chance to gloat at Cameron Josey's expense was clear.

CHAPTER TWENTY FOUR

Lou Chen was obliged to keep Silvia in one of the stations holding cells to await Charlie's arrival on the mainland. Not wishing for him to see her under lock and key, Chen transferred her to the interrogation room and made her copious cups of coffee. Charlie got to the police station just before lunchtime that afternoon, accompanied by Benjamin Bright. Benjamin was asked to wait well away from where Silvia and Charlie were to have their meeting, presumably the last they would ever have. Bright had objected, but Charlie reiterated the Inspector's request—he relented.

From within Chen's office where he and Josey had been going over events, they could see Bright sitting next to the coffee machine in the outer office. It was good to see him impatient and uncomfortable, and so out of his comfort zone; he very obviously wasn't enjoying the slop the machine called coffee.

Josey deliberately stood where Bright could see him pouring a nicer brew from Chen's personal percolator.

'What can we do?' Josey asked Chen one more time.

'Still working on it,' he told him gruffly. 'Thanks to you and your client we are forced to defuse Mr. Bright before we can do anything.'

'Chen, you've got more than enough muscle to scare this guy off without taking on heat.'

'Oh, you think so?'

'I do, he's already running scared.' Josey took his coffee and returned to his seat at the opposite side of the inspector's desk. 'The last thing he wants is cops snooping around his island. He won't press charges; if he does, he'll run the risk of exposing his little scam.'

'If only it were that easy—I can't be seen coercing him in any way.'

'Give me five minutes, I'll coerce the weasel.'

'And get us into more trouble.' Chen dismissed all responsibility by removing a set of handcuffs from a draw and throwing them on his desk. 'Just remember one thing—step out of line again and you will find yourself wearing these.'

Josey knew to respect the delicate position his friend was in.

Chen picked up on that, and added, 'But whatever you are planning; you had better do it quick.' He jabbed a finger at an official looking sheet of paper in front of him. 'Once Bright puts his moniker on this complaint, I am forced to hold Silvia in custody until there is a trial. And, worse, under the circumstances she will not be eligible for bail.'

Josey scooped up the document from Lou's desk and marched toward the door with it. 'When I bring this back,' he offered, 'it'll be confetti.' He left the room and headed straight over to Benjamin Bright.

Chen closed his office blind to avoid becoming a witness, further distancing himself from the *gung-ho* PI.

Silvia sat adjacent to Charlie's chair, electing to cup his disabled hand. 'Are you in love with that Rowlands woman?' she asked patiently.

He shook his head convincingly. 'That's not what this is about.'

'Then what *is* it about. Why can't you just tell me?'

Charlie kept his eyes cast to the floor, digesting her question. Finally facing her he said, 'It's complicated.'

Silvia wiped her eyes and shook her head.

A debilitating knot was tightening in Charlie's throat. 'I'm really sorry for the way things have turned out,' he confessed, 'it's not what I wanted.'

She wrapped her arms around his shoulders and buried her face into his chest, sobbing as she spoke. 'When, you are in that, *trance* - or, whatever it is I saw in that room; does she make love to you in your dreams?'

He gently lifted her up to face him, and said as tenderly as he could. 'It's not real.'

His answer was as good as an admission . . . 'But, at the time,' she whispered, 'while you're, *like that* - it *seems* it is?'

He held her as close as the chair would allow, unable to give her an answer. They stayed like that until the policeman, who had been standing by in the room the whole time, respectfully came forward and interrupted. 'Mrs. Pyrmont. I'm sorry, it's time to go.'

She stood and leant to hold Charlie tight, sensing this would be the last time they ever touched each other. Each second ticked painfully by as a growing reminder their time together was drawing to a close . . .

When she could no longer delay the inevitable she slipped from his grasp, avoiding eye contact as she turned toward the door. 'Good-bye, Charlie,' she said under her breath without looking back.

He hardly heard her. In anger, he clamped his hand over the arm of the chair and wept, lamenting the irony of his self-solicited prison.

His loving wife dare not turn around to see it.

The Inspector stood at the window of his office. On the street below; his visitors were heading their separate ways. His friend Josey was ushering his clients into a cab, while Benjamin Bright was positioning Charlie's chair into the back of the University's special vehicle. Chen let out a deep breath and returned to his desk.
He picked up the torn fragments of the document Josey had somehow convinced Bright not to sign and threw them into the wastepaper bin.

He thought back to the moment Josey had come to grips with the whole episode being over . . .

'A friendly word of advice,' he offered the PI, 'time to cut and run.'

'I can't tell you how unsatisfied that makes me feel,' he answered with a glum face.

'Hmm, I used to be like that. Now, I sleep quite well knowing I still have a cabinet full of uncompleted cases. Your case might not be completed, but it most definitely is over.'

Josey knew he was right, there was nothing more to be done, except get his sad clients back home to carry on their lives the best they could—without Charlie.

Benjamin Bright personally drove Charlie directly to the ferry terminal; he really wanted to know what had been said in the interrogation room with Silvia.

'Do you think she's off your back?' he asked.

'Don't worry,' Charlie murmured, still harboring a broken heart, 'she's gone for-good. Your big secret is safe.'

The faintest smile crept onto Bright's face. He felt certain he would never see Charlie's family again. He was especially pleased that the same might be said of the meddling Cameron Josey.

CHAPTER TWENTY FIVE

The years slipped away, as they must.

Twenty four years ago, Josey and his ex-clients had finally accepted that they would never see Charlie again. Josey had kept his promise to Crestling, calling her every month at first, and then reducing the contacts to every few months a year later. He continued to reach out for the next five years, always inquiring about Charlie's wellbeing, the results of which he would pass on to Silvia. Ironically, four years after their return from China, Charlie's brother Les suffered a massive heart attack and passed away, leaving Silvia totally alone. One day Silvia called and requested that Josey stop giving her the updates, explaining that it was too much of a reminder Charlie was no longer in her life. He respected her wishes, and in so doing began to lose interest himself. For the past fifteen years he hadn't made a single connection, partly because, according to a message Josey received from Inspector

Chen, the University had closed shop and moved deep into China. He hadn't received a call from Joan about the change of address, so he assumed the communication between them was considered, by her—to be over.

Time had been fairly good to Josey; he was now in his sixty-fourth-year and still fit. He made no attempt to suppress his true age by such means as dying his graying temples, or succumbing to the lure of the many unobtrusive face lifts that were around.

Back at the ripe old age of fifty, he had taken a wife ten years his junior. She wasn't just any woman; she was Charlie's brother's ex-wife, *Rebecca*. Although a totally unexpected union, even for Josey, and one that Silvia Pyrmont wasn't at all comfortable with, the situation was at least made tolerable, perhaps even acceptable, by the fact Les had passed away. If he had lived on, would Les have felt the same way as Silvia about this union, or would the union have even taken place. Josey could only hypothesise.

Meeting for the first time at Les's funeral five years earlier, their subsequent marriage could conceivably have appeared inappropriate. Josey felt it was probably this fact that had made Silvia feel so uncomfortable, although she'd never come straight out and said so.

Attracted by Rebecca's great personality and striking good looks, Josey took an immediate shine to her, and her to him, but they didn't connect romantically for at least a year after the funeral. They were married just four years after that. Already with an eleven year old daughter to Les at the time, Rebecca readily agreed with Josey's wish *not to have any children of their own*. Her daughter, Molly, whom she dearly loved, had become like a daughter to Josey anyway, and they quickly became great mates. Molly kept the Pyrmont name, but still called him Dad.

The three of them had settled into the outer suburbs of Sydney in a nice three bedroom house that needed little work. Josey was approaching retirement and was forcing himself to slow down, although he still had a couple of cases in the pipeline. On this particular afternoon he was in his neatly manicured garden at the back of the house cooking prawns on the BBQ in preparation for an expected visitor, part of his new life of relaxation. There was another reason for the BBQ; Molly was celebrating her 25th Birthday.

'Dad!' Molly called from the back verandah.

He turned and shaded his eyes against the sun and saw that his guest had arrived. Molly ushered the man down to be with her stepfather.

'Lou, long-time-no-see,' he said as they shook hands, followed by a bear hug and chummy back slaps.

'Good to see you old friend,' Chen told him.

'Enough with the old,' Josey instructed giving him a shove.

Molly smiled dutifully, but decided these two old fogies would be better left to themselves. 'I'm off to help mum with the salads.'

Josey raised a gleam in his eye when he faced her. 'Thanks, sweetheart.'

'Very nice to meet you Molly,' Chen offered.

She gave him a beautiful shy smile. 'Nice to meet *you*, Mr. Chen.'

They watched her take the garden path with a walk that was destined to melt hearts.

'So, now you are a dad,' Chen said as they watched her leave.

Josey gestured toward a nearby table. 'Come on, sit, we've got a lot to talk about.'

Molly waltzed into the kitchen to join her mother and help with the food preparation. 'How does Dad know him?' she asked.

Rebecca could see the two men through the window. Her answer was warm and reflective. 'Ask him—I'm sure he'd be happy to tell you.' With no time to stand around, she continued slicing into the salad on the cutting board. 'They worked together on a case in China. It was years before my time.'

'He seems like a nice man.'

'Yeah, he does,' Rebecca agreed. 'Apparently they were very close friends, even before the China case.'

Josey and Lou relaxed on cushioned wickerwork chairs, enjoying a drop of Josey's best *Cab-Sav*'.

'So, what can I expect in retirement?' Josey asked.

'Complete and utter boredom I am afraid,' Lou told him sounding blatantly honest about it.

Josey gave him an exaggerated frown. 'That doesn't sound too good.'

Lou laughed and said, 'I guess I should not be saying such things, not when you are on the cusp.'

'No Problem, I've still got a couple of irons in the fire . . . Anyway, I might freelance for a while; you know, do the cases I feel like doing.'

'I am very glad to hear you say that,' Lou revealed as he took a photo from his top pocket and rested it on the table. 'I may have a case that will interest you.'

Josey eyed the photo that Lou was keeping down-turned. 'What's this?' he asked with a keen smirk.

Lou flicked it over as though he were exposing a winning playing card and handed it across.

Josey couldn't understand why Lou was showing him a picture of *Charlie Pyrmont*—back when he was in his early twenties—just the way he would have been before his stroke. He could only assume Lou must be so bored with retirement that he's clutching at straws, trying to find something that would keep him amused, his serious expression said otherwise.

'I hope you're not suggesting what I think you are.'

Chen raised a mischievous grin, beginning to enjoy his friend's response. 'And what is it that you think I am suggesting.'

'Reopening the Charlie Pyrmont case . . . That's what this is about isn't it?'

'Correct,' Chen admitted without any hesitation. He threw back a mouthful of wine and leant forward in his chair. 'When I explain how I got this photograph, you too will want to reopen the Charlie Pyrmont case.'

He had Josey's interest. 'I'm listening.'

Lou sat back and relaxed into his answer, seemingly in no hurry to feed Josey's curiosity. 'Since retiring, I have gained a bit of an interest in photography,' he said sounding like he'd changed the subject.

Josey was compelled to examine the picture more closely, *a very young Charlie Pyrmont,* he thought. Finally he said, 'I still don't get why you're showing me this.'

'Look at the sign in the background.'

Josey focused on the street and the shops in the picture and noticed the letters on most signs were Chinese characters, except for the roman numerals promoting China's New Year.

Josey knew exactly what it meant, and all that his profound astonishment would allow him to say was, 'Bullshit, what the hell are you telling me?'

Lou answered with growing excitement. 'I took that picture one week ago in Nanjing while on holiday with my wife.'

He lifted his eyes to Lou for the explanation the picture promised. 'But, this is Charlie Pyrmont twenty four years ago.'

Lou drank more wine and said, 'Is it? You tell me.'

Josey squinted at the picture. 'How is this possible?'

'As you might expect, I tried to find out. I walked straight toward him to ask that very question.'

'And?' . . .

'As I came near, he saw my wife and me and ran away. I followed for a short distance, but we were no match for his agility.'

'So—he recognised you?'

Lou nodded with arched eyebrows.

Josey studied the picture again. In all his years as a private detective not many things had managed to completely take the wind from him, but this photo definitely did, he could find no logic in what he was seeing. A thought suddenly surfaced. 'This is not some sort of gag is it Lou; you're not so damned bored with retirement you've resorted to practical jokes?'

'This is no joke.'

Josey skulled his wine, poured another to the brim and did the same for Lou.

'Correct me if I am wrong,' Lou said, 'but this can only mean one thing. Everything that the University has claimed is true.'

Like Chen, Josey certainly was surprised by the photo—to say the least, but he wasn't about to accept that the University's claims of miraculous *cures and immortality* were in any way true. 'I tell you Lou, there has to be more to this than meets the eye. I know what you saw, I'm not disputing that, pictures don't usually lie, but don't be too quick to give them the prize. Not just yet.'

'That is exactly what I expected you would say,' Chen divulged. 'That is why I have come to Australia to tell you about this in person. Plus, I would like to offer my services to assist you in your investigation. That is, if you think I can help.' Chen was trying to read the expression on Josey's face. 'I take it you will be following up on this?' he asked with a pinch of doubt.

Josey glanced over his shoulder as if to make sure they were alone. 'Does a Koala Bear shit in the bush?'

Chen beamed - genuinely pleased, yet, maybe with a little apprehension.

Josey put his mind at rest. 'And, there's absolutely no way I'd do it without you, Lou.'

'Good,' Chen said without the excitement Josey was expecting . . . 'However, a thought occurs to me that in all good conscience I must put forward to you.'

'Shoot.'

'What if this young man in the picture, is just a relative to Charlie? Perhaps Charlie had a brother whose son is exactly like his uncle.'

'See, that's why I need you Lou, you still think like a copper. There is another possibility,' Josey added. 'This guy could actually be Charlie's son.'

'I'm sorry; I thought you said he was impotent.'

'Only after his stroke,' Josey pointed out.

Chen immediately understood. 'Oh, I see. He could have had an affair, before his stroke.'

Josey raised his glass to Lou in confirmation. 'That's two scenarios for us to work with, but, neither scenario answers what's going on with all the other desperate hopefuls. In order to answer Charlie's mystery, we pretty much have to find out what's going on with the rest of them. Nothing's really changed in that respect.'

While digesting Josey's comment, Chen tried to enlarge on it, but nothing came to him. 'So,' he said finally, 'when do we start?'

Now Josey appeared hesitant. 'Bit of a problem, the girls and I are about to take an extended trip to Europe. Rebecca's got her long service leave, and Molly has time off waiting to start university.'

Lou shared Josey's disappointment. 'Oh, that is a real shame, because I have no way of knowing how long this young man will stay in Nanjing. We may only have a very narrow window of opportunity to find him.'

Josey considered his point and mulled over his options. 'You're absolutely right Lou. It could be now or never.'

Rebecca was busy swishing away at the contents of a wok on the stove while Molly spiced up the salad with copious amounts of salad dressing. Their attention was drawn away to Josey's voice as he opened the back door and came in. 'How would you feel about a trip to China?' he asked.

The girls paused what they were doing and gawked at him like he had suddenly gone mad. Chen was behind him nodding confirmation that a trip to China was indeed on the cards.

'Right,' Rebecca said, deliberately suppressing her excitement. 'Let's get this onto the table—and then, you boys can tell Molly and me what you're on about.'

Settling back to enjoy some wine at the table; the girls were learning about Inspector Lou Chen, and China—and the change of plans.

'I must say I was looking forward to seeing the Eiffel Tower one more time,' Rebecca admitted, 'but China, well, it'll be different.'

'I think it will be absolutely fantastic,' Molly said enthusiastically.

'Will you be informing Mrs. Pyrmont?' Lou asked.

Josey shook his head decisively. 'No actually; not until we find this guy and talk to him. Silvia insisted I never mention Charlie ever again, and Les—sad to say—passed away twenty years ago.'

Lou was shocked. 'I am very sorry to hear that.'

'Young Molly here is Les's daughter,' Josey told him lightening the news.

Lou looked at beautiful Molly in a new light, 'I had no idea.' A quick calculation told him she would never have known her Uncle Charlie. It then dawned on him who Rebecca was.

'Lou,' Molly piped up changing the subject; she had been asked to use his first name, 'can I see Charlie's picture again?'

'It's not Uncle Charlie,' Rebecca corrected her.

There were amused glances all around as Lou took the photo from his pocket and handed it to Molly.

'He may as well be,' she observed, 'he's identical to the pictures in Mum's album.'

'He's handsome,' she observed after her inspection.

'Perhaps you will get to meet with him,' Chen said without thinking.

Given that they didn't really know what would be discovered about this young mystery man, Josey didn't want to have to deal with the possible ramifications of such a meeting with Molly, who just happened to be pretty attractive herself, and about the same age. 'Lou, let's not go there shall we,' he suggested with eyes on Rebecca to check her demeanor.

It was hard to tell if Chen was embarrassed, or confused by Josey's reaction. He said nothing. They continued talking about their plans to travel to China well past midnight, after which, Chen returned to his hotel. Josey and the girls stayed up for another two hours discussing the cold case and what to expect when they arrived in Nanjing.

CHAPTER TWENTY SIX

L ou settled his visitors into the Zhongshan Hotel, located in the center of Nanjing city, where they had easy access to everything from night markets to western pubs and dance clubs. Josey however wanted to get down to business straight away, and deal with the sightseeing later. He had no objection to the girls doing their own thing. Rebecca had already planned a walking tour of the city, and Molly was more than happy to tag along. Josey received no objections from Chen; he was more than happy to get started. Finding the mystery man was exciting enough for Chen. Besides, he'd already seen Nanjing inside-and-out on his previous visit.

The café where Chen had seen Charlie was within walking distance from the hotel, at an international shopping center on Zhongshan road. Having arrived during Meiyu—Southern China's well-advertised wet season, Chen first took them all to a shop where they could be fitted out with rain coats, hats and boots.

Straight after they acquired their wet weather gear, they put their various plans into action.

It was decided Josey and Chen would separate from the women to investigate the half dozen resorts and *Rehab* places they had found in and around the city.

Josey remained completely adamant that the man the inspector had seen and photographed was not Charlie. Chen of course—knowing what he'd seen with his own eyes—kept his mind open. Josey decided that to keep everybody happy, in future they would refer to the mystery man as Charlie's Doppelgänger. They all agreed, Doppelgänger it was.

On their first day, Josey and Chen went around all the places where they might find evidence of the University.

They found nothing.

The Doppelgänger may have nothing to do with the University, may never have. At best he may just be living in Nanjing, or at worst been making a one off visit when Chen saw him.

The following day, Josey and Lou began their survey in a licensed bar opposite the cafe where they were able to watch via a tinted window. They drank low alcohol beers, but by lunchtime they both felt totally bloated. There had to be another way.

Finally, they decided to take their reconnaissance in turns, each putting in an hour at a time while the other retired to the hire car for a rest. The day turned out to be long, and once again fruitless. When they returned to the hotel with nothing positive to report to the girls, it was decided a newer plan would be needed.

The Zhongshan Hotel perched on the banks of the lower Yangtze River, afforded views of the city set against the water. They'd booked three rooms; one for Josey and Rebecca, and one each for Lou and Molly. Josey and Rebecca's room was chosen to conduct their meeting.

'It's too much of a long shot,' Rebecca mused rhetorically.

Josey stood by the window studying the city high-rise, while Chen sat with his back to a small office desk drinking iced water and deep in thought.

Rebecca and Molly lay sprawled out on the bed.

'Any ideas?' Chen enquired of the group.

'There is one thing we can do,' Josey said without turning, 'but it's a bit risky.'

He came away from the window and stood facing them. 'We talk to the cafe people. Show them Lou's photo of the doppelgänger. See what comes up.'

Rebecca lifted her head off the pillow. 'Why's it risky.'

'It's possible they might know our mystery man well enough to raise an alarm.'

'I think this is worth a try,' Chen told them. 'Well worth the risk. We must learn that he is a regular to the cafe. If he is not, then we are wasting our time.'

'Right,' Josey said closing the discussion with his arm held in the air, 'all those who agree?'

From the group came a categorical agreement. The girls had joined in on the chorus to affirm their interest in finding the doppelgänger, but in reality they were already thinking about their next Nanjing outing.

Josey and Chen pinned all their hopes on establishing the Doppelgänger was indeed a regular. One thing was certain; they had totally exhausted their search for the University of the Next Life. Josey had also checked the web and found, although the Australian web page was still active, there was nothing to indicate the University had set foot anywhere in China. This came as no real surprise, because a base had never been placed on the net in Hong Kong from the start.

'That's it then,' Josey said closing the meeting. 'Have a rest now and we'll all get together for dinner, tomorrow's another day.'

Molly sprang off the bed with such energy it gave her mother a start. 'I'm going out,' she told everyone.

'Where are you going?' Rebecca asked with guarded concern.

'Not far. There's a dance club inside the hotel.'

'What about your dinner?'

'I'll eat later. Right now I'm taking a shower.'

After Molly left to go to the bathroom, Chen could see that Rebecca was worried about Molly going to the dance club alone. 'She will be perfectly safe,' he told her. 'Crime in Nanjing is very low, and the club in this hotel has very good security. If you like I can ask my friend Zou to keep a close watch on her.'

'Would you,' Rebecca said with relief.

'Consider it done.'

The hotel club was like those in any Western city. A mirror ball sent points of light orbiting around the walls while a DJ played mostly American hits. The patrons were a mix of locals and tourists.

Molly swayed toward the bar carrying a persona of untouchability; a woman as good looking as her would surely be already attached. While she could do nothing about the many eyes fixed upon her in the dimly lit club, there was one set of eyes that she welcomed. Zou, the security guard Lou Chen had spoken to on her behalf, was watching her progress intently.

When she slid onto a stool at the bar the bar-man quickly noticed her and came over. She acknowledged him with a quiet nod.

'Haven't seen you here before!' he shouted over the music, 'where you from?' Hotel staff in most tourist spots in China spoke English when dealing with people of European appearance.

'Australia,' she told him.

He was clearly interested in a conversation, the kind of chatter she had no interest in right then—she quickly ordered her drink. 'I'll have a gin and tonic.' To cement her disinterest she turned to face the dance floor.

'Right,' he said, moving off to do his job.

Lou's friend Zou was a rather large man, and could see her across the heads of the dancers. Not a minute had passed before he saw a young Chinese fellow approach and begin a conversation with her. She was smiling, so he assumed she was not being harassed. They spoke for a few minutes, long enough for her to down her drink, then move to the dance floor with him. *Good looking girls are always good dancers*, Zou thought to himself. He also noted the guy she was dancing with was being eyed enviously.

Molly and her acquired partner gyrated about, smiling at each other in a no-contact dance. The bar-man was giving them daggers. She had no idea why she chose to turn to her left at that moment, but if she hadn't, she might never have seen the Doppelgänger making his way out of the club. Molly's partner was noticing the change of expression on her face and became a little concerned. 'Is everything all right?'

'No,' she told him. 'I'm afraid I have to go.'

She left him standing on the floor crestfallen, highly embarrassed. 'Oh come on,' he pleaded, 'really?'

The guard saw her pushing her way through the dancers and could tell something was out of the ordinary. He moved to meet up with her at the exit. 'Is there something wrong, Miss?'

'No, I'm fine,' she told him impatiently, 'I just need to check something.'

He followed her out of the club onto the pavement. She looked left and right, frantically searching for any sign of the doppelgänger.

'Are you sure you are perfectly all right, Miss?' the guard wanted to know.

Shoulders slumped and she let out a frustrated sigh. 'It's nothing. I'm sorry; I thought I saw someone that I know.' She gave the street one more scan, and there he was, getting into a cab.

Don't approach him on your own, her stepfather had said.

The cab began to move off, and instinctively she moved forward to get a clearer perspective on the passenger as the car passed.

The doppelgänger looked straight at her as he slid away in the cab; *he's even more handsome than in his picture,* she thought.

Molly's dance partner came out of the club just as she was going back in. 'What's happening?' he asked, confused.

'Sorry Ling, I'm calling it a night. Maybe I'll see you again.'

He was left open-mouthed as he watched her go back through the club and up to the bar.

She took the doppelgänger's picture from a pocket and held it out for the barman to see. 'You seem good with faces,' she quipped, 'maybe you've seen this guy come in here.'

'Thanks for noticing,' he told her sharply, referring to her underhanded compliment. 'And yes—I have, his name is Brendon Miller. Seen him a few times lately; you a cop or something?'

'*Or something*,' she answered putting the photo back in her pocket . . .

She could see he was slightly put-out over their earlier encounter, and given this new information, she considered it best to keep the barman on-side. 'I'm sorry, I like this guy,' she explained patting the blouse she'd placed the photo in. 'I came in looking for him, but he's blown me off,' she lied. 'I'm calling it a night. Maybe you and I can hook up when you're not quite so on duty.'

The bright smile on the *mere male's* face showed he was taking the belated bait. She held her hand over the pocketed photo, which was right above her left breast, and said, 'If he comes in again, let me know so I can tell him it's over.'

'No worries.' He was wearing an expectant smile.

She gave him a wink and turned to find her dance partner and the security guard had followed her in. They had obviously heard the conversation. 'I'm done for the night, mate,' she told the dancer again, faking tiredness.

The dancer and the guard watched her go to the exit
that led back inside the hotel. The dancer was about to
follow, but the guard took a hold of him.

'I guess this is not your night,' he advised Molly's
dejected dance partner in Chinese. 'European girls,
what can you say. My advice - mingle! Plenty of other
fish just waiting.' His abstruse smile let the guy know
it wasn't a request.

The barman still hadn't wiped *his* smile away. 'You
heard him,' he told the dancer. 'Mingle!'

Molly knocked on her parent's door, but received no
response. Assuming they might still be eating, she
went straight to the hotel dining room anxious to give
them the news. She found them there with Chen in
quite a party mood, being helped along by the red wine
they were consuming.

'You are not going to believe what just happened,'
she announced as she pulled up a spare seat, quickly
gaining their complete attention . . .

'Well go on; tell us,' her mother commanded excitedly.

'I just saw the doppelgänger.'

This news came totally unexpected, especially by
Rebecca, who had opened her eyes into large saucers.
'At the club?'

'Is he still there?' Josey was keen to know.

'No he's gone, but his eyes were right on me. God,
he's really gorgeous.'

'Hey, he might be your uncle.' Rebecca said as
though she suddenly thought it might be somehow
possible. 'Did you talk to him?'

Molly was still laughing at her mother's suggestion he could be her uncle. 'No, he left in a cab.'

Josey brightened. 'Please tell me you got the cab's number,' he said ignoring what he considered was a moment of insanity from his wife.

Molly nodded and gave him thumbs up with a wink. 'You might not need it though; he's been seen in the club a fair bit; calls himself, *Brendon Miller*.'

Josey couldn't hide his excitement, *this is progress*. He was feeling a little pride in his stepdaughter too.

Molly got back to gushing over the doppelgänger. 'You can't believe how much of a lookalike this guy is. He really is the spitting image of Uncle Charlie's picture.'

'It's only a picture, Molly.'

'Wait till you see him Mum. That's all I'm saying.'

'I for one can't wait to do just that,' Josey promised, 'but right now, you deserve a drink.' He poured her a red wine and held up his glass in a salute—the others followed. 'To *doppelgänger Miller*,' he offered. They clinked glasses and chimed, 'To doppelgänger Miller,' and then took a hearty drink.

'I'm pleased to see you reason the doppelgänger isn't Charlie.' Josey said to Molly.

'He better not be,' Molly moaned, 'because he can put his shoes under my bed anytime. He's quite hot.'

Chen gave everyone a cautious glance to see their reactions, Rebecca was looking truly horrified.

'I'm joking Mum,' Molly said with a laugh.

Her mother gave a visible sigh of relief and felt a little foolish.

But then, with a cheeky grin, Chen added fuel to the fire. 'Also, remember that at best, he is your *cousin*.'

Molly mimicked disappointment. 'Thanks Lou, I'm still kind of hoping he isn't related at all.'

Her mother rekindled her horror.

'Still joking Mum.' Molly said.

'You better be,' she warned with a wry grin.

CHAPTER TWENTY SEVEN

Molly was relieved to find her biggest fan, the man behind the bar from the night before, didn't appear to be on duty. She sat next to a window that faced onto the street, studying the cabs as they came in and dropped off passengers. Most people gave the club a wide berth and headed straight for the hotel lobby, the night was still comparatively young in club-speak.

She was getting plenty of attention, and she hoped her admirers would continue to maintain their distance. To help achieve this she placed an extra drink on the table in the hope it would provide the illusion someone was with her. She knew the longer she sat there with no one picking up that drink, the less effective the ploy would become.

She pulled her cell phone from a small purse and fired in a message with her thumbs.

Josey responded to the incoming text.

Rebecca recognised her daughters call tone. 'Is she okay?'

'She's fine.' He passed the phone over for her to read.

'Still no sign, Molly,' she read out loud.

It had been an hour. Almost impossible not to have finished her drink, and presumably her onlookers were already considering the recipient of the other drink was a *no-show*.

A pretty young Chinese woman approached Chen's special security guard and tugged at his massive arm. He leant down and she spoke close to his ear to be heard over the music. The large man nodded an approval and moved through the crowd like an icebreaker with the girl in his wake. On reaching Molly's table he said, 'Excuse me Miss, *Ling Po* asks if you would like some company.'

Molly was a little surprised at the offer, but it was just what she needed. 'Oh, hello,' Molly said with a warm smile.

Her newfound friend laid eyes on the extra drink and frowned.

'No, that's all right, my friend is not coming.' Molly gestured to the seat opposite. 'Please.'

This got a smile. 'Oh, thank you.' Ling Po sat and stared at the decoy whisky as if it were poison.

Molly pulled the drink to her side of the table and said, 'What would you like?'

The girl was politely embarrassed. 'I do not drink alcohol.'

'We'll get something soft,' Molly said looking at Zou.

Zou, who had been waiting to see if things remained amicable, waved a nearby waiter over and told him,

'My friends would like some iced water and Pepsi for their table.'

The waiter nodded and hurried away.

'All right?' Zou inquired of, Molly.

'Perfect.'

With a satisfied beam he slipped away to return to his observation post. Once there, he saw that the girls seemed to be hitting it off. He stayed on them until the waiter returned to the table with the iced water and Pepsi.

At the table the waiter filled Ling Po's glass with the Pepsi and left.

'You are very generous,' Ling Po told Molly.

'It's a pleasure, but I have to be honest with you, I was very pleased you joined me because I don't want men asking me to dance.'

The girl wasn't concerned at hearing this, but she did lose the smile as she asked out of pure interest, 'Do you prefer to dance with a woman?'

Molly burst out laughing.

Ling Po was startled. 'Did I make you laugh?'

Molly controlled herself to say, 'you did, but in a nice way.'

Ling Po said nothing, opting to sip on her Pepsi.

Molly followed suit, then said, 'I'm sorry, I owe you a proper explanation.'

She took the Doppelgänger's photo from her purse and held it up. 'The fact is I'm waiting for this man, but I think he may have stood me up.'

The photo seemed to surprise Ling Po. 'Oh, I think that it is I who owe *you* an explanation.'

Molly's heart skipped a beat. *What on earth does she mean—?*

'It seems you are both looking for each other.'

Molly began to panic. *Why would he be looking for me?*

'Have you known him for very long?' the Chinese girl asked.

Molly tried to think of a quick answer, but nothing came. 'No, actually I have never met him.'

Ling Po sucked on her straw until her glass of Pepsi was emptied. She tried to speak, but extradited a resounding burp instead. She giggled and said, 'I will get him for you.'

'He's here?' *Oh my God—what will I say to him?*

Ling Po had a blank expression on her face. 'I will bring him.'

She was up and gone before Molly could stop her. Molly decided on a quick text in her absence.

Josey and Rebecca responded to Molly's call tone. Josey answered and read the text for Rebecca, 'Might be about to make contact.'

'What does she mean *might be*?' she asked, 'Text her back.'

'Not unless she gives us another text,' Josey insisted, which was fortunate, because Ling Po was already returning with the Doppelgänger in tow. As they came closer, a wave of nerves took hold of Molly. She asked herself the same question again, *what will I say to him?*

She turned toward the window to hide her distress, quickly downing the last two thirds of her drink.

'Ling says you want to talk to me.'

His voice was deep, and Australian. She turned to face him and thought, *he sounds as good as he looks.*

'Ling says it's *you* who wants to talk with *me*,' she said recovering her confidence seamlessly.

'I will leave you now,' Ling Po offered ahead of introducing them to each other. 'Brendon - Molly'.

'Thank you Ling,' he told her politely.

She left and he took her place at the table.

Up close, even in this dim light, Molly could see his eyes were as blue as those in the picture. She thought he had a very calm manner about him - sort of, *no-threat*. All the shots she'd seen of Uncle Charlie were coming to life right in front of her, right down to his calm expression.

He presented an open palm toward her. 'You go first.'

He made it sound like whatever it was she wanted, he was willing to fully cooperate.

It was far too early to blurt out her real reason for wanting to talk with the doppelgänger. She would have to lie. 'You'll probably think I'm being too forward,' she said, sounding as apologetic as possible, 'but I saw you here last night leaving in a cab.' She checked the street as a distraction. 'I guess I, um, wanted to see you again.'

Oh God, she thought in panic, *did Ling tell him about Charlie's photograph?*

That could bring her story undone — either way she wasn't fibbing about wishing for a revisit. On turning to face him she found his expression hadn't changed, still calm - inviting.

'Ditto,' he admitted.

Knowing he must realise she couldn't possibly have forgotten the way they had locked eyes last night, and *with no mention of the photograph* she thought, *Good;* then said, 'Oh, right.'

He gave a perfect smile. 'Don't be embarrassed.'

For what seemed like minutes to Molly, they just smiled at each other, their silence replaced by the loud dance music. Her head was beginning to whirl in response to the booze and the Coke—which she had drank too quickly.

'Would you like to get some fresh air,' he asked in the nick of time.

She released a relaxing breath. 'That would be great.'

The security guard watched the couple make their way toward the door and exit onto the street. He placed a call to Lou Chen as he slipped the Doppelgänger's photograph from his pocket. 'Your girl has just left the club with the young man,' he said in Chinese.

'He is the one in the photograph?' Lou probed.

'Yes. It is definitely him.'

'Does she seem happy to go with him?'

'Yes, she seems happy. They have not left the front of the hotel.'

'Very good, Zou, please let me know if they look like doing so.'

'Yes, of course.'

The inspector disconnected.

Molly and the Doppelgänger chatted happily among the night revelers in the cool night air. A light rain had begun, wetting the road and painting the city lights deep into an inverted subterranean world.

'We won't be taking a walk tonight,' he said stating the obvious, since they had no rain coats.

'Well it *is* the wet season,' she said keeping him in the corner of her eye.

'Right; . . . you know, I'm surprised tourists come here at *all* this time of year.'

She allowed a muffled giggle.

He quickly grasped her point wasn't intended to be taken so seriously - not to mention his response was somewhat insulting to her as a tourist. He backpedaled. 'Sorry, I didn't mean to make out you don't know what you're doing.'

'Apology accepted,' she said with mock indignation.

He showed his perfect teeth and chuckled at her fresh sense of humor.

. . . 'Do you live in Nanjing?' Molly inquired feeling confident the time was right to start probing for the truth about the Doppelgänger.

'Temporarily; my home is in Beijing, but I come down here months at a time on business . . . *You*, been here before?'

'No; first time to China.'

'Why Nanjing?'

Good question, Molly thought, *Best to tell a half truth.* 'My father's here on business as well. I'm just along for the ride.'

'What business is your father in?'

Molly was beginning to wonder who was interrogating who, but she was always able to backslide into embarrassment when the occasion demanded, what she was really feeling was panic.

He thought he saw her discomfort and a need to be let off the hook. 'It's sensitive, right,' he suggested.

She relaxed. 'You're very intuitive.'

'Tell you what—how about we settle in at the hotel bar, we can have a dryer conversation and get to know each other.' He woke up to what he'd said. 'Oh shit, you know what I mean.'

'Sounds good, let's hit the bar and have a *dryer* conversation,' she agreed laughing. He may have turned red; she wasn't quite sure with the surrounding multi-coloured lights hitting his beautiful face.

Chen was in Josey and Rebecca's room advising them of Molly's unexpected success in making contact with the Doppelgänger.

'Cam, why can't we just go down and confront him,' Rebecca suggested.

'Because if we scare him off and he walks away; we might lose him forever.'

'Well I'm not comfortable with her being on her own with him; we have no idea what he might be capable of.'

'You should dismiss your worry,' Chen assured her, 'the hotel—including the bar—has security cameras on at all times. I have spoken with the officers and they have promised to advise if they leave. They have told me that they can keep her in sight no matter where she goes in the hotel.'

'What if she leaves the hotel?' Rebecca asked.

'Then,' he said looking at Josey, 'I presume we will intervene.'

Josey nodded. 'Correct.'

'You're enjoying this aren't you,' Rebecca said to her husband.

'After twenty years; you *betcha!*'

Molly and the Doppelgänger were getting along just fine after downing a couple of rounds from the bar.

'Given I'm not at liberty to talk about my father's business,' Molly mused, 'I suppose I shouldn't be asking what *you* get up to.'

Molly clearly knew she was becoming increasingly inquisitive about who this person really was, but she was also desperate to end her role as an undercover investigator as soon as possible.

Her detective stepfather had to be right about the doppelgänger of course, this man couldn't possibly be Charlie Pyrmont, that was just common sense, for that matter, was his name really Brendon Miller; he was so identical to pictures she'd seen of her Uncle Charlie it was becoming increasingly hard to believe it wasn't him. One thing she didn't have is the benefit of knowing what Charlie sounded like; she wished her father was here for that alone.

The doppelgänger could see Molly was becoming uneasy. 'Are you feeling okay?'

She needed this to come to a head. 'Not really,' she admitted. 'Brendon, there's something I need to ask you, but I don't quite know how to start—'

A text came in on his cell, instantly interrupting the conversation. 'Sorry,' he apologised taking the phone from his pocket to read the message:

Get out of the hotel they're onto you.
Joan.

The worried expression that had swiftly swept across Brendon's face made her ask, 'Something wrong?'

'It's not safe for us to be together,' he announced nervously as he stood to leave.

His answer was completely cryptic, but she could see he was extremely scared. 'I have to go. Don't try and follow.'

He gave her a kiss on the cheek and walked away.

'Where are you going?' she called after him.

'Somewhere that will keep you and the others safe!' He entered the lift. 'Once Silvia's here I'll find you!' The doors slid closed.

A man watching the hotel security monitors watched on with interest . . . He saw Molly make her way to the lift then exit down the stairs, where monitor 3 picked her up . . . The monitor covering the Bar caught his attention again; two Caucasian men were entering in a hurry, continuing on down the same set of stairs that Molly had used . . .

He saw Molly enter the car-park on monitor 4. Back on 3, the two guys were following.

In the car park, unaware she was under surveillance, Molly searched for any sign of the Doppelgänger. She called out, but got no answer. She heard the two men who were following enter from behind—saw their interest was in her. Instinctively, she ran.

They followed with guns drawn.

On monitor 4, the surveillance officer saw a puff of smoke. He barked into the in-house emergency line, reporting it directly to the hotel security men. 'Gunfire on B1; get someone down there; take backup!'

In the Garage another shot rang out, chipping into a concrete pillar as Molly took cover behind it.

'Hey!' a voice echoed from somewhere else. Molly turned to see the Doppelgänger waving at the gunmen.

They sent bullets spitting in his direction. One gunman waved the other man toward Molly while he moved in on Miller.

More voices rang out. Security had arrived—heavily armed.

While shots were exchanged, the Doppelgänger took the opportunity to run and get Molly away from it. They left via a fire-escape to reach the floor below, B2—where he had a car waiting. To reach the exit they had to drive through the middle of the gunfight. The Doppelgänger had Molly lay flat on the seat and did his best to keep himself as low as possible. A couple of bullets were close calls, smashing through the cabin as the car sped toward the exit.

With a lurid screech and a bellowing cloud of rubber Miller's car squealed onto the street and raced away, the spectacle watched on by throngs of pedestrians with mixed expressions.

Miller took the car a couple of blocks before Molly suggested he slow down. He half turned in his seat to make sure no one was following, and seeing the-coast-was-clear, did as she wanted.

'Do you want to tell me what the hell that was all about?' she asked catching her breath.

'Something I needed to keep you out of.'

'That much I get. Question is; why is someone trying to kill you; for that matter, who the fuck *are* you?' She was scared; it made the hard question all the easier to ask.

He checked the rearview mirror and said, 'First we have to get ourselves to somewhere safe. Then I can explain everything.'

Molly had very mixed feelings about going with the doppelgänger to wherever he was taking her. She'd only just started feeling reasonably comfortable calling him Brendon, but now she really wanted to get out of his car and find her own way back to safety, contact her parents to let them know she's all right. There was that, but she needed to find out who this Doppelgänger really is and she thought she was close to doing that. That was the excuse she gave herself anyway. Deep down in her playful soul she was attracted to him, *big time*. She said finally, 'Just tell me who you are—like, right *fucking* now?'

He checked the mirror again. 'Who do you think I am?' he said answering with a question.

There was one thing she was absolutely certain of; he wasn't just a freakish look-alike. He was obviously much more—*But what?*

He thought he knew her mind. 'I'm not who you think I am.'

'And who's that?' she stumbled feeling exhilaration over the possibilities.

He smiled knowingly. 'Your Uncle.'

Molly was gob-smacked at learning she was the one under the microscope. Rolling her eyes she told him, 'As much sense as that makes, I have to ask again; who the hell are you then?'

'The big question,' he said sounding like there might not be an answer.

Molly pressed on. 'You do get that you're exactly like him—right?'

He didn't hesitate answering. 'Yes; just as he was twenty years ago.'

He's Charlie's son, she thought, *has to be!* So she said, 'Tell me your Charlie's son.'

'You could say that.' He was being evasive.

'What the hell's that supposed to mean?'

He once again checked to see no one was following, and made no attempt to answer . . .

The penny dropped, but not the one she mostly wanted. 'Our meeting was no accident, was it—?'

'*No accident,*' he admitted. 'For twenty years Charlie kept the family under surveillance, never letting me lose sight that I was part of it. After letting your friend the inspector get a picture of me, I was pretty much expecting, *hoping,* that someone would come. That's why I started hanging around the hotel—it's close to where he first saw me.'

'If you wanted to make contact, why did you run away from Inspector Chen?'

'I wasn't running from *him.* The people who are after me now, they showed up just behind where Chen was standing when he took the photograph. I had to leave in a hurry.'

Molly wasn't letting it go. 'All right, Charlie's got to be your father - that's obviously the only reasonable possibility; so, who's your mother?'

They had just made it onto the freeway leading out of the city toward the mountains. 'Well; Are you going to tell me?' she prodded.

'Not someone you'd know,' he told her.

As Lou answered his cell phone, it drew the attention of Cameron and Rebecca.

'Yes,' Lou announced.

He listened, and then said, 'I beg your pardon.'

They could see Chen had just received some really bad news.

'What is it, Chen?' Josey asked nervously.

He pocketed the phone and faced Molly's parents to deliver the message. 'The doppelgänger has left the hotel.'

He could see the stress on Rebecca's face and wished he didn't have to tell her the rest.

'Molly has left with him.'

'What?' Rebecca squealed from a pinched throat.

Josey was ashen faced.

In the hotel security center, Chen was surrounded by several local Police. Josey and Rebecca watched on nervously as he engaged in an animated conversation with a plain clothes man, obviously the one in charge of the investigation. The conversation ended and Chen came over to report what was happening.

He was beyond stressed.

'This is getting worse by the minute,' he told them.

Rebecca's heart jumped. 'What could be worse than having your daughter shot at?'

Chen's face said it all—Molly was in the worst kind of trouble.

'Inspector Chong, he is saying our Doppelgänger, Brendon Miller, is wanted for murder.'

'What?' Josey chimed, 'Who?'

Chen didn't know how to break it to them. He drew a deep breath and told them, 'He has supposedly killed his *father*!'

'Oh my God,' Rebecca breathed, 'he's going to kill my little girl.'

'We don't know that, Beck,' Josey snapped.

'We should never have let her do this. I should never have let you bring her here.'

Chen leaped to Josey's defense. 'Perhaps it's me you should blame.'

Rebecca was struggling to control her nerves. 'Why were these people shooting at Molly? She hasn't done anything.'

Josey was lost for words. If Molly were to be hurt, he would never forgive himself.

'The Police recognised our Doppelganger from the security camera,' Chen continued, 'but they have no idea who the gunmen are.'

Josey's cell rang, giving him a sudden surge of hope. 'It's her,' he announced with relief, as he read out the text in a low voice. 'I'm safe don't worry explain later. Brendon wants to see Silvia. Let us know if you can get her to come. M.'

'How do we know he didn't send that himself?' Rebecca asked, unable to relax. 'He could have already killed—'

Josey cut her off. 'She's fine,' he said showing her the text message. 'She's signed with a capital 'M'. I told her to do that if she ever needed to let us know she's okay.'

Rebecca managed a smile and hooked her arm in his. A great weight had been lifted.

'She seems comfortable calling him, Brendon, that's a good sign.'

His comment relaxed her just a little more. 'Sorry, sweetheart.'

He patted her hand and asked Chen, 'They tell you anything else?'

'Enough to know the murdered man is definitely Charlie, disabled, aged in his early forties.'

'I guess that answers one question,' Josey said unable to hide his disappointment. It wasn't the fact that *the Doppelganger wasn't Charlie*, or that *Charlie hadn't achieved immortality* - these things Josey had already figured - it was more that *Charlie's death heralded the end to a search that had spanned over more than two decades*.

A myriad of thoughts swam through his mind, chief among them—Charlie's Widow.

The plain clothes Policeman came over and spoke in English. 'Was that call from your daughter, perhaps?' He could see they looked a little more relaxed than a moment ago.

Josey put on his gravest face and cancelled the cop's doubt convincingly. 'No regrettably, we are becoming very concerned for her safety.'

The Policeman was sympathetic, but dubious. 'Have you any idea why your daughter has become involved with this man?' The footage from the club and the bar had provided the police with enough to know she was.

'No idea,' Josey lied.

Chong could find no concrete reason to argue, and said, 'Well, try not to worry, I have made it clear to my men she is not to be harmed; at least not by us.'

Chen gave Josey a glance that was easy to read, *he's a cop; what can I say.*

Josey's attention was drawn away to the array of monitors the police were studying. The security officer was zooming in and out of the recorded images, bringing up detail on faces. 'Chen, help me out,' he said as he pulled away and moved closer to get a better look.

The other's followed, including Inspector Chong.

'Ask him to back it up,' Josey said to Chen.

Chen repeated the request in Chinese, and the man did as he was asked, reversing the playback.

On the screen, the gunmen are hurrying backwards out of their getaway car.

'Stop there!' Josey called.

The operator understood; and froze the image.

'Can he take it in closer to the driver?'

Chen reiterated—the driver's face enlarged.

'You're chasing the wrong man,' Josey told Chong. 'That's your man right there. I think you'll find he's not only responsible for killing Charlie Pyrmont, he's now trying to kill the one man he thinks knows it.'

The inspector became extremely interested. 'You know this man?'

'It's been twenty years,' Josey admitted, 'but yes, I know him—his name is *Benjamin Bright*.

The name meant nothing to the police, but Chen and Rebecca understood one thing more than anything. Molly might not be as safe as they thought.

CHAPTER TWENTY EIGHT

The elevator lifted Molly and her doppelgänger to the top floor without a word being spoken between them. Accompanying this virtual stranger to his potential hideaway felt wrong on so many levels, but her expectations were totally devouring all reasonable caution.

The doors opened and they stepped out into a lavish room with a large window affording a magnificent view of the countryside. In the far distance a severe storm hung over Nanjing City.

'No one will find us here,' he told her.

She wasn't sure if that was reassuring or alarming. The unease showed.

'You've nothing at all to fear from me,' he promised.

Both soaked in sweat, a shiver swept through her - partly due to stress.

'Let's get you into a shower.'

A new shudder shook her to the bone.

'On your own,' he smartly supplemented. 'I have two bathrooms.' He led her to hers and gestured for her to help herself. 'You'll find all you need and a clean bathrobe while your clothes dry. After we've cleaned up, I'll explain everything.'

No turning back now, she told herself as she smiled and edged past him.

Hearing the door lock brought an amused grin to his face as he made his way to the other bathroom, stripping off as he went.

She paused, listening, wondering what he might be doing. Assuming the door that she then heard closing was the second bathroom; she relaxed and quickly peeled off her damp clothes to get into the shower.

With the warmth of the water chasing away her chill, she felt comfortable and safe somehow. It was hard to believe she had actually found him, the mysterious Doppelgänger. Even more surprising, she was now alone with him in his apartment.

She couldn't wait to see the looks on her parents' faces when they asked their mandatory questions;

'Was he a gentleman?'

'Did you behave yourself?'

Their imaginations would run wild. Perhaps with good reason, she wasn't sure she knew the answers to these questions herself at this point.

Molly wasn't inexperienced when it came to the subject of sex, but she hadn't been particularly promiscuous in her encounters, not that her parents would know one way or the other. Here in this place with Brendon, she was already of a mind to push any concerns about who the Doppelgänger is, neatly into the background.

When Molly came out from the shower, she found Brendon clad in a matching white bath robe, working away in the kitchen.

'Hope you like Italian,' he offered.

'Perfect.'

He put on his best Italian accent and told her, 'I'm making a *Torn Pasta with Tomato Sugo*. Do you know it?'

She was smiling and studying the layout of the room. 'Straccetti di pasta sugo di pomodore,' she responded in perfect Italian.

He laughed and continued cooking.

Molly was attracted to several family photos that hung on the wall; one in particular caught her eye, a picture of her Uncle Charlie and Brendon together. *Must have been taken no more than a year ago,* she thought.

'Why do the police think you killed your father?' This she had learnt from him even before they'd reached his *hideaway,* as he had called it.

'I was set up by the University.'

Brendon had come out from the kitchen and was standing right behind her. He handed her a glass of wine and there was a moment when his arm touched hers. She felt a spark.

'These people are extremely dangerous,' he told her as she kept studying the photos. 'That's why I had to get you somewhere safe.'

She took a sip of wine and said, 'So, who *did* kill your father?'

'Has anyone mentioned the name, Joan Crestling to you?'

'No. Was it her?'

'No, Joan is a good friend. She was the one who sent me the text at the hotel. Joan's in just as much trouble as I am. Even before we got away from the University, she warned us her husband's life was in danger. Both of them desperately wanted out of the program, but it was made clear that wasn't an option. She couldn't explain it exactly, but she just knew they were in danger.' He pointed to one of the pictures. 'That's the two of them there.'

'Is her husband all right?' she asked.

'Richard, I'm afraid not. They murdered him too.'

Molly faced him with her mouth opened in shock. 'Why haven't you explained this to the police?'

'The guy who runs the place is very ruthless, and very clever, they don't leave a shred of evidence, other than something to incriminate someone else. They set Joan up just as they did me.'

'Why are people being killed?'

'Self-preservation; You've got to understand, what they were doing at the University was highly illegal. I think they thought the laws in the future would be relaxed, but that hasn't happened. They've stopped now. Things got too hot.'

'And, what *were* they doing?'

'Certain aspects can be seen as something good. It's what makes people want to stay there of their own free will.'

'But they're not allowed to leave,' Molly summarised. 'That can't be seen as good.'

He drew her attention to another photo on the wall - a shot of Charlie, with Brendon aged about seven. 'We were happy back then. In fact life was good most of the time, but later on; some of us wanted to get out into the world.'

'Can you tell me why you're being so hesitant about what was done in that place?'

'When I said I'd explain everything, I wasn't quite telling the whole truth,' Brendon confessed. 'Parts of what went on have to wait for Silvia. She has to be the first to know.'

CHAPTER TWENTY NINE

Brendon's Penthouse was located on the 50th floor of the *Pinnacle building*, a slender white spire at the edge of the city that had been blessed with lots of security against people just walking in off the street. Feeling safe - for the time being at least - they kept their heads low for the next week while trying to work out a plan of action, one that wouldn't see Brendon immediately thrown into prison, or endanger the lives of Molly and her family. Once a day Molly would send a text to her parents letting them know she was fine, and to make sure *they* were, always signing off with the letter 'M'. Her calls were untraceable because the University had no Intel on any of the associated phones, including Brendon's.

As the days went by, Molly and Brendon became explicitly close in mind and body. Not like cousins, more like friends—very *close* friends. They both knew where this friendship was going. It was inevitable. It came at the end of their week of hibernation, the day the police investigation had advanced to the point where arrests at the University were about to be made. Police had gained Intel from Chen and Josey about the organisation, and they were able to fill in the blanks, one of which was to exonerate Miller and Crestling for Pyrmont's murder. Arthur Crestling's murder case was also put to bed.

The news that the police now believed Brendan was innocent of his father's murder, developed into a call for celebration, which led to a swim in the apartment's indoor pool.

Already in the water; Brendan waited in his birthday suit. Swimming in the nude had been agreed upon, but she still hesitated—as eager as she was.

'Would you like me to turn around while you come in?' he asked.

'Yes please,' she told him with relief.

Once he'd turned, Molly removed her white toweling gown and took the stairs down into the pool. 'Nice,' she said as the warm and inviting water swirled around her body, offering a little modesty.

He turned and admired her raw beauty beneath the surface, breasts dancing in and out of clarity. 'You're very attractive,' he told her with blunt honesty.

She felt panic set in. What had she let herself in for? She knew if this gorgeous man came close enough to touch her, she would not be able to prevent giving herself up to him—cousin or not. She was becoming so excited by the prospect that she found herself wanting to initiate the process.

But, he kept his distance.

That answers one question for my parents.

'Are you much of a swimmer?' he asked.

She grinned. 'I'm no slow coach, why, do you want to race?'

He launched into a powerful swim.

Molly was up for the challenge, swimming after him. By the time they were half way down the pool she had drawn level, only to be presented with a distraction that threatened to spoil her chances of an easy win. She made the mistake of keeping her head underwater to admire his muscular physique, that and *his generous member doing its own thing like a magnificent slug*, which she couldn't help marveling.

Seeing the funny side, she brought her head up for air and a raucous laugh, taking in a little water. This allowed Brendon to touch the wall at the end of the pool before her.

Molly was still laughing when she arrived in a small tidal wave beside him.

'Do you always break into uncontrollable laughter when you swim?'

'It depends on what I see underwater,' she confessed through continued amusement.

In an instant he was up against her, aroused, pressing hard against her stomach. He sank lower in the water and she sensed his manhood sliding down to reach the mouth of her loins. Once there, she lowered onto him, receiving him, receiving the tentacles of pleasure that invaded her limbs and torso, forever reaching deeper, pervading her shoulders, arms and fingers to their tips. She arched back, accepting kisses she could barely feel above the total ecstasy that was being injected into every cell in her body . . .

An hour later the storm that had hung over Nanjing City had made it to the Pinnacle. A small two-seated helicopter set down inside the white circle on the roof of the apartment, churning the rain into a mini cyclone. While the pilot stayed within his machine, Benjamin Bright alighted to the tarmac and ran for cover under the spinning blades. The ruckus made by the arriving chopper had brought the rooftop security officer from his control room.

Bright came running out of the rain as the man appeared at the heavy metal door that opened onto the roof—

She felt the sex was all about *her* pleasure, not just a sexual release for *him*. Her body began to twitch with the throws of orgasm, and then, and only then did he allow his juices to flow . . . relaxed in the knowledge they had experienced perfect sex*; not something that happens to everybody*.

Past experiences helped her recognise that this was something special.

And yet, *potentially forbidden*.

The helicopter pilot watched from the cabin as Bright and the Security officer engaged in a conversation. The security guard wasn't too happy about them being there. He tried to close the door, pushing at bright to prevent him from following. The pilot saw an orange flash and the man fell limp. Bright was looking toward the chopper and drawing circles in the air, indicating the pilot should keep the motor running.

Brendon lifted from the pool, his beautiful body fully revealed. She had no regrets about what had happened between them, and hoped it wouldn't be their first and final encounter. She watched him dry, unashamedly and comfortably in his nakedness. He slipped into his shorts and poured two glasses of champagne from a bottle that had been sitting on a small table by the pool. He brought one to her and sat with his legs dangling in the water.

A call came in on the in-house phone . . .

Brendon picked it up off the table and answered in fluent Chinese.

Molly was beginning to hate the invasive nature of phone calls, but whatever was being said on the other end of the line had Brendon extremely worried—it was that same fear she had seen in the bar at the hotel.

'Get dressed!' he told Molly as he put the phone down. 'That was security. There's been some sort of trouble on the roof; we need to get out of here.'

In double time, Molly and Brendon were dressed and ready to go. Brendon rummaged in a draw and pulled out a pistol. 'Get the lift,' he suggested as he loaded bullets into the weapon.

Sensing the urgency she didn't need to be told twice. The sight of the gun assured her something seriously dangerous was happening and asked no questions.

As she entered the small corridor that headed to the elevator, a man came through the door that comes in from the roof, which Brendon told her was kept locked. He had a key in his hand. 'Are you security?' she asked nervously.

Brendon heard Molly's voice, followed by a man's. When he came rushing into the corridor, a chill hit him

the moment he saw Benjamin Bright holding Molly
with a gun pressed to her neck. Knowing how ruthless
this man had become, a quick decision was needed if
they were to have any chance of getting out of this
alive. His mind raced, adrenalin pumped. With Bright
holding Molly from behind there was no clear shot to
be had, but he knew this innocent girl's safety was
paramount. Her life was in his hands—

He pointed his gun at the roof and fired, opening up
the sprinkler system. A follow-up shot provided just
enough time for him to lunge and pull Molly from her
captor's grip.

Bright had stumbled, but still was between them and
the elevator; the only way out now was via the stairs
that wound to the roof. To keep Bright down long
enough to get away, Brendon fired a volley of shots in
his general direction. They scurried onto the stairwell
and ran for their lives. There was no way of knowing
what lay ahead of them; the roof could be swarming
with armed men for all they knew. The first obstacle
they came across was the security guard sprawled and
bled-out on the stairs, shot dead.

Bright could be heard entering onto the L-shaped
staircase behind them. Ahead, the roaring spin of
chopper blades amalgamated with cracking blasts of
thunder. They hastily stepped around the dead man and
ran toward the open doorway above, their only escape
hatch — dubious as it was.

The pilot stiffened as the couple came running onto
the windswept helipad. Lack of visibility due to the
torrent might have been the reason he saw no sign of
Bright, but it looked like *the guy with the girl* was
running toward the chopper with a gun aimed. He

As they watched it recede from sight, Brendon asked Josey, 'How did you figure out to come, we'd kept this place secret as you know?'

Josey pointed to Crestling, who had just appeared in the doorway of the stairwell, veiled by the storm, carried there on her wheelchair by one of Inspector Chong's burley cops. She was recognised immediately. Her face hadn't changed. And sadly, nor had her disability. 'That would be *her* doing,' he told Brendon with a glint in his eye.

'How'd *she* know?'

'She's an incredible woman.'

'That, I know.'

Molly was under Miller's arm, holding him captive, appropriately bemused by her stepfather's obvious shine for Joan Crestling.

Seemingly unaware, they were all dripping wet.

'Let's go over and have a chat with her,' Josey suggested.

Brendon reached for his back and flinched when he took a step.

'Are you hurt?'

'No I'm fine, let's do it.'

Beneath the awning at the top of the stairs, Joan wore a pleased smile as she watched them approached. 'You haven't aged a day,' she told Cam.

Josey bent and gave her a peck on the lips. 'That was my line.'

'Oh, still the charmer I see.' She held her hand out to Brendon. 'Sweetheart, thank God you're all right.'

'Thanks to you and the detective.'

She looked about as if someone might be missing. 'Where's Bright? The police told me he was up here shooting.'

They glanced over to the parapet before turning back to her, Josey electing to explain, 'You've missed him; he was in a hurry to get to the pavement.'

She took only a moment to understand his meaning, and then in light of the person they were referring to, the irreverent comment sat quite well with her. 'Benjamin Bright was a monster in the end; I just hope no one got hurt when he met his fate.'

Neither Josey nor Brendon wanted to go into the gory details, but suffice to say the body now lay atop the concrete awning above the building's entrance.

'Mr. Miller,' Chen announced as he interrupted their reunion. 'You and I need to have a talk about what has happened here.'

Expecting police involvement he held his hands out to be cuffed, 'Of course.'

Josey had his eyes on Chen to gage his reaction, he needn't have worried. 'That won't be necessary Mr. Miller. We are well aware of the situation. Just a few routine questions and you'll be free to go.'

'Thank you, Inspector - I appreciate it. He leant to the chair and thanked his friend with a heartfelt hug. Then gripping Josey's hand he almost shook it off. 'I'll see you two later,' he prompted hopefully.

Shedding an almost undetectable tear Joan told him 'You will, sweetheart,' Joan affirmed.

'Later, guys - I owe you both.'

Molly was clinging to him like a magnet. Josey smiled, tickled at Molly's not so secret affection for the doppelgänger.

'Is it all right if I go with him to the police station,' she asked panning her head between Josey and the inspector.

As far as Josey was concerned, she didn't have to ask. 'Go ahead, cherry pie.' He said looking across at Chen, 'if it's okay with the inspector.'

'*The Inspector* has no objection,' Chen conceded.

Molly thanked Josey with a heartfelt embrace. 'You're the best dad ever.'

'I hope I'll be as popular with your mother,' he responded jestingly.

'It's like looking at Charlie,' Josey pointed out to Joan as they watched the unlikely lovers leave with the police.

'Oh, poor Charlie,' she said pensively, 'it's so sad what that mongrel did to him.'

'And Richard,' he pointed out.

She became teary at the mention of her husband's name.

'I'm really sorry for your loss, Joan.'

She dismissed it with a wave of her hand. Feeling just as concerned for Charlie's wife she asked, 'How is Silvia?'

Typical of Joan Josey thought, a woman in the same boat with time for the worries of others. 'I've spoken to her on the phone, to tell her about Charlie; she broke down, understandably.'

'She must be heartbroken.'

'She's arriving in Nanjing tomorrow. You might get to see her. You two have a lot in common.'

She looked disappointed. 'I will get to see her, but it will have to wait till were both back home. I leave for Australia tonight. I can't stay here.'

'Yes, I understand. Joan, let's make it a threesome; I couldn't be closer to this thing if I tried. I need a little closure myself.'

'You are a wonderful man, Mr. Josey, and I need to apologise for the way I acted. If only I'd listened to you.'

'No, no — you absolutely did the right thing staying with Richard. At least you got to be together.'

Recognising he was right, she offered him her hand, which he took, toting an appreciative kiss to her cheek, simply for knowing her.

She pulled him in close, speaking through tears that made her words illegible.

'Joan, what is it?'

She forced herself to gather control. 'We're not out of the woods yet,' she uttered under her breath.

'Why — what do you mean?'

'Bright's son is as big a monster as his father.'

A cold chill rippled through Josey.

'The bastard brainwashed his two kids into believing what he was doing was for the good of all humanity, a scientific breakthrough that would make them all rich. My Charlie loved Joanne and Brian; they were such sweet little things before their father got his claws into them. As adults, they were so – poisoned, that they were coerced into committing murder.'

'That's the most disgusting thing I've ever heard,' Josey said.

'I know, right.'

'Please don't tell me it was one of them who killed Charlie.'

She shook her head as if to remove the memory from her mind . . . 'It was Brian, he shot Charlie while he sat in his chair.'

'My God . . . and the girl?'

Joan burst into tears. 'Joanne was pressed to believe Richard was a threat, I can't bring myself to say what she did to him, to my beautiful man,'

Josey thought if there was any doubt that Bright and his children needed to be punished for their crimes, that doubt was now lifted.

Squeezing Josey's hand she warned, 'You have to be careful; now that their father has been killed they'll be after revenge, their extremely dangerous people, Cam. Be watchful — for the sake of your family, because I promise you, they'll stop at nothing.'

Josey was left with the thought that getting out of China would be a very sound idea, but with Silvia coming, a departure would have to wait — but not for long.

The Immortality Connection

CHAPTER THIRTY

Josey and Rebecca stood chatting on the porch of the information center at Yuhuatai Park Cemetary. Spits of rain heralded the arrival of yet another bad storm. Veins of lightning danced within dark, swirling clouds, thunder, seconds behind announcing the closeness of the danger.

'We picked a good day for this,' Rebecca observed.

'With what Joan told me, the weather might be our greatest friend.'

'Are we doing the right thing bringing Silvia here?'

'Because of the danger?'

'That too — no, I mean, seeing-Miller.'

'I hear you, but she's spent years attempting to wipe Charlie from her mind. Fact is, she's made quite a leap of faith in agreeing to come. I think it proves she never really got over him; this might give her some closure. She flies out in a couple of days, so we can't really wait.'

'Do we have to do it *here*—in the open?'

The doppelgänger has something to tell her, and needs it done here. Unless she goes through with this we might never learn the truth. Let's just see what happens.'

They fell silent when Chen stepped out onto the porch with Silvia on his arm. Twenty years had aged her in a way that made her look drawn and weighted down. Maybe it was a complete lack of dress sense, or maybe it was her lack of interest in that sort of thing after losing Charlie. She obviously wasn't working to attract another man.

'Are you feeling comfortable?' Josey asked Silvia as they drew up beside them.

'I'm fine' . . . she wasn't.

They had no sooner set foot from under the awning when the heavens opened.

'Would you like to wait for the storm to pass?' Chen offered worrying about the state of the sky.

'No. Let's get this over with.'

It wasn't hard to hear the bitterness in her voice.

Chen raised an umbrella over Silvia, while Josey and Rebecca shared their own. With the wet season in play, they had all come dressed in long rain coats and rubber boots to the knee.

They made their way along a concrete path lined with camellia bushes, void of flowers now, but loaded with buds awaiting the spring. At the end of the path they came to an open grass area where people had laid out masses of artificial flowers that glowed in the grayish light—impervious to sun and rain. A few took flight on gusts of wind.

They walked past the fake blooms for a hundred yards and stopped where no flowers *ever* stood. At their feet, a shiny brass plaque, awash with exploding crowns of water, defiantly stood up to the torrential downpour.

Silvia bent down onto her knees to better see what was written on its fresh face. As she scanned the words, salty tears fell unnoticed.

Silvia
Believe that I never stopped loving you
Charlie

The plaque showed that Charlie had died just a year before. What it didn't show, was that he had been murdered by the son of the very man who promised him an able-bodied life.

Silvia knew that immortality had never been on the cards, even Charlie, along with all the other University subjects, had always been aware it was intended to be seen as a ruse by the outside world in order to cover up the reality — but not *this* reality.

With Chen's help, Silvia stood, but her gaze remained on Charlie's vow of love. She spoke so softly that no one heard what she said over the sound of the rain pounding against the umbrellas.

'What was that, sweetheart?' Josey inquired as he leaned closer.

'Too little, too late!' she repeated in a louder voice. Drawing her eyes from the plaque she added. 'Let's leave here.'

Chen started back along the path with Silvia on his arm, keeping his silence. Josey and Rebecca followed, sharing an unspoken thought with a glance.

They'd walked only half way back to where Chen had parked the hire car, when Silvia froze on the spot. 'Holly Jesus;—do you see him?'

They all turned in the direction she had pointed, and to where she now gazed into the diminishing gloom where the doppelgänger had stood.

Another line of lightning relit the graveyard, bringing the doppelgänger back into view, again standing by the tree where she had first seen him—Molly at his side.

'Silvia!' he called out over the storm.

She faced Rebecca, her slightly estranged sister-in-law, the mother of Molly, as if she'd know how to respond to Molly being with the doppelgänger.

'He's not a ghost,' Rebecca assured her with an indefinable coldness, 'that much I can promise you.'

After all the years that had passed since Rebecca had left Charlie's brother Les, there was still a degree of discomfort between the two women. Silvia had never understood how Rebecca could so easily move into the arms of Cameron Josey, another man so soon after the death of her husband.

'I know he's not a bloody ghost,' Silvia said with annoyance, 'I'm not stupid. But why is Molly holding him like that, as though he is some sort of *boyfriend*?' She looked ready to explode with anger. 'That *wretched* Rowlands woman is his mother isn't she!'

Even Josey was taken aback by Silvia's sudden rage.

'No way he's her kid,' Rebecca said, holding onto her indifference.

This information made Silvia all the more annoyed. 'Who is then?'

'Maybe he had an affair,' Rebecca responded, 'before his stroke.' She'd got that idea from Josey.

The glare Silvia gave Rebecca was ferocious. 'Oh, you'd love that wouldn't you,' Silvia spat out, 'but not everyone's like you.'

'Charming,' Rebecca quipped, knowing full well the woman had a knack for bringing out the worst in her.

'Hey, let's all calm down,' Josey demanded.

Rebecca knew he was right and wasn't without regret for sparking, but she wasn't finished. 'If you'd taken the time to notice,' she announced to Silvia without any sign of sensitivity, 'after his stroke, Charlie's sex life was over - he couldn't have had a kid with her or anybody else; your husband was impotent.'

Silvia was so suddenly shocked, that Rebecca found herself feeling guilty for being so blunt with the facts.

Josey knew his wife well enough not to preach when she had something on her chest that needed to be said.

Although the two women had a mutual dislike for each other, Rebecca couldn't help feeling a little sorry. It was probably too late for that, especially coming from the one person on earth Silvia had close to nil respect for. She told her, 'Give up the anger, Silvia. Why not take a risk for once.'

Surprisingly, Rebecca's bluntness sank in, Silvia stepped out into the rain and warily walked toward the doppelgänger; Chen, catching up in a couple of steps with the umbrella.

Walking arm in arm toward her through water an inch deep, the doppelgänger and Molly appeared to be lovers, their affection for each other seemed more so the closer they came. When they were face to face and umbrellas were touching at their rims, Silvia could not believe her eyes, the beautiful man standing before her was exactly as she remembered her young husband from twenty years ago, back when Charlie was whole.

'My God,' she said, looking into his eyes. 'Who *are* you?'

It was the question he had been expecting. 'That's why I'm here, to tell you who I am.' . . . He caught the inspector's eye for a moment, and then reached out to Silvia with an open palm, an invitation to accept the unacceptable. Brendon knew the problem she had with him. For her, this was not even close to a happy reunion with her beloved husband. His invitation to forgive was full of *hope*, and nothing more, there was no crystal ball predicting how the future would pan out.

With vision blurred by rain and tears, the image of the Doppelgänger swam before her as might a dream. She had dreamt of Charlie like this, unable to bring him into focus, or to touch him, no matter how hard she tried. Perhaps now she could, even though she knew it wasn't him, in fact her mind was torn between what she saw and what she knew. What she *saw* was a man who appeared to be Charlie, whereas what she *knew,* in reality, was that her beautiful man lay alone and forgotten in the ground nearby.

Tentatively, Silvia's arm extended from beneath the umbrella, slowly reaching out to touch. Their fingers met in the pouring rain, creating a charge of energy that was real. This was the closest she'd felt to Charlie since he left her two decades ago . . .

She convulsed and broke into tears, and without thinking he enveloped her firmly in his arms, stifling the sound of her sobs against his chest. His own tears then flowed.

Molly took charge of the umbrella and gathered with them. She wanted to cry too, but managed to push the urge away, and to think about finding cover, a thought amplified by a sudden flash and a burst of thunder. 'Let's get out of this,' she pressed.

Chen faced Josey to see if he was comfortable with what was happening. Josey nodded, because really, this couldn't be ending any other way.

Huddled beneath the large but inadequate umbrella, the doppelgänger and the two women made it into the dubious cover of an atrium laced with a flowerless jasmine vine. Silvia - wet, shivering, and embraced by Miller's futile attempt to still her emotions, relived the memory of Charlie's protective arms.

Chen joined Josey and Rebecca as lightning smacked the ground nearby. They flinched, hair stood on end and ears rang—the ferocious storm above seemingly the only clear and present danger . . .

But, the unmistakable romping beat of helicopter rotors forced a rethink, and a refocus on the sky for a different reason. Given the risk to aircraft in severe weather, its arrival was odd, equating to either an insane pilot, or . . .

It sounds near to the ground, behind the trees, Josey thought. The shifting wind and rain was throwing the sound—

Then it dawned. 'We need to move—Run!'

They were about to learn why *running* was a very excellent suggestion.

On a razor's edge following their recent experiences with the University, everyone knew who was crazy enough to be flying that helicopter.

Brendon had Silvia and Molly heading for his parked car a hundred yards away.

The machine lifted into view, twitching above the tree tops in the wind like a giant dragon-fly.

Gunshots spewed from its open doorway!

For the targets below, a cluster of trees were their only chance of escape, their only protection against the deadly downpour of bullets and rain, evidenced by the watery explosions on the ground around them. They ran, just hoping the tiny missiles wouldn't bite into their flesh at any moment to bring them down. Each moment *alive* was a moment cherished.

Josey, Rebecca and Chen's predicament was a whole lot less impending by the fact they were behind the focus of the onslaught.

Up ahead, the others were almost to their car, and silent prayers begged no one would suddenly fall.

Minds raced . . . movement became surreal.

With the pendulum of times gone, and hopes of times to come, everyone had their own private thoughts and memories rewinding . . .

Rebecca, her eyes fixed on her young daughter running for her life up ahead, felt that if anything happens to her, she will hold Cam responsible. She carried guilt too; and regret for the way she had treated Silvia over the years . . .

Josey, was already holding himself responsible, not just for bringing his stepdaughter into this, but his wife and the inspector as well.

As for the Inspector, he was wishing he had the entire Nanjing Police Force here to back him up, and that he had perhaps never met Detective Cameron Josey.

Molly saw her mother and step father, running for their lives with the policeman, who had taken his pistol out and was shooting into the sky . . .
I don't want to lose anyone, she thought, not tonight.

Silvia, she was of two minds, part of her wished a bullet would pierce her heart to take her to her beloved husband; another part wished to live long enough to explain the young man at her side.

The Doppelganger, Brendon Miller, was holding himself entirely responsible for everyone. If he hadn't allowed himself to be seen by the policeman that day, none of this would be happening.

When the inspector and Co reached Chen's hire car, Brendon was already fishtailing out through the front gate of the cemetery in his black Nissan, the chopper twitching through the storm in hot pursuit.

Chen had been a patrol policeman in the busy streets of Hong Kong back in the day, and in as much as he was a skilled driver, he didn't like car chases, he knew they could end badly . . .

He planted his foot anyway, wishing he had the security of a wailing siren.

'Let's not kill anybody!' Josey yelled voicing his fear of the speed Chen was doing.

As they speared from the cemetery and onto the roadway, Brendon's car was seen making a right-hand turn about two hundred yards up ahead.

The helicopter was being held back, challenged by overhead power-lines. It was only narrowly avoiding the almost invisible black strands, inviting a constant chance of disaster, *if only!*

Chen's car roared at frightening speed toward the sharp corner and negotiated the bend in a controlled broadside.

As if Josey wasn't feeling nervous enough about the outcome of a car chase in Nanjing, the type he was certain they hardly ever saw, when Chen brought the broadside under control at the end of the bend, greater fears materialised.

The Nissan had crashed.

There was another car involved; a much heavier four-wheel-drive vehicle.

Chen jammed on the brakes, bringing the car into a screeching skid; Josey was on the bitumen before the locked up wheels came to a standstill, running toward the wrecks.

People were staggering from the second car shouting something in Chinese, but Josey had no idea what they were saying.

Chen picked up on what had them so alarmed and ran toward the Nissan yelling. 'Their telling us there's a fire!'

Josey looked up to the sound of the chopper closing in. 'That's not our only problem!' He saw it loom out of the rain, thirty feet above their heads.

Another lethal shower of bullets rained down.

Chen pulled his service revolver and handed Josey a backup pistol, the one he'd been holding under police orders following the incident on the roof of the Pinnacle. They both started firing. A bullet meant for the shooter caught the pilot.

The helicopter went into a wild spin.

The Nissan shifted, adding a new problem, it had been balancing on its side, and now gravity brought it to its roof.

New flames erupted from the underside of the engine bay.

The out of control chopper was falling toward them. Rotation was slowing the descent, but it was getting seriously close to the ground—to the disabled wrecks and the people still in them.

Dropping onto his haunches next to the Nissan, Josey shoved half his body in through the smashed window to check out the status.

Molly had her head bent forward, unconscious at best. Brendon was hard up against the steering wheel struggling to get out of his seat belt, Silvia seemed unhurt and conscious.

Smoke filled the cabin, forcing Josey to work almost blind. He wriggled all the way in through the broken glass of the window and wrestled with Brendon's belt until it clicked open. Visibility had quickly diminished to zero. He had no idea how hurt Molly might be, but getting her out was a priority, even with the very real risk of moving her causing further injury.

The throbbing sound of the descending chopper was ever present, getting louder—closer.

'Help Silvia,' Brendon shouted. 'I'll get Molly.'

Josey realised in his mind's eye that Brendon did have a better chance of getting to Molly between the front seats, so he concentrated on Silvia, un-clipping her belt and dragging her free.

Chen was eyeing the massive chunk of metal and fuel descending from the sky, now perilously close to the wreckage on the road. He saw Josey and Silvia appear out of the smoke plume, running clear of the upturned vehicle.

'Get the hell out!' Chen screamed.

Brendon followed with Molly, who appeared to be unconscious.

With a metal-crunching crash, the tail rotor clipped the back of Brendon's car.

There was a loud pop from the car's underside as fumes ignited, spreading an even bigger fire the length of the tailpipe - dangerously close to the fuel tanks.

None of this stopped Josey returning to the carnage to help Chen get the other two as far away from the growing threat as possible—

The tank exploded!

Seething heat shot over their heads as they kept to their feet.

The cockpit of the doomed aircraft swept into the stricken Nissan and exploded on impact.

Shrapnel gouged out chunks of earth from the grassy bank where Josey and the others had barely made it to.

Brendon went down – *hit;* a piece of the burning metal had mercilessly found its target.

While the fires fulminated, the doppelgänger and Molly were being dragged further away from the emitting heat and the possibility of more explosions.

Molly started coming around and panicked when she saw Brendon covered in blood - passed out, or dead, she didn't know.

Chen felt for a pulse. 'Sweetheart, he's alive.'

Josey's relief was palpable. 'Small mercies.'

Molly cradled Brendon's head on her lap, taking on the task of his personal nurse.

Coming off his phone Chen told them, 'Ambulance is on the way.'

People from the other vehicle had made it to safety, and were consoling each other away from the accident.

There were no further explosions to emanate from the wreckage, which continued to burn as they sat by Brendon Miller's side, watching and anxiously waiting for the ambulance and the police to arrive.

Molly kept talking to Miller in an attempt to bring him round, doing her best to stem the flow of blood with the torn off hem of her blouse.

Silvia appeared to be in shock.

Josey put his arm around her. 'We're all safe.'

She looked over at Miller. 'He said he was honoring a promise he made to Charlie. Since you seem to be the one who knows everything that's going on; maybe you know what he meant?'

Josey didn't respond to Silvia's edgy comment, explanations could wait.

Chen recognised a look on his friend's face that he'd seen before. *He knows something*, he thought.

One thing they all knew was that the two people in the helicopter were clearly dead, their bodies trapped inside the burning wreckage. They also knew that they were the hellions from the University, Joanne and Brian. An ensuing investigation would go on to raise serious questions about Benjamin Bright and his secret organisation.

Many answers were yet to come to light, but come they would. The most alarming statistic being the death of Benjamin Bright's two brainwashed children, the occupants of the doomed helicopter.

CHAPTER THIRTY ONE

The doppelgänger survived the accident, albeit with a fracture to the skull and a deep wound to his back, he thankfully had no concussion and no swelling of the brain. Awake and sitting up in bed, a large glass window afforded him a view of the nurses' station and the corridor that led to the elevators, where his family and friends were grouped in wait. Inspector Chen and Rebecca were sitting on a bench about a meter away from where Silvia stood talking with Molly. He was thankful *everyone* had survived.

A nurse fussed around with his saline drip. From a seat on the other side of the bed, Josey had been filling in the patient on some of the things he couldn't recall. Although Brendon remembered the events leading up to the collision, and being rescued by Josey from the fire, the events just before the crash were hazy.

He hadn't forgotten he still had things to say to Silvia. 'How much does she know?' he asked looking at her through the window.

'I get that you wanted to tell her yourself,' Josey said, 'but I've had to tell her the whole thing. I hope you don't mind.'

Turning to the detective, he asked, 'You did well to work it out. Does she believe it?'

Josey searched for a diplomatic way to answer him, he opened his mouth to say something, but in the end just drew in air.

'I understand. It's a lot to take in.'

Sensing the tiredness in her patient's voice, the nurse took hold of his wrist to check his pulse. 'Do you feel up-to seeing your other visitors, Mr. Miller?' She was a pleasant Chinese lady in her fifties and spoke English as well as anybody.

'I'm fine.'

'All right,' she decided turning her attention to Josey. 'One at a time.'

'Thank you nurse.' Josey stood to leave.

The nurse gave a bow and moved away to call in the next visitor.

'We'll talk again after you've rested,' Josey told Brendon before following the nurse from the room.

'Nurse,' Brendon called after her.

Josey squeezed past as the nurse turned at the door to see what her patient wanted.

'Can you send in my mother first?'

'Yes; of course.'

The nurse stepped from Brendon's hospital room and surveyed the remaining visitors to guess who might be the mother. She glanced over at Rebecca, then back to Silvia. 'He has said he would like to see his mother.'

'Don't look at me,' Silvia said with sudden ferocity.

Embarrassed, the nurse turned her attention to Rebecca, but received a head shake.

Josey moved away from Silvia and ushered the nurse out-of-ear-shot . . .

'The situation is a little complicated,' he told her in a whisper. 'The woman I was standing with is the one he wants to see. Leave it to me; I'll make sure she goes in.'

The nurse was only too eager to pass the task to Josey. She bowed and hurried away.

When he turned to see the irritated expression on Silvia's face, Josey wasn't at all sure he could deliver his promise. Molly sensed his uncertainty and felt she had to do something to help.

Moving in next to Silvia, she kept her voice low and exclusive. 'I know it's hard for you, aunt, but you needn't be his mother if that's what you want, just be his friend . . . He really is quite a nice guy.'

'Yes, I can see *you* like him,' she supposed quick as a whip.

Silvia could see Miller watching her intently. She saw him struggle to sit up in bed, then wave at her to come in. 'Why does he insist on thinking I could be his mother?' Silvia protested.

Molly moved around to look her aunt in the eye. 'Maybe you're the only one who *can* be.'

Silvia felt a little ashamed that a girl half her age should be offering advice.

'Do you understand?' Molly pleaded.

Silvia finally nodded with a weak smile; mainly to avoid being so blatantly psychoanalysed.

Moving reluctantly into the hospital room, she stopped at the foot of the bed and just stared at him.

'No one can possibly imagine,' she said . . . sounding as though it were the end of the sentence.

'Imagine what?' he asked her gently.

'What it's like to see a young man who is the mirror image of a husband from two decades ago; a husband now dead.'

She moved slowly around his bed until she was just a few feet away from his gorgeous face, a face that hadn't changed in twenty years. 'Everything about you is identical to my Charlie; *my beautiful man.*'

What she did next was beyond her control, she found herself reaching out to touch his cheek. It wouldn't have been too big a stretch for her to abandon what she understood about this young man, and to then fantasise that he really was her UN-aged husband. But that was something she would never allow. Reason told her that neither would he.

'You're not my son,' she finally told him as she drew her hand away from his face. She was immediately aware the comment had cut into him, and although she saw the hurt, had more to add. 'And, no-matter what you may think, or however you want to twist it, you're not Charlie's either.'

Tears streamed instantly onto his cheeks. She was ripping his heart apart. 'What am I then?' he asked in an uncertain whisper.

She backed away from him and stopped at the foot of the bed. 'What you are,' she told him with conviction, 'is a, *freak.*'

The emotion that struck Miller right then sent his life monitor off the scale. He began gasping for air. Silvia couldn't help the despair that suddenly swam over her, knowing she was the cause of what was happening to him. She moved out of the way as the nurse ran in to assist, followed by a doctor who quickly placed an oxygen mask on the patients face.

Silvia ran from the room into Josey's arms.

Rebecca moved across to the window and watched the hospital staff trying to stabilise their distraught patient. On hearing Silvia sobbing behind her, she turned and asked, 'What the hell did you say to him.'

Josey wasn't comfortable with his wife's tone. 'Cool it Rebecca.'

She backed off, but her disbelief at Silvia's behavior was still apparent.

Josey walked Silvia toward the elevators, away from the tension that hung in the air like a dense fog.

'That was uncalled for, Mum,' Molly told Rebecca once they were far enough away from Chen.

'I know she can't handle what he is,' Rebecca said, 'but God—what the hell did she say in there to get him so upset—'

Chen came over and butted in. 'I think we should all leave here for now. We'll come back later to see how he is.'

'I'm staying,' Molly insisted.

'Sure. You stay with your new boyfriend,' Rebecca told her, apparently just as unimpressed with Molly's infatuation as Silvia - at least they had that in common.

Chen felt embarrassed. 'Call us when they get him settled,' he said to Molly.

Josey had taken Silvia into the hospital canteen for coffee. Rebecca put on the brakes when she saw them huddled in conversation. 'Let's go outside,' she told Chen.

He understood why she wouldn't want to join her husband and x-sister-in-law at that moment, and they left.

'What goddamn right do these people have to do this?' Silvia asked Josey.

'I know you think it's wrong, but all I can say to you is this; he's here, and your Charlie gave him life.'

'And destroyed mine in the process.'

Josey exhaled, 'Brendon told me that Charlie had no choice about keeping everything a secret. And, I know that was extremely hard for you. Whatever else you believe though; know that what Charlie did was a sacrifice. That baby I saw in the window twenty years ago was a precious, innocent beginning. Brendon's beginning. That baby was Charlie's flesh and blood; and his alone. I know you hate to hear that Charlie's offspring is - you know . . .'

'A *fucking* Clone,' Silvia offered, screwing up her face. 'You can't even say the word yourself.'

Josey refuted her quickly, 'Would you rather have continued believing he was the son of Lisa Rowlands?'

This last point reached inside her. She buried her face in her hand.

He continued to try and reason with her, to accept the reality. 'Brendon has no mother. This is why he looks to you with such passion. He needs you. Just like any person, he needs a mother.'

'He's unnatural—'

'Maybe,' Josey said diplomatically. 'But there are so many ways now that a human being can come into this world, that the only thing left to consider is the actual person that does come. How a life gets here may be the last thing that matters.'

'It's against God,' she blurted out through the tears.

Faith; it wasn't an area Josey wanted to get into, but perhaps it was the one thing that might break through the wall she was putting up. He gently took her hand away from her face and said, 'If that were a fact, do you think *your-god* would have allowed Brendon to be born?'

Her expression told him he had lifted some of the guilt from her mind, and superstition from her heart—he was happy with that. If he was making an immoral judgment about God's acceptance of manmade clones, he decided he would apologise to God later.

It wasn't some flippant promise either, because when all was said and done, Cameron Josey was a believer, in something—he just didn't know what it was. He was certainly accepting of the idea something existed beyond death. That's why he constantly talked to *Fredie*, his dead partner.

He believed the door to that something was death itself; and for him, for the time being, that could wait.

He felt while there was life of any kind, life had to be respected, and protected . . .

Above all, loved.

CHAPTER THIRTY TWO

Silvia was back in her restful house in Australia, perched on the edge of the deep valley that Charlie had loved so much.

But this day, she was invited to the Josey's for one of the many family gatherings that would follow.

Silvia nursed the newborn and sang a song to him.

'Nan's really spoiling you,' Brendon's voice said from behind.

'Hold your tongue,' she told him jokingly, 'he's my little boy, and he loves to hear me sing, don't you, sweetheart.'

Brendon snuggled in to Molly, the proud mum of Brendon's baby. 'She's really adjusted well,' Molly whispered to her husband. 'You wouldn't know she was the same woman from ten months ago.'

'None of us are the same,' he pointed out. 'No *pun* intended.'

Rebecca's voice resonated from the kitchen. 'Come and get it!'